He was only supposed to make contact with her, but now he had to save her life...

The kitchen was a shambles. Delgado met the first Sig with a strike to the throat, the man folded down, his larynx crushed. The other man shot again, missed both times. By that time, Delgado cleared leather and popped him twice. The Sig crashed to the floor. Del was dimly aware of the crash as the front door gave.

If it's a standard Sig team they're waiting for the points to get her out the front door. They must have identified the dad and the other woman through the window. If it wasn't for Henderson calling me we might already be caught. They think Rowan's upstairs. That'll give me a few seconds to get her out of here.

He looked for Rowan. She had scrambled forward on her knees and was by the butcher-block table, holding her father's limp body. *"No!"* She probably thought she was screaming, but the only thing coming out was a choked whisper.

Delgado leaned down. His hand closed around her arm. "Move," he barked. "Come on, Rowan! You can't help them now."

The woman—Hilary—lay crumpled on the floor, her sleek dark head a mess of hamburger. The Major had taken one in the chest and lay unmoving in Rowan's arms. She shook him, frantically, still making that choked mewling noise that tore at Delgado's heart. "Come *on!* " he said. "They'll be coming down the stairs and sweeping the house next. Come on, Rowan!"

She looked up at him, her eyes red and brimming with tears. "What's *happening?*"

He hauled her up, trying to be gentle, and remembered she had bare feet. *Can't afford to holster the gun, might have to drop another Sig if they have units waiting on the side.* He bent and hefted her over his shoulder. "Sorry, Rowan," he said, and his boots crunched over broken glass. "Goddamn."

There was a shuddering impact, probably against a bedroom door upstairs, that shook the whole house. No time to calm her down. No time to do *anything* but get her out. Cold hit his skin in a wave, and his entire body felt full of electric prickles. Danger— and *her.* She wasn't screaming, but she was struggling ineffectually, beating at his back and trying to twist free.

"I'm sorry, Rowan," he said again, and moved faster.

For Linda Kichline, editor and friend,
who is far better than I deserve at both.

Acknowledgements

The first big "thank you" goes to my husband James and my children MoMo and Pickle. Without their steadfast love and support, none of this would be possible. Special thanks are also due to my mother Paula and grandfather Jim, who take my weird ruminations about explosives and gunshots in stride—because after all, authors are strange people, right? A big thank-you goes out to my father, Joe, who taught me how to change the oil in my own car, and my sisters Tricia and Alison, whose love and support have never wavered.

Thank you to Joe Zeutenhorst, who is always good for a plot line or two. Also big thanks to Jess Hartley, fellow author and true-blue friend; and to Janine Davis, whose conversation is like a fine meal with good wine.

These acknowledgements would not be complete without mentioning two people: Linda Kichline and Miriam Kriss. Miriam, you are one of my first and best readers and the best agent in the universe (at least in my particular opinion). And to Linda Kichline—fellow author, wonderful editor, and even better friend—thank you for believing in me, and putting up with me. It's anyone's guess which is harder. I know we were together in another life, kiddo, there's just no other explanation. This is your book, Linda, most of all.

Last but most certainly not least, my enduring and heartfelt thanks to all my Readers. You are who I write for, and an author couldn't ask for a more dedicated and wonderful bunch. Let me thank you in the way you like best: by telling you a story.

Other Books by Lilith Saintcrow

Dark Watcher
Storm Watcher

Coming Soon
Hunter-Healer
Fire Watcher

The Society

***

Lilith Saintcrow

ImaJinn
Books

The Society
Published by ImaJinn Books

ISBN: 1-933417-58-7

10 9 8 7 6 5 4 3 2 1

PUBLISHER'S NOTE:
This book is a work of fiction. Names, characters, places and incidents are products of the author's imagination or are used fictitiously. Any resemblance to actual events or locales or persons, living or dead, is entirely coincidental.

Books are available at quantity discounts when used to promote products or services. For information please write to: Marketing Division, ImaJinn Books, P.O. Box 545, Canon City, CO 81215-0545, or call toll free 1-877-625-3592.

Cover design by Patricia Lazarus

ImaJinn Books
P.O. Box 545, Canon City, CO 81215-0545
Toll Free: 1-877-625-3592
http://www.imajinnbooks.com

"...it's like someone took a knife baby, edgy and dull
And cut a six-inch valley through the middle of my soul
At night I wake up with the sheets soaking wet
And a freight train running in the middle of my head
Only you can cool my desire
I'm on fire."
—Bruce Springsteen

Militae species amor est.
—Ovid

PART ONE

One

It was, as Rowan's best friend Hilary often said, a day of small mishaps turning into complete disasters.

First, Tuna didn't start. The aging Volvo sedan didn't even click when Rowan turned the key that morning, so it became a mad dash to get to the bus stop. That made her twenty minutes late to work—and she was lucky it wasn't twice that—which made the head nurse, Wendy Yamakari, a little piqued. Rowan had been so discombobulated she'd spent a good fifteen minutes of her lunch break crying in the bathroom, more out of sheer frustration than anything else.

Then, as usual when she was upset, the patients started to react. Benny started to scream halfway through the shift, and not even Rowan's calm voice could help him. They had to wrestle him to the ground and use Thorazine. Siegfried slipped back into catatonia, and Marshall was found smoking a cigarette by the fire door, completely naked. Rodney had another of his episodes in the middle of dinner, and the food thrown had a marvelously energizing effect on every other patient in the cafeteria.

As a result, Rowan was two hours late getting home, bone-tired, and had to walk eight blocks from the bus stop. Her purse strap had snapped, and to crown the whole damn day, her shoelace had snapped too *and* she had a pounding headache.

So when she saw the lights in the abandoned Taylor house on Smyrna Avenue, she was tempted to just let the whole thing lie. Who cared what kids were up to in there? It was three weeks to Halloween, and the strange people were already coming out and doing odd things. Rowan should know; she had a whole ward full of them at work.

But then she thought she saw a flicker of flame in one of the house's upper windows, and that decided her. She'd take a look. If they had a candle or something in there it was a fire hazard, and if she passed by and something happened later, she'd never forgive herself.

So she made her way through the broken-down gate and up the weedy driveway, shivering under the October chill and going cautiously, pushing back a few stray strands of hair that had come loose during the struggle with poor Benny. Her thick-soled nurse's shoes made little noise against the dry cracked concrete, and she had her cell phone out, with 911 on speed dial. *It will probably be nothing,* she thought, *and you'll feel stupid, won't you? But better to feel stupid than to have some teenager die in a house fire because they wanted to do some Halloween woo-woo.*

She was tempted—oh, very tempted—to let go a little, maybe *look* ahead and see who was in the house, but that would have been a violation of privacy. Hearing what other people were thinking was a curse at best, and a double curse at worst. She had worked too hard and come too far to risk exposing what she was to a bunch of drunken teens.

The laurel hedge had gone wild, bending over the low, broken fence and screening her from sight. Once she was all the way up the driveway, she thought maybe she was mistaken. The upper windows of the crumbling old Victorian house were dark and broken, dusty and watchful. *I wish the city would level this place,* she thought irritably. *It's a hazard to life and limb. All those kids with rocks can't wait to break a window or two, and daring each other to sleep here—someone's going to get hurt.*

It was more than that, of course. The house sent a cold chill up Rowan's spine. The kids whispered, like Rowan supposed they did about every old abandoned house, that the Taylor house was haunted, that someone had been murdered there, and if you slept there you'd go mad. Rowan didn't know about going mad. She'd seen enough madness to doubt that one night in a rickety old house could drive you into it, but still…

The place looked creepy, and it raised goose flesh up and down Rowan's arms.

Will you just quit it? she told herself. *Next you'll be believing in ghosts and fairy tales. Be rational for once, Rowan!*

So when she came around the corner and looked at the flagstoned front walk, weeds forcing up through the stones and drifts of fallen leaves lying dry and whispering to either side, she was completely unprepared for what she saw.

A sleek black van was parked on the front walk, its windows blind with privacy-tinting. There was a faint smell of ozone in the air, and flickering candlelight shone out of the broken windows on the first floor. She contemplated this for a second before someone stepped out the front door, making the rickety porch groan.

Rowan ducked back so the overgrown hedge hid her from view. *What on earth is going on here?* She looked down at her cell phone tucked in her hand. Her purse, clutched against her other side, shifted a little bit.

Instinct insisted she hide, and it was so clear and unavoidable her heart began to pound. She'd only felt it two or three times in her life, but each time it had proved valuable. Whatever was going on there was likely to be uncomfortable, dangerous, or both. Most likely both.

I'm going to take another look, she decided, *just to see if I should call the police. Who knows, maybe someone's bought the old wreck?* But the chill touching her nape mocked her. Who would buy this place? It had stood empty for at least twenty years, even though urban development was going on all around it.

Rowan peeked around the hedge.

Candlelight still flickered in the windows. She heard the faint echo of footsteps and a low indistinct murmur of voices.

Someone scuffed on the other side of the van. Rowan's heart leapt into her mouth. She thought of retreating, but she hesitated, curiosity and civic duty warring with caution.

"Hello there," someone said, very low, almost whispering.

Rowan jumped guiltily.

A shadow slid out from behind the van, and her dark-adapted eyes made him out to be a man, taller than her, dressed in a hip-length coat and a pair of jeans. He had both his hands up, like people on TV did when the police had them at gunpoint. "Don't be frightened," he said. "I won't hurt you."

That was strange enough to nail her in place for a few more seconds. Clutching her purse under one arm and her cell phone in her other hand, she searched through all the words she knew. None seemed applicable. "Hi," she settled for. "This must seem really strange to you."

"Well, we're out here in the middle of the night, so maybe we're the strange ones," he said. "You wondered what was going on?"

"Well, yeah," she admitted. "Look, this house is a firetrap, and it's abandoned. High school kids play around in here, and it's not safe. So I thought I should check it out."

He nodded. "We're investigators, and electric flashlights will interrupt our equipment. And if we worked during the day there'd be a whole bunch of gawkers." He stood stock-still. Rowan could make out dark hair, cut short, and the glitter of eyes.

Gawkers? Like me? Rowan had the totally inappropriate

urge to giggle madly. "Look," she said, "this is awfully weird."
"I know." A shadow of amusement in his voice. "You should
hear us trying to explain this line of work to our mothers."
"What did you say you were investigating?" she asked
carefully.
"I didn't. But I'll tell you. We're parapsychology investigators.
We're attached to the University of—"
That was enough for Rowan. She backed up, goose flesh
rippling all the way down her back and spilling down her legs,
prickles of chill running along her skin. Chill and a type of
electricity that made her entire body tighten. "Oh," she said. "I'm
sorry. Nice to meet you."
"Hey, wait a second," he began, but she bolted.
She ran down the driveway, clutching her purse and her cell
phone, made it through the ramshackle gate and halfway down
the block, her heart pounding and her side aching, a stitch grabbing
all the way from her left hip almost up to her shoulder. The house
on Smyrna Avenue was only four blocks from home. She ran
those four blocks, turning right on Ninth Street, running as if the
devil was after her, clambering up her own steps and desperately
fumbling her keys out of her pocket. It seemed to take forever to
get the door open, and when she finally made it inside she threw
the two dead bolts and stood, her ribs heaving, gasping for breath,
her silent, dark house closing comfortingly around her. *Dad must
be asleep,* she thought, and dropped her purse on the floor next to
the door. *God, oh my God. Parapsychology. Oh my God. Please,
God. Please.*
She had been so careful, ever since she'd figured out she was
different. She'd avoided anything that might even be faintly
considered unorthodox. She'd never even checked out a library
book on that sort of stuff, never watched any of the "Unsolved
Mysteries" shows or anything else like that.
We're parapsychology investigators. He'd said it so calmly,
too. Hopefully he wouldn't recognize her. Hopefully none of their
"instruments" had done anything funny while she was there like
some other electronic things. When she was upset, she could
literally short out small appliances.
She'd stay away from that house, now. Completely away.
She couldn't risk it.
The lamp was on, its warm, mellow glow comforting,
showing the familiar foyer and the stairs going up, the hall closet's
door slightly open, and a painting of her mother hung on the wall.

Everything was normal, familiar, and *safe*. Her heart finally slowed down, and she kicked her shoes off, not caring that the careful knot she'd put in her shoelace was flopping back and forth. "That was a close one," she muttered.

"Everything okay?" Her father's voice drifted down from upstairs.

Rowan gave another guilty start. "Fine, Dad," she called. "I'll be up in a minute."

"No, go and get some dinner. I'm only reading in bed. How was work?"

"Long and embarrassing, Dad," she answered, searching for a light tone. "Did you figure out what was wrong with Tuna?"

"The starter's gone. Hilary dropped by, and we went to the auto parts store and got a new one." His whisky-rough voice echoed in the stairwell. "Get something to eat, honey. I'll be up for a while."

Hilary had gone to high school with Rowan, and was one of the few people she felt completely comfortable with. "Okay," she called back. "Do you need anything?"

"Just a good night kiss from my girl," he replied. "But you eat first, honey. I made chicken soup."

"Sounds good. I'll be up in a few." Rowan picked up her purse from the floor and set it on the table by the front door. *Of course they wouldn't know you're different, Ro,* she chided herself, taking a deep breath and slipping out of her coat. *Nobody knows. It's okay. You'll never see them again. You're safe. You did the right thing.*

She went down the hall into the kitchen, flipping on the light and blinking. The kitchen was neat and clean—two deep-green bowls drip-drying on the rack, the green countertops wiped, a Crock-Pot sitting next to canisters of flour and sugar. It smelled heavenly—garlic and chicken—and Rowan was suddenly aware she was starving.

Ten minutes later, carrying a tray up the stairs, she had a thought that made her stop and almost drop the tray. *How did they get the van on the front walk like that?* Another chill raced up her spine. *Just forget about it, Rowan. If you just ignore it, it'll go away.*

She made it to the top of the stairs and carried her tray into her dad's room.

Major Henry Price lay in bed, his crisp blue pajamas immaculate, a textbook on military history facedown on his lap.

His short, graying hair was slightly mussed, and Rowan smiled at him. "Hey, Dad. How was your day?"

"Oh, I skinned my knuckles on that damn car of yours," he replied cheerfully, smiling. His bedside lamp with its green shade was set at precisely the right angle. "We should buy you a new one."

"As soon as we pay off the house, Dad. We're mighty close." Rowan set the tray down, then kissed her father's cheek. He smelled, as always, of lemon after-shave. "What are you reading about?"

"Oh, just going over some old battles." Her father's green eyes followed her as she settled down in her usual chair and picked up her mug of soup. "You look pale, sweetie. Did something happen?"

"Oh, I just had an irrational moment on the way home. Ran four blocks." Rowan shrugged. "It was a weird day at work, Dad. Even weirder than usual."

"Well, you were in a mood when you left," he pointed out, settling his horn-rimmed reading glasses on his nose and returning to his book. "Every once in a while a day comes along where it's just better to stay in bed."

"Tell me about it," Rowan said, rolling her eyes. "I'm off tomorrow. I'll help you put the starter in."

"Mmh. I already did it, sweetheart. The car works fine. I just finished about an hour ago, and it was too late to pick you up from work. I called, and that Sickwitzer woman—"

"Sistowicz," Rowan corrected automatically, around a mouthful of chicken.

"Sickwitzer," her father promptly agreed. "Well, she said you'd already left."

Rowan crumbled a saltine into her soup. "Thanks for the thought, anyway. I hate riding the bus."

"Mm. Good for the environment." Her father grinned, and Rowan was startled into a laugh. She was already forgetting the Taylor house. By the time she finished her soup and got ready for bed, she was humming. She had two whole days off, and her car was fixed.

Life was good.

Two

"Are you sure?" Henderson said, settling the camera back in its spot. The older man closed the case, flipped the locks down, and glanced up at Delgado.

"Pretty damn sure, General. The instruments went crazy." Delgado shrugged. "She bolted, so I followed her home."

"And?"

"Nice house, about four blocks from here. No security. She's not government." Delgado folded his arms. Catherine brushed past him, her Mohawk nodding. *Thank God our mystery girl didn't see that,* he thought humorlessly. *Might've scared her off even sooner.*

The woman had just appeared out of nowhere as he'd stepped outside to scan the perimeter. She'd blown out the alarms he'd set up, whether by chance or skill, he wasn't sure, but he was beginning to think chance.

Of course she's psi. The instruments were going nuts. And it felt like a jolt of electricity—she's definitely got some talent. Some talent? Lots of talent.

Only one thing bothered him. She'd bolted as if the hounds of hell were after her. He'd been projecting reassurance as hard as he could, but she'd grown more visibly jittery during the whole conversation and finally run away. "I deliberately tried to be nonthreatening," he said, as Cath fitted her telem rig into its carrying case.

Catherine snorted, her nose-rings glittering. "Since when?"

He ignored the gibe, as usual.

"We should check it out," Henderson said. "If she's got that much talent, we want to recruit her. If she's government, we need her neutralized. I want to test some more of the telem rigs here and iron out that bug in the flux phasing."

"We could do that back at HQ," Delgado offered, knowing they couldn't. It was his job to make the suggestion.

"Not bloody likely," the older man said. "If there's any leakage we'll have Sigma on our tail in no time. And if this woman is psi enough to bust through our perimeter and knock you into a tizzy, Sigma will find her."

Delgado shrugged. He hadn't been able to see much except pale blonde hair, glowing in the uncertain light, and the sparkle of her eyes. She'd been clutching something in her hand, and he'd identified a cell phone and eased his hand away from his gun. She hadn't noticed. Hadn't had a clue. Civilian. *Then why did she run?* Something about this bothered him. She'd been buttoned-down so tightly she was practically invisible, which meant at least *some* training. But then why had she run away?

He'd waited until the downstairs lights had turned off, and then made a recon of the house. Nice little two-story affair, old like all the houses in this neighborhood, with a slightly shaggy garden, a clean, green kitchen seen through a bay window. Whoever she was, she was a neat little soul. There were thorny bushes underneath all her windows, which made it a little difficult, but he'd detected no invisible traps or defenses. That made it even more of a puzzle.

"Okay," Henderson said. "Let's roll back to base and get some chow, team. We'll work out a surveillance on this woman for a few days and see what we can suss out."

"I'll stay," Delgado offered. "If there's a leak on the telems and it brings Sigma here, they'll try to scoop her up. She's all over the spectrum, General."

Henderson actually paused for a few seconds. "You got it," he said finally. "Your instincts are too good to disregard, Del. I'll send Zeke over with a car and some chow for you, ten-four?"

Delgado nodded. "Got it. If Sigma shows?"

"Scoop her first and bring her." Henderson didn't sound happy. The white patch over his right temple glowed in the darkness as he slid behind the wheel of the van. Cath slammed the back doors and leapt into the passenger seat. "And Del, if she's government, get rid of her quietly. We've got to get these rigs running."

"Ten-four." Delgado backed away, fading into the laurel hedge as the van started with a swift purr. Henderson pulled out carefully, and in a moment all that was left was the smell of exhaust and a dark, abandoned house.

This place gives me the creeps, Delgado thought, looking up at the shattered windows. It was right on a ley line, and there had been a murder committed here in the 1920s. Since then the place had been amplifying and reverberating with psychic turmoil. In another few years it might have active poltergeist phenomenon, which made it the perfect place to test the rigs. The only wrinkle in the otherwise smooth operation had been the sudden appearance of the woman.

Isn't that the usual story, he thought, smiling. Nobody would see it here. And if anyone else in the Society ever saw him smile, they might well find a wall to protect their back. Not that he would shoot a fellow operative in the back, but the taint of Sigma was a hard thing for them to get over. Besides, his talent wasn't warm or fuzzy, it was flat-out dangerous, and he didn't have any gift for making himself liked.

Delgado flitted through the dark, empty streets as if they were enemy territory. He found a good sheltered spot to watch the woman's house from across the street, lying under a hedge, the branches obscuring him from sight. It was cold, but not unbearable. Thank God it hadn't rained for a while. If he had to lie in the mud, he'd never hear the end of it.

The mailbox said "Price" in neat, even lettering, but there was no mail inside that would give him a clue. He let himself relax a little, slowing his breath, waiting, but he could see no telltale shimmer in the air around the house. Which meant either she was fantastically good or untrained. Either way it was going to be one hell of a hassle. If Henderson decided to recruit her, he'd probably send Yoshi to make contact. Yoshi was the most nonthreatening.

Delgado settled himself for a long night, watching Miss Price's house.

Three

Rowan carried her coffee cup out the front door, yawning and shivering in the early-morning chill. The paper lay out in the driveway, and she scooped it up, digging her toes through her pink fuzzy slippers into the concrete. Another yawn overcame her as she turned to go back into the house.

The sun was up, making her squint as she glanced over the yard. Frost edged the grass, and her roses were bare and leafless. She finished yawning, contemplating her front yard, and started up the driveway again. She stopped halfway to the house, something nagging at her. Some instinct warning her, but that was silly. *Keep your head out of the clouds, Ro,* she thought, and continued on.

The sense of being watched returned as she put her slippered foot on the first porch step. She stopped and looked over her shoulder, scanning the street.

Nobody there.

I'm probably just nervous from last night, she thought, and shook her head, taking a sip of coffee. It was too cold to stand out in her front yard woolgathering. Her breath plumed in the air while she made her way back up the porch steps and into the house. The Major had raked all the leaves into piles, preparing to get them into the compost heap. The sight of the bare, leafless trees made her feel a little sad. But that was silly too.

"Paper, Dad," she said, coming into the kitchen and dropping a kiss atop her father's steel gray head. He growled, and she set the paper in front of him and poured him a cup of coffee, adding a little milk. *I drank so much black coffee it hurts m'gut,* he said sometimes, shaking his head. *But I can't give it up, so I cut it with a little milk. Sissy.*

And Rowan would always laugh. *Not a sissy, Daddy. Just a softie.*

By long agreement, neither of them spoke again until they had both finished a cup of coffee. The Major read the business section while Rowan read the comics. Then she got up and scrambled some eggs, made his toast the way he liked it—almost burned—and poured him a glass of orange juice. When that was done, she made her own toast—barely browned—poured more coffee, and settled down at the kitchen table with her well-thumbed *Compleat Shakespeare* while her father digested the rest of the paper, spreading it across the butcher-block table with complete abandon. It was the only messiness he allowed himself.

She was deep in the wilds of *Othello* when the sense of being watched returned, making her shiver. She hurriedly took a sip of coffee to cover it, but her father's green eyes came up over the rim of the International section of the paper and fastened on her. "Rowan?"

She waved a hand at him. "Nothing, Daddy."

He folded the paper and set it aside. "You look pale, sweetheart. Is it one of your feelings?"

Rowan felt heat rise to her cheeks. "Dad." Her tone was firm. "You know I don't believe in that junk." *Or I only wish I didn't.*

"Well, is it?"

"I just feel like I'm being watched, that's all," she admitted, setting her coffee cup down and scratching at her neck. Her conscience pricked her. Why hadn't she told her father about the Taylor house last night?

Because I don't want to worry him, she told herself firmly. *It was nothing, just some college kids doing a stunt.*

Something nagged at her, though. Some uneasy feeling. Rowan finally sighed and met her father's eyes squarely. "I'm uneasy," she said. "I don't know, Dad."

"Well, pay attention to that feeling," he said, returning to his paper. "More there than you know, princess."

Rowan suppressed a sigh. For a former Marine and such a precise man, her father was certainly in love with woo-woo. He read all sorts of books on psychic phenomena, listened to radio shows about the unknown and subscribed to magazines about New Age stuff. Rowan felt a smile tugging at the corners of her mouth. *Well, he's earned a little eccentricity, hasn't he? And ever since Mom died, he's been getting more and more into this stuff. I think it's comforting for him. Probably harmless, too.* She took another drink of coffee. *It's nothing, Rowan. Just ignore it. You don't need a bunch of weirdness messing up your life.*

She settled back into Shakespeare's comforting rhythms, trying to ignore the persistent feeling of being tickled right on her nape. Eventually it would go away. It always did.

Four

"Holy Christ," Zeke breathed, the binoculars almost lost in his beefy paws. He handed the 'nocs over, elbowing Delgado in the process. "Take a look at *that*."

Delgado did. He whistled, a long low sound.

The blue van was parked just west of the Price house, looking old and neglected from the outside. Inside, the computer screens in the back cast an eerie green glow over the darkness. But in the front, morning sunlight poured through the privacy-tinted windows and gave both men a clear view of the house.

The woman shuffled out the front door, a steaming mug in her hand. She was slim, slightly less than average height, and lost in a bulky plaid bathrobe, with fussy, fuzzy pink slippers on her feet. A long fall of slightly curling ash-blonde hair glowed in the clear winter sunlight, and even from here Delgado could tell she was pretty. When he focused the 'nocs, he found himself looking at clear pale skin, an aristocratic nose, great cheekbones, and a flawless mouth. Dark circles under her eyes only served to underscore how green they were. The robe showed a fascinating slice of white décolletage, and Delgado dropped the 'nocs. "Damn," he said.

Her voice was slightly husky, he remembered. A contralto, when it wasn't squeaky with fear. He'd been almost close enough to touch her last night.

"You got *that* right." Zeke shook his bullet head. "She's a live wire, Del. Look at this." He held up a scanner.

The handheld Matheson unit was going crazy, colored spikes shifting on the screen, the dial at the bottom twisted all the way into the red. Zeke's dark eyes were wide and worried. He scratched at his chest through the black T-shirt with blunt fingers. His many-times-broken nose wrinkled a little.

Delgado sighed. "Christ," he said, and dug in his breast pocket for the cell phone. He dialed, his eyes still nailed to the woman, who had straightened and was shuffling back to the house. "Look at that. Looks *and* talent."

It was a bad joke, but Zeke laughed anyway, whistling through his mashed nose. Humor helped.

The phone crackled in Delgado's ear. "Henderson," the old man barked.

"General, we've got a live wire," he answered, with no preamble. "She's picking up her morning paper and nearly blowing all the circuits in Zeke's unit. Looks like she's got a helluva lot of raw Talent, but she's virtually untrained."

"Where's the dial?" Henderson asked. He sounded a lot less cranky and a lot more awake.

"Over in the red." Delgado watcher her, his mouth suddenly dry for no good reason. "You should see this, General. The goddamn thing looks like smoke should be coming off it."

The woman paused at her porch steps and glanced down the street. She seemed to be listening for something.

The van's shielded, he thought, *but I'll bet you ten thousand she can feel us anyway. Goddamn.* "I think she might know we're watching, too," he added.

The General was silent for a moment. "Let's just hope Sigma isn't on our tails," he said finally. "I'll have Yoshi step up his monitoring. Make contact as soon as possible, Del. Don't let Zeke approach her. He'll freak her out if she's that sensitive."

"Wait a minute—why me?" It took him by surprise, so much so that the question came out stunned instead of calm. He would spook her too. His own particular Talent made him unpopular around other psis. It was as if they could smell the danger he carried.

Delgado took a deep breath, his eyes fixed on the woman, who seemed to be staring right at them. Then she shook her head, as if dislodging a thought, and went back into the house, shuffling in the ridiculous slippers. *God, she's beautiful. Why does she wear that shit? Then again, if she came out in silk and high heels it might cause traffic accidents.*

"Because Cath'll frighten her, so will Brewster," Henderson answered, "and I need Yoshi to work on those rigs. We've *got* to get them up and running. Use those interrogation techniques you're so proud of. Besides, if Sigma gets there, you're the best bet to extract her from them. Bring her in, Del, and work fast. Got it?"

"Yeah, I got it." He suppressed the urge to swear. Those were all valid points, but if she was half as sensitive as the scanner said, he was the one most likely to spook her. *Goddammit, what's wrong with me?* "How long do I have?"

"Forty-eight hours max. We'll get you a dossier in two. I'll get those rigs working and we can blow this town. Be careful, okay?"

"Absolutely," Delgado answered, staring intently at the house. He hung up.

"What's the word?" Zeke asked.

"You're supposed to stay out of the picture. I'm supposed to recruit her in forty-eight hours. And keep a weather eye out for Sigma, because the telems still aren't finished and might be leaking."

"Yeah? And when do you walk on water?" Zeke sniggered. "You get all the great jobs. Bet those legs go all the way up to her chin." He picked up the 'nocs and scanned the house again.

"She's probably a nice girl," Delgado said absently. "Watch your mouth, okay?" There was a long silence. Zeke was pale when Del glanced over at him. "What?"

"Nothin'," the big guy said. "I didn't know, Del. Okay?"

Is he sweating? Jesus. Does he think I'm going to turn on him? "It's not a big deal, Zeke. Chill."

"Yeah. I'm gonna go monitor, okay?"

"Sounds good. Tell me as soon as we get the doss on her."

"You got it."

Zeke didn't have to worry. His Talent made him impervious to psionic attack. Delgado couldn't crack him if he tried. Still, Zeke was nervous. They usually were.

Delgado slid over into the driver's seat. "All right, Miss Price," he said. "Come on out and show me that pretty face again."

Five

"Hey, Dad. I'm going for a run and then we can do some errands," Rowan braced her foot on the second step, tying her shoe. *Let's hope the laces don't break,* she thought sourly, and made sure her MP3 player was securely clipped to her sports bra.

"Ruin your knees running like that," he called back. Rowan grinned.

"I run on a track, Dad. And I wear proper shoes. My knees are fine."

"Be careful." He shuffled out of the kitchen, holding his coffee cup. "I'll be ready by the time you get back."

"No hurry." She bounced up to him and gave him a kiss on his leathery cheek. This close, she could see the deep crow's feet near his eyes and grooves at the corners of his mouth, the ravages of time on his face. "We've got all day. Be good."

"You too, princess. Did you stretch out?" He sounded worried.

"Of course I did, Dad." She rolled her eyes, sounding like a teenager again for the first time in a good twelve years. "I'll be back in an hour or a little less."

"Be safe, sweetheart."

She gave him another kiss and went out the front door. The cold made her suck in a quick breath, since she was wearing tight bike shorts. She got to the sidewalk, her hands stuffed in the pockets of her running jacket.

When she made it to the corner, she glanced at the Howell's house. There was a blue van parked out front, a rundown thing. Maybe someone was visiting. Rowan settled the earpieces in her ears and punched the "Play" button.

Ten minutes later, she was at the high school, cutting through the soccer field and heading for the track, her arms swinging and her breath coming in long deep swells, pluming in the chill air. As soon as she hit the track her stride lengthened, and she began to run.

Running was the best. Her feet pounded the track as she paced herself, a Bach cello suite echoing in her ears. As usual, the outside world fell away, her attention narrowing to the steady beat of her feet on the track, the rhythm of her breath, aching in her calves, her pulse pounding in her wrists and throat.

Her ponytail bounced and her hands curled into fists.

By the time the music shifted through Chopin and into techno, she was sweating freely, steaming in the chill air, everything left behind her. Work, worry, her father's trembling hands, the waves of other people's emotions threatening to drown her, all left behind. The patients on the ward, their insanity burrowing inside her skin, her own freakish abilities threatening to escape her control—all of it was left in the dust as she stretched herself out and let herself fly, or the closest to flying she could reach.

Nine laps later, when the music slipped back through its cycle and turned into Debussy's *Clair de Lune*, she slowed regretfully, but her breath came in harsh tearing gulps and her legs were on fire. She tore the ponytail holder out of her hair, walked around the track until Satie's *Gymnopedie* came through the earpieces, and then she turned toward home.

Deep breaths. Deep breaths, keep breathing...

Her mood had lightened considerably. Her hair bannered back on the breeze as she slowly walked back home, feeling the burn in her legs and side. The stitch on her left side returned, but it receded as she breathed through it.

The blue van was still there. *Why am I looking at that?* she wondered, walking past it. *It just looks wrong. But that's silly, Rowan. Stop it. You've got a day of errands to run and dinner to cook. So just stop being an idiot, okay?*

Still, the van bothered her...and goose flesh slid down her back again. Maybe it was just the cold.

She bounced up the porch steps and into the house. "It's me, Dad," she called.

"Hey, princess. How was the run?"

"Fabulous." She took a deep breath in. It smelled like garlic. "Are you making more chicken soup?"

"And some bread," he called back. "Hilary's coming for dinner."

Bless you, Dad. "Sounds good." It had been at least a week since she and Hil had indulged in a good gossip session. Maybe they could go out to a movie. She unclipped the MP3 player and wound up the earplug cord. "How's Tuna?"

"Fine and frisky," Dad said. "Should be no trouble. Hey, Hilary wanted you to call her back."

She always wants me to call her back. We've been burning up the phone lines since fourth grade. Should have bought stock in the phone company. "I will, right after my shower."

He made a sound of assent, and Rowan bounced up the stairs, suddenly feeling lighter and freer than she had in a long time. Everything was going to be all right. On a crisp winter morning with an endless blue sky, a morning run and a day of errands was the best of all possible worlds.

Still, the blue van nagged her. Maybe she would call the police and have them check it out, especially since she was so concerned with her civic duty lately.

Yeah, and have them think I'm a nosy Nellie. And maybe have them find out about me.

Better nosy than sorry about it, though. And if she called from a pay phone, they wouldn't be able to find out about her. Rowan knew better than to mistrust her instincts. Hadn't they warned her of danger last night? And like an idiot, she'd just gone blithely ahead.

If the van's still there tomorrow, I'll call the cops from a pay phone. Just to have them check it out.

Six

Delgado quietly shut the van door. Every time they left the shelter of the vehicle, it upped their chances of being seen. But he couldn't drive the van after the woman, so shadowing her on foot was the only option he had.

She walked through her neighborhood to the high school, cut through a soccer field, and took to a track, running slowly at first, saving her energy. After about fifteen minutes she started to really go for it, long ash-turned-golden ponytail glowing in the sun, legs flashing, her face blank with effort. *Running with headphones,* he thought dryly, standing in the cover of a cedar tree whose branches made a nice little tent. His breath made a white cloud in the air. *Doesn't she know anything about safety? Then again, it's broad daylight, and she's a civilian. Still, though.*

The thought of anyone watching her while she ran so blithe and unconcerned made his fingers tighten on the 'nocs. *Don't be ridiculous,* he thought, *and don't get emotionally attached to a subject. She could be government. She could be anything. Just because she's psi doesn't mean she's on our side.*

She finally slowed after a while, walked around the track twice, her arms swinging and her shoulders less tense, and then headed for home. She didn't look back, and Delgado didn't sense she was aware of him. You knew after a while if your subject was nervous or suspicious.

He let himself back into the van and was greeted with a file folder and Zeke's grin. "Hey, old son," the big man said. "Enjoy yourself?"

"Exercise never looked so good," Delgado replied dryly. "What's the word?"

"Well, she's not government. That's good. There's the doss." Zeke shifted in the too-small chair

"I can see that. I suppose you already took a look."

"Just a peek. Curiosity."

"And?"

"Enjoy."

Zeke took over watching the house while Delgado settled down with the dossier.

Rowan Price, thirty, never married, psychiatric nurse and counselor at Santiago County Mental Hospital. Lived with her father, a certain Major Henry Price, decorated for bravery, discharged with honor. Mother died five years ago—stroke. No arrest record, good credit, no lawsuits—not even a library fine. Worked her way through school.

What's a psi this sensitive doing in a mental hospital as one of the staff? It would be more likely for her to be a patient. He flipped through the rest of it—mortgage on the house almost paid off, Daddy's last medical checkup. The old man had a heart condition. Her health was clean—she went in for a physical every year. How cautious of her. Other than some slight problems with low blood pressure and hypoglycemia, she was extraordinarily healthy.

There were even some pages from her employee file. Delgado scanned them. She'd turned down a promotion twice, citing her need to be available to care for her aging father. Despite that, her reviews were marked "excellent" except for one, from a certain Wendy Yamakari, head nurse. Yamakari apparently had it in for Rowan.

That wasn't half as interesting as the comments section on the reviews.

Rowan has a real gift for working with patients.

Calming, soothing.

Just like magic.

A psionic nurse, working quietly away in a mental hospital, trying to help the patients.

So why had she bolted last night?

Chances were, she was completely untrained. How was she keeping herself together, especially under the onslaught her job must represent?

"Curiouser and curiouser," he muttered, looking at a grainy employee photo of her. She wasn't smiling, but she was still pretty, her eyes wide and obviously luminous, her hair pulled severely back. "Well, Miss Price. You're certainly an odd duck."

"Del? Someone's leaving." Zeke twisted around in the front seat. "The garage door's opening."

"Who?"

Zeke lifted the 'nocs, waited. "Looks like both of them."

"Okay. Let me out. You follow them. I'm going to recon the house." It was a sudden decision, one that he might regret later. "Don't let anything happen to her, Zeke."

"Course not." The van started with a swift purr.

"I mean it. Anything goes down, you keep her skin whole."

"I *got* it, Del. You coming or not?"

"No. I want to see where she sleeps." Delgado slid out of the van, his little bag of tricks already strapped on. Messenger bags coming into style had been good news for covert operations. "Good luck."

"And you." Zeke drove away, keeping under the speed limit, drifting after the ancient, silvery Volvo station wagon. Delgado waited a little while, scanning the street from the shelter of a convenient laurel hedge. Nothing out of tune, even to his senses. He called in, but Henderson's voice mail came on.

Something must be going down, he thought, listening to the passionless electronic voice recite the number. After the beep, he paused for a second. "This is Del," he said. "Instinct's taken over. Doing some recon. Zeke's got the subject. Call me if necessary." Then he switched the phone to "vibrate" and stuffed it in his front jacket pocket.

It was child's play to penetrate the back yard: neat garden-boxes and a well-maintained, slightly shabby lawn that would be shaded by old oak trees and a high juniper hedge in summer. The back door, as he'd guessed, only had one deadbolt, and a few moments with picks made the lock yield. The whole house was empty and open, no invisible defenses except for the natural "static" surrounding people's houses. How a psi could stand to live here was beyond him.

A pretty kitchen with deep-green countertops, matching towels, and dishes piled in the sink met his inspection. Delgado's fingers itched to touch, even through latex gloves. He overrode the urge; it was weakness. *Why did I come down on Zeke?* He looked down at the coffee cups in the sink. They were blue and gray pottery mugs, handmade, obviously well-loved. *He knows his job. I shouldn't have said that. I don't even know this woman.* There was a rack of herbs in terra cotta pots set in the bay window, and an airplane plant hung over the counter by the back door. The plants glowed with health.

The house was comfortable rather than chic, overstuffed chairs, potted plants, soothing colors, very few sharp edges or avant-garde touches. A painting of a woman with long brown hair and hazel eyes hung in the foyer, watching the door with a benevolent smile. She looked enough like Rowan that Delgado guessed she was a family member. A ficus stood next to the stairs in a brass pot, green and succulent.

He went up the stairs slowly, savoring the feel of the house. Normal. Safe. A haven.

What the hell are you doing? You're not going to get anything from this. She's a civilian.

He told that voice to take a long hike and it went quietly, with very little fuss. His conscience usually did.

At the top of the stairs—the banister had been carefully repaired, probably by dear old dad—a hall led to two bedrooms, a bathroom, and a small niche filled with bookshelves.

He tried the nearest room first. A military-neat bed with a plain headboard, shelves of books on military history and strategy shared space with New Age titles, psychic phenomena, and weird occurrences. Dad was a believer. There was an old-fashioned lamp with a green shade on his nightstand and a closet of neatly pressed suits, a duty uniform swathed in plastic, a Navy storage locker labeled *PRICE* held up four pairs of shoes. A pair of boots stood obediently on the closet floor next to the storage locker. The dresser held a mirror, an old ceramic washbasin, a Wandering Jew in a blue pot, and pictures in plain frames. Some of the pictures were of a smiling little blonde girl—Rowan. The other pictures were of the woman painted downstairs. Mom, then.

Delgado moved down the hall. The bathroom was spic-and-span, done in cream with touches of wine-red, the smell of soap still hanging in the air. The shower curtain was still wet. *She took a shower here,* he thought, examining the bar of soap. Bubble-gum toothpaste. Three different types of feminine shampoo—evidently she took her hair seriously. Dad apparently used Vitalis. There were some bath salts in the mirrored cabinet, but most of the space was taken up with medications for Dad's heart condition and the various ills of aging. The linen closet built into the wall held towels and sundries.

Now for what he'd been waiting for.

Delgado entered what should be her room.

Bingo.

Her exercise wear was thrown across the top of a plastic laundry basket that held crumpled nurse's scrubs. He took a deep lung full of the air here—this was where she slept. *Christ, I'm really getting attached, aren't I? That isn't good.* There was a breath of perfume, a female smell, his heart pounded against his ribs. He wondered what it would be like to hear her even breathing, to feel that pale hair brushing against his face.

A missionary bedstead of plain pine, its severe lines softened by a white down comforter and a white lace spread, lay rumpled and open. Her sheets were a sunny yellow, and the walls were painted the same color. Even in the dead of winter, the room would glow with sunlight. Four bookshelves, made of the same unvarnished pine, held books and African violets. A philodendron hung in the window, its leaves glowing green. There was also a large healthy mother-in-law's-tongue plant set in a yellow pot between the dresser and the window.

Delgado examined the books, his hands behind his back. Poetry. Lots of poetry. Medieval history. Medical textbooks, a DSM, a Tabor's, Gray's Anatomy, PDR, NDR, guides to prescription drugs, a Mosby's, several books on nursing and psychiatry. No fiction, no science fiction, nothing on paranormal phenomena, nothing on psychics, nothing on the occult.

That was *very* interesting.

There was a definite section on ancient Rome, and some biographies—Churchill, Catherine the Great, Anäis Nin—a small section of modern history, and a smattering of books on death and grieving.

Does she even know she's psi? She has to. There's no way she couldn't. So what is this? She's obviously well-educated.

Her dresser held the first clutter he had seen in the house, a jumble of perfumes, a hairbrush with strands of ash-blond hair attached, a few crystal necklaces, earrings tossed in a small ceramic dish. A small rosewood jewelry box held a strand of pearls, two diamond necklaces, two wedding rings—both antique, probably heirlooms—an East Santiago High School class ring, a pair of antique ruby earrings, her father's dog tags, and a few bits of rhinestone costume jewelry from the twenties. There were a few crumpled bits of paper, a Mason jar almost full of spare change, an old driver's license…and a clear glass paperweight, bubbles frozen forever. There was no mirror in her room, which he also found intriguing. The picture forming from her possessions was a very interesting one.

Her closet held several different pairs of scrubs, some dress shirts, slacks, a few business suits. No dresses, and no heels, either. Her shoes were serviceable nurse-shoes, sneakers, sandals, and one pair of engineer boots that had seen heavy use. Boxes in the back of her closet were labeled: *Estate, Bills, Taxes, Personal, Photos,* and *Diaries.*

He ached to open up the "Diaries" box or the one labeled "Personal," but he didn't have time. She could come back at any moment. Zeke might not be able to call and warn him. However, the "Diaries" box gave him a clue. A few moments of searching found a red Miquelruis notebook in the drawer of her nightstand. He stood, his feet placed carefully on either side of her fuzzy pink slippers dropped carelessly next to the bed, and opened the book, feeling a twinge of conscience that he hadn't felt in years. *I have to know,* he told himself. *I have to know so I can keep her safe.*

Her writing was firm and clear, beautiful just like the rest of her. He scanned through accounts of days spent on a psych ward, patients identified only by first initials, fellow nurses given titles like "Sourface" and "Sleepy," and wondered if Rowan had any idea how desperate she sounded.

—managed to calm him down, but not before Head Hatchet yelled at him to stop being such a baby, which just made it worse. The woman has no compassion, she could see he was suffering, she just wanted to get to lunch. I did, too, but I couldn't have eaten anything if I hadn't made sure he was okay. He just wants to feel like someone's listening, they all do. Why is that so hard for people to understand?

—guess I am going crazy. If I didn't know I was mostly sane and that it's a repetitious objective phenomenon I would sign myself in. But it seems to work, so I just keep waiting for the day everything comes crashing down. Making no sense. Don't have to make sense here, it's just my rambleramble.

—The thing I can't understand is, if Dad's right and these "feelings" are real, which they seem to be, why can't everyone have them? I just want to be normal. Please God, make me normal.

—DON'T THINK OF UNPLEASANT THINGS. This was written in capitals, underlined, taking up a whole page.

—Hilary tried to fix me up with another one of her "friends" tonight. Disaster. He looked like a snake and acted like one, too, swallowing his chicken cordon bleu whole and yapping about his ex-girlfriend the weightlifter—

Delgado's breast pocket vibrated, startling him. He closed the diary, placed it precisely back, and then closed the drawer. There were a few other items in there—tissues, a battered romance novel with a ripped cover, a small bottle of sleeping pills—that would bear further examination later if he had time.

"Delgado," he said into the phone.

"You want the bad news or the bad news?" Henderson said.

"Christ, you mean I've got a choice?"

"Sigma's in town. Looks like the telem leakage brought them."

"Fuck." Del's stomach flipped. He forced it down.

"Yeah. They're doing sweeps. Haven't found a goddamn thing yet, but it's a matter of time before they trace us to that house. And once they're in the neighborhood—"

"They'll find her." Delgado crossed to the window and looked out. Her window looked south onto the back yard, sunlight making a rectangle on the hardwood floor, filmy white drapes on either side. "Goddammit."

"How powerful is she, Del?"

"Too powerful to let Sigma get their claws in. You know what they do to the strong ones. But this one's fragile, General. Doesn't even know what she is. Thinks she might be crazy."

"How soon can you bring her in?"

"Depends on her. Don't want to spook her."

There was a long, crackling silence. Delgado had never said anything even remotely like this to the old man about a potential. "Are you personally involved with this one, Del?"

"I guess so," he answered. "I don't know why. Just instinct, maybe."

"Be careful. But if it comes down to it, bring her in kicking and screaming."

Relieved, Delgado let out a short breath. "You got it. What's the bad news?"

"I still haven't ironed out that bug yet," the General said heavily. "And Blake's team lost another operative."

"Fuck." That made the second in two months. Sigma was hunting them down like dogs.

"Yeah. Look, I've got to go put out a few fires. Can you spare Zeke? I need manpower."

"Sure. Just leave me some wheels. I'd hate to have to steal."

"You got it. Be careful."

"Absolutely." Delgado hung up.

It wouldn't be more than forty-eight hours at most before Sigma found her if they started scanning in sweeps out from the abandoned house. She was less than four blocks away—right in their critical zone. They would scoop her up, fill her full of Zed, and brainwipe her as soon as they realized she was an untrained psi. She'd spend the rest of her life with a Sigma handler, doing work for the black side of the government.

The thought called up an irrational flare of anger. *You don't even know this woman,* he cautioned himself. *You don't know anything yet. And really, Delgado, you've done everything but sniff her panties now. You're sick. Do your job and get the hell out of here.*

He wondered why she didn't have any pets while he bugged her bedroom and the kitchen, and he spent another few minutes locking the back door and setting up a few countermeasures that should at least keep her from random Sigma probes. If they were doing concentrated sweeps the counters wouldn't be very useful, but at least he'd know once Sigma came calling. Unless she did as she'd done last night and blew out the probes.

How am I going to make contact with her? She's well-insulated, if I read her right, not a lot of social contact outside her job and her father. And she's sensitive. I'll probably rub her raw. He retreated down the street, deep in thought, the used latex gloves stuffed back in his bag. *How the hell am I going to make contact without spooking her?*

His phone buzzed again. He ducked into an alley between two fences and flipped it open. "Delgado."

"Del?" It was Zeke. "Get your ass out here, man. We got problems."

It took less than a second for his brain to click into "work" mode. "Where?"

"Corner of…Maple and Seventeenth, Shop'N'Save parking lot. I've marked a Sig transport, Del."

Delgado took a deep breath. His heartbeat slowed, adrenaline copper on his tongue, iron training smashing down his body's instant reaction to the news. "Okay. Are they engaged, or surveilling?"

"Surveil, it looks like. Jesus Christ. Jesus *Christ.*"

"Relax, Zeke. There's a bike I can boost and be there in minutes. Just monitor them. If they go from surveil to engaging, or if you even *think* they might, call me again, okay?"

"You got it," was Zeke's reply. He still sounded pale. "I'll call you if they move."

"How long ago did Rowan go into the store?" He was

already scanning the empty street, planning his approach.

"Thirty-six minutes. Jesus. Jesus God, there's Sigs here."

"Relax, Zeke. They could just be hungry." Delgado hung up, and took out his wallet. It was time to do something just a little bit illegal.

Two minutes later, five hundred dollars were left in an envelope in a mailbox, and Delgado had stolen a motorcycle. The money would help whoever actually owned the bike—he hoped.

Seven

"I don't know," Rowan said, holding up two packages of brownie mix and eyeing them critically. "I guess so." Muzak drifted through the brightly lit aisles, a soupy rendition of *Stairway To Heaven.*

"Well, Marta—at the bridge club, you know—says he's a very nice boy. And he's asked Marta about you." Her father rested his trembling hands on the cart. His red suspenders matched his red socks, and his sports jacket with a hole on the collar was his traditional grocery-shopping outfit. "Get the ones with nuts, sweetie. You know how I like those."

"I'll add real nuts to the mix, Dad," she replied absently, putting a box back, taking two of the other brand and dropping them into the basket. She tucked a strand of hair behind her ear. "I'm not going on another blind date."

"It's not a blind date if you've already dated him. Are those the ones with nuts?"

"I'll *add* nuts, Dad. I've got a whole bag of walnuts at home. Look, the man's an ass. He spent our entire last date talking about his job." *And how big his dick is. Always thinking about teenage girls. The guy was an oily jerk. I don't care if he is Marta's nephew, I'm never going near him again. Makes my skin crawl.* She shivered, pushing away the memory.

"Well, you make men a little nervous, princess. You're a very beautiful girl."

"Yeah, Dad. That's why they're beating down my door, right?" *Stop it,* she told herself, pretending not to see when her father snuck another box of brownie mix into the cart. *Don't be mean to him. It's not his fault you're too picky, Rowan.* "We need milk and tortilla chips and some bottled water, and some frozen vegetables."

"You should have made a list." he said, a mischievous smile crinkling his face. His eyes sparkled.

"I did make a list," Rowan replied, tapping her temple. "It's up here. Come on, slowpoke." The conversation was so familiar she barely had to pay attention.

Which was a good thing, because she was severely distracted. It wasn't often that she wandered while driving, or had trouble choosing *brownie mix*, for God's sake. But her former good mood had fled, and her head seemed stuffed with cotton. She was also shivering, even though the supermarket wasn't cold, and her father, who felt chills far more than she did, was comfortable enough in his sport jacket. Goose flesh ran in waves down her back.

They managed to get through the rest of the store without mishap, and Rowan paid with her debit card. Between her job and her dad's Social Security and pension, they were both supported and could even save a little, which meant that maybe they *could* afford a new car. Tuna was an old trooper, but Rowan was getting tired of the frequent breakdowns. A hundred and sixty thousand miles was a good enough lifespan for a car, anyway, but Tuna had been her mom's car.

The thought of her mother sent a spear through Rowan's heart. Outwardly, she was holding her father's elbow as a pimpled young clerk pushed their cart out to the car for them. She made small talk, kissing her father's cheek and patting his arm after she unlocked his door. Inside, she was thinking of how her mom had just fallen over, tumbled to the ground between one word and the next, dead of a massive stroke. It had been painless, Rowan supposed. But still, the thought of her mother made Rowan's chest ache and her eyes fill with tears.

Why didn't I know, if I know all these other useless things? The thought still tortured her. If she could help her patients, why hadn't she been able to help her mother?

She helped the clerk load the paper bags into the trunk and thanked him, and tried to ignore the feverish worry cascading out of the boy.

Fucking Dee stiffed me for a dime, got to get the money, how'm I gonna get the money—The blast of thought caught her off-guard, and she leaned against Tuna's battered silver side for a moment, taking a deep breath. Dad slammed his door and locked it, so she had to hurry. It was cold and she wanted the—

"Come with me, miss," a man said, his hand closing around her elbow. Her head began to pound, horrible twisting needles pushing through her temples.

She was so stunned by the pain that he had dragged her a whole three steps away from the car before she started to struggle.

Eight

Christ, Delgado thought, *they must really be desperate to try that.*

He had ditched the bike in a convenient street side space and entered the supermarket parking lot on foot, his cheeks and eyes stinging from riding without a helmet. His hair was probably a mess. None of that mattered. The only thing that mattered was that a tall, balding Sig had grabbed Rowan Price's arm and was dragging her toward a low black van with two antennae, the standard-issue Sigma workhorse vehicle. This was messy, even for them.

How many of them in there? he thought, before his brain started clicking over alternatives.

The most efficient alternative—putting a bullet in the Sig's head—was immediately discarded. Too noisy, too messy, and above all, it would frighten her. Escalating this to a firefight would possibly involve the civilian authorities, something neither the Sig nor Delgado wanted. Waiting and watching to mark where the Sigs took her would give him valuable information, but it wasn't an option. The thought of her being bundled into that van was suddenly unbearable. That left calling down the civilian authorities—already a no-no—and injecting himself into the situation as a wildcard, which was what he was planning to do.

His cell phone buzzed. Delgado ignored it.

"Let *go* of me!" Rowan's voice was clearly audible, and clearly panicked. The parking lot was oddly clear, just a scattering of parked cars. Of course, it was late on a weekday morning, and not many people did their shopping in this time frame, which was probably why she'd chosen to come now. She could get through the store quickly and not tire out dear old dad. "Hey! Stop it! Leg*go*—"

Blond hair tumbled around her face. She wore jeans, a camel coat, and a white dress shirt. Delgado's stride lengthened into a run. He marked one Sig, but the van was running, so there had to be at least one more. Unless the Sig was planning on getting her into the van, downing her, and then driving away.

Just one dragging her. Could he be alone? What do you think, God, am I lucky today? It's against regs for a Sig to go out alone.

The buzzing in his breast pocket stopped. *Good,* he thought, clinically, before the switch flipped inside his head and he started operating purely on cold, trained reflex.

He reached them just as Rowan inhaled to scream and her father opened up the passenger door of the old battered Volvo. The Sig hadn't gotten her more than ten steps away from her car and had his other hand in his pocket, probably searching for a hypo. The black van was parked across the aisle, lights off but engine running. Was someone else in there? He needed to know, but he had no way to check quickly. He could *scan,* but that would take too much time and distract him.

"Hey," Rowan yelled. *"Help! Help!"*

Hang in there, angel, Delgado thought. *Help's on the way.* "Hey!" he shouted, his voice cracking through the chill air. "Hey, what're you doing? *Hey!"*

The Sig—balding, gray-black trench coat, big, bulbous blue eyes and red cheeks—literally jumped, as if someone had smacked him. The guilty start gave Rowan the chance to thrash her arm out of his grasp. She stumbled back and Delgado, without thinking about it, caught her arm as he drew level with them. One quick movement and the Sig stumbled, his knee giving under the force of Delgado's kick. Rowan, staring up at Delgado, gasped.

This close, she wasn't just pretty.

She was stunning.

Her eyes, clear green, had a darker ring around the iris. Her pupils, dilated with fear, made them seem unnaturally dark. There were high fever-spot blotches of color on her flawless cheeks, and her pale hair tangled over her forehead, catching the winter sunlight and throwing it back with a vengeance.

Delgado didn't have time to look. He pulled her away from the Sig, who was limping back for the van. "Are you okay?" he asked pitching his voice with just the right note of worry. *I'm a concerned citizen. I just saw a guy trying to drag a woman off. I'm just a normal guy doing a good deed.* "Hey, what was that? What's going on? Are you all right?" His other hand curled around the Glock in its hidden holster. If the Sigs made any trouble he would have to escalate the situation. His weight shifted, ready to shove her down into cover if necessary.

The Sig made it to the van, bundled in, and the engine roared. Delgado pulled her back as the van screeched by, almost tearing off a few bumpers. He noted the plate number out of habit, though it wouldn't help. He watched as the van leaned around the corner and rocketed out into the street, cutting off a cab and a maroon minivan. *Jesus Christ, I'm lucky. They could have taken both of*

us. Good thing they don't know who I am. He looked down at her.
She only reached his collarbone and was staring after the
black van. Her face was printed with a priceless mixture of shock,
anger, and dazed incomprehension. "Are you all right?" he
repeated, hearing the genuine concern in his voice. *Oh, shit,* he
thought, *I'm actually emotionally involved with this. Christ, what's
happening to me?*

His pulse pounded, and his breath came in short gasps. He
felt like he'd just run a marathon. It wasn't combat—he was in
good shape. It was *her.* The thought of her dragged into that van
and pumped full of sedation to keep her quiet until they could get
her to an installation and start to break her made his heart feel
like it was trying to break out through his ribs and do a cancan.

"I—I think so," she answered, in a stunned, breathless voice.
"What the *hell—*"

"Rowan? *Rowan!*" Her father shuffled up. Delgado dropped
her arm, scanning the parking lot. The blue van sat on the other
end, silent and apparently deserted. Good. Zeke knew better than
to interfere.

What a golden fucking opportunity, he thought. *Play it careful,
Delgado. Please. Play it very fucking careful here.* "That was
weird," he said. "That guy was trying to drag you off or something.
Are you okay?"

"My arm," she said, rubbing where the Sig had grabbed her.
"He really had a grip on me. God. I…I…"

"Who the hell are you?" Major Price barked at Delgado, who
stepped back, raising his hands in a classic *Hey man, I'm harmless*
stance.

It was too risky. *Forgive me,* he thought, and used just a little
push.

Major Price took a step back, his eyes blinking. That small of
a *push* wouldn't cause much pain—just a slight headache, nothing
severe. Dear old dad was vulnerable to psychic assault, it seemed.
The intelligent normals usually were.

Great.

"I saw him dragging her," Delgado answered smoothly, deftly
snapping free from the *push.* Dad was on his side now. "She didn't
look like it was consensual, so I—"

"Dad," Rowan interrupted, "he probably saved my life." And
then her eyes were on him, looking straight through him, and
every hair on Delgado's body threatened to stand straight up.
"Thanks."

"No problem," he managed. His entire body felt as if it was dipped in electricity. Had she felt him *pushing* her father? No. Delgado was experienced enough to avoid that. *Jesus, what's she doing?*

"What were they doing?" her father asked. "What happened?" "Some guy told me to come with him," she said. "I think he bruised my arm. He was dragging me toward a van." Rowan laughed, a breathless, brittle sound. "And this man came out and scared him off."

Major Price regarded Delgado for a long moment. *He's not psychic, barely on the scale. Where did she get it from?* he wondered, and let his eyes shift over to Rowan, as if helpless. It was only half an act. Being this close to her was like standing in the path of a lightning bolt. His fingers itched to touch her cheek, he wanted to curl his hands into fists to stop the persistent aching itch. He had never in his life wanted to touch a woman this badly.

Finally, the old man extended his hand, the *push* reverberating inside Delgado's skull. If he'd used any more power, the old man might have had a real headache instead of just a sick, faint feeling and a slight twinge around his temples. "Thank you, Mr.—"

"Delgado," Delgado said, quietly. No reason not to give his name. He was going to recruit Rowan anyway.

Rowan stared at him, her eyebrows drawing together. *Do I sound familiar? No, I don't. And she didn't see me last night. It was too dark.* "You look familiar," she said. "Have I met you before?"

"I don't think so. I'd certainly remember that," he answered, shaking her father's hand. *If she touches me, it'll spook her. Got to avoid that.*

"Price," the old man said. His eyes were very sharp, a lighter green than Rowan's, but piercing. His grip was firm, professional, no-nonsense. "Henry Price. This is my daughter Rowan."

Delgado nodded. "You look cold," he said to her. She was still staring at him, her mouth tilting down at the corners. "Both of you. You'll catch cold out here." He gently extricated himself from Price's handshake. It wouldn't do to break Daddy's wrist.

"The police—" Rowan began.

"I don't know if they can do anything," Delgado said. "Did you get the license plate?" *I doubt you did, angel. You were too busy screaming.*

"I—" She was *staring* at him. "No, I didn't," she finished abruptly. "But—"

Delgado nodded. Wondered what her skin would feel like. "Well, glad to help. Look, I'm in a hurry, I've got to go."

"But the *police*," Rowan protested, just like a good little Girl Scout.

"No police," the old man said suddenly, giving her a warning look. Delgado almost sighed, relieved. The *push* had worked. "Thank you, sir. Rowan, give the nice man our phone number. What can we do to thank you, Mr. Delgado?"

"Okay, Dad," she said, obediently, finally looking down to dig in her brown canvas purse. She was obviously stunned.

"Well…" Delgado weighed the situation, found it precarious. "I'd like to take Miss Price out to dinner." He managed a light tone. "This hardly seems like a good way to introduce myself, though."

"We're having dinner tonight," the old man said. "Can we invite you over to thank you for saving Rowan's life?"

"Dad," Rowan protested weakly. Was she *blushing?* Delgado forced himself not to look. *Can it really be that easy? What did I do to deserve this kind of luck?*

"Give him our address too, Rowan. Dinner's at seven tonight. Can we invite you, Mr. Delgado?"

"I'll reshuffle my schedule," he answered. "I'd love to. I'm just glad I was here to help. That guy looked like he meant business." *You have no idea how close you were to losing your daughter, Major. No idea. And I'm the luckiest sonuvabitch on Earth. This was a godsend. Jesus God, I wish I could touch her— her arm, maybe, or just her hand.*

Rowan handed him a slip of paper with her familiar clear, firm writing on it. "Can we at least exchange numbers?" she asked shyly, shaking her long hair back. "I just feel so—I'm sorry. It's not every day I get grabbed in a parking lot."

"If I give you my number, will you promise to call?" He was already digging in his own messenger bag for a piece of paper and a pen. Metal shifted inside the bag. *What would she do if I pulled out a grenade or a scanner? I can't believe I'm trying to flirt with her. This is so fucking wrong.*

"Dad." She appealed to the Major, but his eyes were twinkling. He looked proud.

"Take the man's number, Rowan." He folded his arms, and Rowan sighed. The sigh made her mouth turn down and turned her into a pensively pretty woman.

Delgado wrote his cell phone number down on a handy slip

of blank white paper, using the pen that had a tiny digital camera concealed in the shaft. "Call me if you need anything," he said. "Anything at all. I'm sorry it had to be this way, but I'm glad to meet you, Miss Price."

She nodded, accepting the paper and rubbing at her arm as if it ached. *Did he bruise her? This was sloppy, even for a Sigma,* he thought, vaguely uneasy. He scanned the parking lot—nothing but Zeke in the blue van. Zeke would be jamming signals, taping, and erasing the store's security footage, if it was possible. If it wasn't, Del would go in and take care of it. Later.

"Likewise," she said, with a polite smile. "Thank you." Now she looked directly into his eyes, and his entire body tingled again. *What the hell is going on? I just gave a civilian a private Society drop-number. Jesus Christ, what am I DOING?* "I think you might have saved my life. Who knows what that guy wanted?"

Delgado found himself nodding. "I'm glad I was here to help," he repeated, and watched as she took her father's arm.

"Come on, Dad," she said. "Let's get you into the car before you freeze to death. Nice to meet you, Justin."

Delgado froze. *I didn't tell her. I couldn't have told her. Oh, my God.*

Neither of them noticed. He took a deep breath. *Goddamn,* he thought. *Goddamn, she's dangerous.* "Nice to meet you too, Rowan," he said, and watched her help her father into the car. He watched until she was safely in the silver station wagon and had backed out. She waved through her window before she pulled away.

As soon as she was out of sight, he crossed the parking lot and clambered into the blue van. "What the hell—" Zeke started.

"I've got an invitation to dinner at the Price residence tonight," Delgado answered shortly. "Get Henderson on the wire, Zeke. Sigma just tried to grab our girl. And since I just blew my cover, they're going to be back in droves soon. We need a workable plan, and I need some strategy help." He looked out the front window at the parking lot, still eerily calm. "And we've got another problem, too. I think I really like her."

Nine

Rowan's hands shook. She pulled into the garage, almost clipping the mirror off the driver's side. Sudden darkness filled the car, startling after the winter sunlight outside. "I'm glad we got the shopping done," she said unsteadily. It was the first either of them had spoken.

"Rowan?" Her father sounded worried. "Sweetheart, are you okay?"

"I'm not okay, Dad. I just got attacked in the parking lot, and I can't even go to the police because I didn't get the license number and someone might find out what kind of a freak I am and—"

Her father reached over and laid his fingers on her wrist. Rowan shut her eyes. His familiar mental aura wrapped around her like a cloud of after-shave and boot polish, an astringent smell she remembered from childhood. Her head hurt; she drowned in the wash of her father's worry and attention.

"I didn't say not to call the police because of *you*, Rowan." Her father sighed. "Sweetheart, you're shaking."

"I can't believe you invited him over for dinner," she mumbled, taking a deep breath. Of course her father didn't think she was a freak. He was supportive of and enchanted by her freakish talents. She'd always been his little princess.

But he wasn't acting like himself. And that man—Delgado...

"Well, he's military," he said, as if that explained everything.

That wasn't like her practical, suspicious Daddy.

"How do you know?" She finally opened her eyes and looked at him. "And why should that matter? We should have called the police. If that man tries to kidnap someone else—"

"They won't come back to the Shop'N'Save," her father replied, with maddening illogic. "And we military brats can always tell each other. He was almost in parade rest, Ro."

I think I'm going to throw up, she thought, distantly. *I'm in shock.* "I don't feel so good, Dad," she said. "I think I want to go lie down. Let's get the groceries inside."

"I invited him to dinner because he stopped that man from dragging you off," he said. "I couldn't get there in time. I'm an old man, princess, and I couldn't help you. *He* could—and did. He looks like a very nice man."

"Fine," she said. "I'm sorry, Dad. I just want to lie down. My arm hurts and I think I'm going to throw up."

"I'll get the groceries inside," he said promptly. Rowan cut the engine and pressed a button on the garage-door opener. Darkness fell inch by inch, until the glow of the garage lamp was the only light.

"No," she said, "But you can help. Then I think I'll go lie down."

He was silent as she carried the groceries in and helped her put everything away. He was also quiet when she finished folding the paper bags and stacked them in the pantry. He said nothing when she climbed the stairs and flung herself facedown on her bed, dropping her coat on the floor.

Dry-eyed, she hugged a pillow and started to shake. Her arm ached—the kidnapper's fingers had been like iron claws. But that wasn't quite why she was shaking now. She was shaking because she couldn't get the mental image to go away.

He was tall, taller than her, and had stubborn dark hair cut like her father's, military-short. His eyes were hazel, and very flat, under charcoal lashes. He had a nice face, even cheekbones and a firm mouth—and her heart hammered even now to think of the electric jolt that had gone through her at his nearness.

His voice sounded familiar, and she didn't know why. He didn't *look* familiar.

She couldn't even remember what he'd been wearing, beyond a dark coat and a messenger-style bag. He looked like a student, maybe, or one of the young IT professionals who wore casual-classy to work.

She'd been stunned, hadn't even realized what was happening. Not until the van had screeched away and the man—Delgado—had looked down at her, dropping her arm as if it burned him. *Are you okay?* Her heart had threatened to burst out through her ribs. Electricity had smashed through her veins. Her entire body had started to sing.

And Dad had made her give him their phone number. *He might call. He might even come for dinner. Oh, my God. Oh, my God. I never...NEVER...act this way. I almost got kidnapped. God, I almost got kidnapped. Why? Why me?*

It took a long time, but she was finally able to produce a few tears. The crying brought no relief, only made her feel even more terrified and foolish. *What was he going to do to me? I could have gotten raped and killed. I would have never seen Dad again, or Hilary, or any of my patients. Never gone running again, never done anything again. Thank God that man was there. Thank God.*

She lay there, staring at the sunlight slanting through her bedroom window. *I could have died,* she thought, over and over again. *I could have died. Could have died. Could have died.*

The most disturbing thing wasn't that someone had tried to kidnap her. The most disturbing thing was that Rowan hadn't *sensed* him. He'd been almost invisible to her, no betraying blast of thought, no wash of emotion, just a blank wall, only Rowan's nausea and headache alerting her that something bad was about to happen. Delgado. She'd felt him, something electric, not a feeling she'd ever had before, but it could have been his adrenaline. The kidnapper had been completely "silent" to her freakish senses.

Rowan lost track of how long she laid there, falling into a kind of trance. Oddly enough, she felt…well, almost safe here in her bedroom, lying on her bed. Nothing could possibly happen to her here.

Yeah, right.

She lay curled on the bed, watching dust dance through the bar of sunlight from her window, her head revolving miserably, her stomach revolving just as quickly. *I must be finally going crazy,* she thought. *I didn't hear him at all. I didn't hear a single thing. He might as well have been invisible. Is he like me? Did I almost get kidnapped by some freak like me? Is that what I have to look forward to?*

Yet she'd felt her rescuer. All the way down to her bones.

Rowan groaned, buried her face in the pillow and took long, deep breaths until she fell into an uneasy, twilit sleep.

***

"Ro?" Familiar voice. Someone shaking her shoulder. Smell of fresh-baked bread. "Ro?"

Rowan struggled up to consciousness. Hilary sat on the bed, stroking her shoulder, occasionally jiggling her a bit. Hilary's soft hip pressed into Rowan's side. "Wake up, sleepyhead. It's time for dinner."

"Mmmargh," Rowan managed. "Jeez. I fell asleep."

"Obviously. Your dad called me. He said you almost got snatched in the Shop'N'Save parking lot. You okay?"

Trust Hilary to go straight to the point.

Hilary's short black bob swung as she moved, standing so Rowan could sit up. Hil put her hands on her hips and glared down through the dimness—the short winter twilight had fallen, and Rowan's room was now dark. Hil's eyes glittered, gold hoops swung against her pale cheeks. "Well?" she demanded, impatiently. She was six months younger than Rowan, but somehow always managed to look like the older sister.

"I'm fine," Rowan said, yawning and rubbing at her eyes. "Just a bit shaken up. Some guy tried to grab me and stuff me in a van. Another guy frightened him off. It was really scary."

"Why didn't you call the cops? Or store security?" Hilary's heels tapped against the floorboards as she stalked up to Rowan's nightstand and turned on the light with one efficient click. Rowan yawned again, blinking in the sudden light.

Hil's black eyes snapped with furious fire. "Rowan? Do you *hear* me?"

"Dad said no cops. We didn't get the license number of the van." Rowan stretched. She pushed up the sleeve of her white dress shirt and examined her arm.

Four fat bands of bruising, the mark of his thumb too, ground deep into her upper arm. The bruises were red-purple, just beginning to get some good color.

"Jesus Christ," Hil breathed. "The guy that grabbed you did that?"

Rowan nodded. "He meant business. It was like something out of a movie, Hil. I could have ended up dead."

"This is serious," Hilary stated. "My God, you need to call the police."

Rowan shrugged. She couldn't tell Hilary why she wouldn't call the cops—they might find out what she was. She'd avoided trouble all her life, flown under the radar, and wasn't about to break cover now. "I doubt they'll be able to help."

"But what if this guy snatches someone else?" Hilary persisted. "You could have valuable information."

"I didn't see *anything*, Hil. One minute I was getting in the car, the next minute he had me halfway across the parking lot. It happened so *fast*. If that other guy hadn't come along..." Rowan shivered.

Hil must have just come from work. Her gray wool skirt hit just above the knee, and her jacket was unbuttoned. Her usually sleek hair was mussed as if she'd run her fingers back through it once too often. "I guess so," she said darkly, "but what if the guy that rescued you was in on it?"

"Oh, not another conspiracy," Rowan moaned. "For God's sake, Hilary, talk about something else! What happened at work today?"

"Oh, two murders and an ongoing arson investigation. Hot copy all the way around," Hilary chirped, throwing herself down on the bed again, narrowly missing Rowan's feet. She kicked her heels off and stretched her feet, sighing a little. It was a familiar gesture, they'd spent half their teenage years sitting on each other's beds, gossiping and giggling. "I came over as soon as your dad called me. I was really worried about you."

"I'm fine. I just won't go to the Shop'N'Save alone anytime soon." Rowan combed her fingers back through her hair, wincing as she found tangles. Her mouth tasted like foul copper—all that adrenaline, sleeping during the day, and bile. Her stomach flipped and settled again. "Really, I'm okay."

"I don't think so." Hil's square-jawed face was too striking to be called pretty. The shadow of crimson lipstick still hung on her full lips, and her tastefully-arched eyebrows raised a little as she examined Rowan's face. "You've got that pale starey look. You been hearing things again?"

"I'm not crazy, Hil." Rowan slid her feet off the bed. Making it to her feet, she decided she wasn't going to fall over. She made it across the room and started digging for a pair of sweatpants and a T-shirt. The only thing worse than sleeping in jeans was *running* in jeans.

"I never said you were. You might want to comb your hair," Hil said laconically. "You've got a guest, you know."

Rowan froze.

"Nice-looking guy. I don't go for the clean-cut ones, but he's very polite. Showed up at seven sharp with a handful of flowers and a bottle of very unpretentious domestic wine. He's even now making small talk in the kitchen with Henry." It sounded like she was restraining laughter only by sheer force of will. "Trust you to meet a hero in a parking lot, sweets."

Rowan cursed. Not very inventively, but it got the job done. She rested her forehead against her top dresser drawer, leaning over and taking deep breaths all the way down to her stomach. "Christ," she whispered. "Why now? And what happened to being suspicious?"

"Oh, for God's sake, you haven't had a date in aeons. Loosen up a little, will ya?" Hilary swung her legs easily, holding her arms up and admiring her red-lacquered fingernails.

"You just finished reminding me that I was attacked in a parking lot, asked me if this guy was perhaps a part of it, and now you want me to loosen up?"

"Well," Hilary remarked practically, "you said you were feeling fine." When Rowan glared at her, she said, "There, there's the Ro I remember. Welcome back, sweetie. You were looking kind of dazed there for a minute."

"I wonder why." Rowan rescued another pair of jeans and a black sweater from the dresser's depths. "I'm being interrogated by the Herald's star crime reporter."

"You're not going to wear *that*, are you?"

"Yes, I am."

"At least comb your hair."

"Shut up."

"A little bit of lip gloss wouldn't hurt either."

"Hilary, I'm *warning* you—"

Hilary bounced up to her feet. Rowan was in the process of struggling into the sweater, her back turned to the bed, but she heard the bedsprings creak. "You really scared me, Ro. Henry sounded dire. I'm glad you're okay."

"Me too." Rowan finished pulling the sweater down and turned, freeing her hair from the collar with a few practiced yanks. Hilary stood, her hands on her hips, and shook her head.

"I don't know what I'm going to do with you," she said mournfully. "There's a hunk downstairs, and you won't even put on any lip gloss."

"I'm not on the market. Why are you and Dad so determined to marry me off?"

"Oh, so we can shack up as secret lovers," Hilary said breezily, as Rowan slid into clean jeans and tossed her old ones in the laundry basket. "You know he's the only man I've ever really loved. Tragic, isn't it."

As usual, Hil only sounded halfway teasing. "Soap-opera tragic." Rowan gave her hair a few swipes with the brush before grabbing a scrunchie and tossing the whole damn mess into a ponytail. "I'll pay you five bucks to get rid of this guy," she added.

"And miss all the fun and your inevitable discomfort? No

way. You're stuck with this one, honey. Now, come on, before your dad gets out the shotgun and scares him off." But Hil's eyes were a little too bright. The crackling acerbic wash of worry spread out from her in waves. Rowan stopped and held out her arms.

The two of them stood, hugging each other, for a long time. "I was really worried about you, kiddo," Hilary said finally, her voice suspiciously thick.

Rowan's throat was tight. "Thanks. I'm fine, but...thanks."

"Don't you dare leave me, Ro."

"I won't." Rowan took a deep breath. Her stomach settled and her head cleared. "I promise."

"Good," Hilary sniffed, untangling herself firmly and decisively. She stepped back and ran a critical eye down Rowan's outfit, wiping at the tear-tracks on her pale cheeks. "Now do something with your hair, for the love of God, and hurry up. I'll delay him as long as I can."

That made Rowan laugh. "Not interested. Why don't you see if you can find out what branch of the military he served in?"

"Absolutely," Hil said over her shoulder as she exited. "Don't take too long, Rowan. I'm hungry, and supper's almost ready."

Ten

Things were going well.

The Major was deep in a rendition of Dieppe, German troop movements and casualties, while Delgado nodded and made small remarks. It was standard interrogation technique, listening, making the subject feel important. Most people loved to talk, either about themselves or about their obsessions.

The other woman—Hilary Baum, a reporter and Rowan's friend—had gone upstairs to wake Rowan up after fixing Delgado with a piercing, dark gaze. Delgado, aware he was being measured, suffered it. He'd expected that Rowan would retreat after the morning's events. He'd even expected the Major's war stories and casual measuring questions—where had Delgado served, what branch of the military, commanding officers, what type of discharge?

He answered carefully, sticking to the truths that wouldn't raise any more questions. The Major didn't need to know he'd been tipped straight into Sigma because of his scores. They exchanged stories about basic training, and the Major finally gave him a bottle of beer and settled into a lecture on military history.

Hilary came back, barefoot, her smooth dark hair shining as she pulled out a chair at the kitchen table and helped herself to a cracker from the platter the Major had set out. "She'll be down in a sec. I made her comb her hair."

"Miracles do happen," the Major said with a sly glance at Delgado.

Christ, he thought. *He thinks I'm eligible. So does this other woman, apparently. I'm passing their tests, but when she comes downstairs, how am I going to handle it?* He took a sip of beer. "I suppose she was pretty upset," he offered.

Hilary actually giggled. She was a very pretty woman, a smooth façade of professionalism over a type of boiling sensuality he would have found pleasant if he hadn't been waiting for…what? What was he waiting for, exactly? "She seems to have recovered. So, why didn't anyone call the police? That guy could be abducting someone else by now."

Delgado almost choked on his beer. *She's smart,* he thought, and set the bottle down. "Well," he said, "I didn't get the license plate number, so I didn't have anything useful to tell them. "

Not that I'd go anywhere near a police station, he thought, and his eyes met the Major's.

The older man was studying him closely. "Well," he said, "we didn't get a license plate number, and we didn't really see anything important. I'm just glad Rowan's okay." There was some other message in the man's green eyes, but Delgado couldn't decipher it. Maybe it was the residue of the *push*, making the Major feel chummy with him.

"That's the truth," Hilary said, taking another cracker. "If anything happened to Rowan, I'd be *really* upset." She gave him a meaningful glance, then bounced up to her feet, crossing to the fridge. "Do you have any white wine, Henry?"

"Bottom shelf," the Major replied. He was still trying to signal something to Delgado, who didn't have a clue. His cell phone buzzed in his breast pocket.

He extracted it and glanced at the number.

Shit. "Excuse me a second," he said, rising smoothly from the chair. "I have to take this."

"No problem," the Major said politely, still trying to telegraph something with wiggling eyebrows. *What the hell is going on now?*

He walked into the living room and flipped the phone open. "Delgado," he said cautiously.

"Move it up, Del," Henderson said. The old man sounded exhausted. "They found the haunted house. Cath and Zeke barely made it out. They're doing sweeps. What are you doing in there?"

"Haven't made secondary contact yet," Delgado said quietly. "How much time do I have?"

A short pause, sound of fingers on a keyboard. That would be Yoshi. Then Henderson's tone changed. "None. They're moving in. Christ, Delgado, get out of there."

Not without her, he thought. "We'll see," he said.

"Don't go funky on me, Del. I need you. Get the fuck *out* of there."

"Not without my subject."

"Del—"

His entire skin tightened with electricity. *There she is. She's coming downstairs. How can I sense her today, when I couldn't last night?* "Got to go," he said. "I'll call you back."

Then he hung up on the old man. *Sorry about that, General,* he thought. *But no Sig's going to get his filthy hands on her again.* He turned the phone off and looked down at the sleek black plastic. *How the hell am I going to do this?*

"Hi," Rowan said. "Dad said you were in here...oh." She saw the cell phone in his hand. "I'm sorry, I—"

"No, I'm done," he said, slipping it back into his pocket. "How are you feeling?"

She looked...well, unearthly. The circles under her eyes were still there, but her eyes were clear and unshadowed now. Her pale hair, pulled back into a ponytail, begged to be touched. The flush of sleep was still on her cheeks, and she wore a black V-neck sweater that only served to make her skin look even more translucent, her collarbones more fragile. Jeans and pretty bare feet completed the picture, and Delgado almost forgot the Sigma net closing around them. His entire body felt dipped in electric sugar, his nerves resounding with her nearness. *What is wrong with me? I just went against orders and hung up on Henderson. And what am I going to do? How am I going to get her out of here and to a clean house?*

She yawned. "Good," she said. "I wanted to say thanks, you know. For...for saving my life. I didn't realize until later that...well, anything could have happened." Evidently nervous, she shifted from foot to foot, her cheeks even more flushed. *Why? Am I having some sort of effect on her? I hope so.*

He realized he was staring into her eyes, fascinated. "Anytime," he said. "I'm just glad I was there." *God, am I ever glad I was there. If they'd taken you—*

"Are you..." She trailed off, glanced around the room, nervously. "I mean, my dad said...He didn't call the police. He said you were military."

Several things about Henry's signaling fell into place. *Damn. He's more observant than I thought, or I bled through with the push.* Delgado realized he was moving forward, his hands buzzing and tingling with the need to touch her. He stopped himself just in time, six feet away from her. "Oh," he said. "I had no idea he noticed." Then he could have slapped himself, because something crossed her face.

"You seem really familiar. Are you sure I haven't—" She trailed off again, comprehension flooding her face.

Oh, no. His hands actually physically hurt, itching and throbbing.

"You were at the Taylor house last night," she said, and her cheeks drained of all color. "Why are you following me?"

He was about to start talking when two things happened at once. The first thing was a crash and tinkle of broken glass as the teargas canisters were lobbed through the front window. The second event was the sudden death of the lights.

Damn Sigs, coming in under dampers. He was already moving. "Don't breathe," he yelled. "Gas! *Hold your breath!*" He had her by the waist, swinging her around, his body between hers and the window in case they fired. *They won't. They want her alive. How am I going to do this with three civilians? Goddammit, I should have just snatched her myself.*

Then he was scrambling, half-dragging her, as she screamed breathlessly. The hallway was utterly dark. He lifted her off her feet and dragged her toward the kitchen. His lungs burned. *Clear air there, take a breath, hold it.*

Two coughing sounds. *Shots fired. Goddammit.* Delgado's pupils expanded to catch any stray gleam of light. Gas drifted through the air, sucking back through the broken window. The back door was open. Cold air kissed his skin. He clamped his hand over Rowan's mouth. "Stay *quiet*," he hissed in her ear. "I'll take care of you, Rowan, just *stay quiet.* Please."

She didn't respond. If she started to choke on the gas, he would have that to worry about as well.

The kitchen was a shambles. Delgado met the first Sig with a strike to the throat, the man folded down, his larynx crushed. The other man shot again, missed both times. By that time, Delgado cleared leather and popped him twice. The Sig crashed to the floor. Del was dimly aware of the crash as the front door gave. *If it's a standard Sig team they're waiting for the points to get her out the front door. They must have identified the dad and the other woman through the window. If it wasn't for Henderson calling me we might already be caught. They think Rowan's upstairs. That'll give me a few seconds to get her out of here.*

He looked for Rowan. She had scrambled forward on her knees and was by the butcher-block table, holding her father's limp body. "*No!*" She probably thought she was screaming, but the only thing coming out was a choked whisper.

Delgado leaned down. His hand closed around her arm. "Move," he barked. "Come on, Rowan! You can't help them now."

The woman—Hilary—lay crumpled on the floor, her sleek dark head a mess of hamburger. The Major had taken one in the chest and lay unmoving in Rowan's arms. She shook him, frantically, still making that choked mewling noise that tore at Delgado's heart. "Come *on*!" he said. "They'll be coming down the stairs and sweeping the house next. Come on, Rowan!"

She looked up at him, her eyes red and brimming with tears. "What's *happening*?"

He hauled her up, trying to be gentle, and remembered she had bare feet. *Can't afford to holster the gun, might have to drop another Sig if they have units waiting on the side.* He bent and hefted her over his shoulder. "Sorry, Rowan," he said, and his boots crunched over broken glass. "Goddamn."

There was a shuddering impact, probably against a bedroom door upstairs, that shook the whole house. No time to calm her down. No time to do *anything* but get her out. Cold hit his skin in a wave, and his entire body felt full of electric prickles. Danger—and *her*. She wasn't screaming, but she was struggling ineffectually, beating at his back and trying to twist free.

"I'm sorry, Rowan," he said again, and moved faster.

Eleven

Everything was going too fast for Rowan. He opened the car door and dumped her onto the seat, almost bashing her head against the edge of the doorway.

"Move over," he said, and she blindly scrambled for the passenger side. The car was black, a two-door model. She made it to the other side and started frantically scrabbling at the door lock. It wouldn't budge.

At that moment, all the fight went out of Rowan, like water going down a drain. She actually felt her will to resist slip away. Her hand dropped down, and she pulled her knees up on the seat and hugged them, making herself as small as possible. Tears slid hotly down her cheeks. There was a limit to what she could do, and what exactly did this man want? It was a nightmare, only a nightmare.

He dropped into the driver's side. Rowan took a deep, shuddering breath and stared out the windshield. Her feet ached with the cold. *Daddy.* Her shocked brain reeled.

There was a huge black van with a trailer parked in front of her house, its lights turned off. Her house was completely dark, the front window broken. *Oh, God, Daddy.*

The man closed the car door. "Got to get moving," he said. "Are you hurt? Rowan? *Are you hurt?"* He didn't precisely yell, but his tone was harsh. He dug in his jacket pocket and produced his cell phone.

"N-n-n-" Rowan shivered. She couldn't finish the word. The car was cold, and her feet were bare. The sweater did nothing to keep her warm. Her teeth started to chatter. She stared as shadows detached themselves from the van and tramped through her front yard, surrounding her house. Now there were lights—flashlight beams. She saw a light flicker upstairs.

They're searching the house, she thought. *Searching for what? For what? Why would someone want anything in our house?*

"It's Delgado," the man said into the cell phone. "I need a diversion. The Sigs have cleared the house. Two casualties." A pause. "No, I got us both out. No net, just a single unit on primary penetration. They just now sent in the net. Don't give me a goddamn editorial, General. Give me some *help.*"

They shot my Daddy, she thought, and Delgado glanced over at her. She shivered, pulling away from his gaze. *They shot my Daddy. Oh my God.*

"She's in shock, and I'm not too goddamn happy either. Get me out of here, General." Another pause. "Okay." He hung up. "We're going to wait for a distraction," he said quietly. "Then we can get out of here. Are you hurt?"

She shook her head, numbly. "Daddy," she whispered. His blood still coated her hands. They had shot him in the chest. Shot her Daddy. "What the hell is happening to me?"

"They want you, Rowan," he said quietly. She got the strange idea he was trying to be soothing. "Because of what you can do. They're Sigma, a black-sector government division. They take psionics and drug them, brainwash them and turn them into weapons. Nasty."

It was as if he was speaking a foreign language. Rowan blinked at him, then stared out the windshield at her house. "Why do they want *me?*" she heard herself ask.

"Because you're very special, Rowan. Don't worry. I'm going to take care of you." His eyes moved smoothly over the house and the black van.

"Who *are* you?" she whispered. "What have you done?"

"I didn't do anything, Rowan. They tried to pick you up this morning, and I stopped them. I didn't think they would take a risk like this so soon in the game. They must want you very badly. I'm sorry. I really am. You don't deserve this." He didn't look at her; he was too busy watching the house. "Sorry about dragging you, too, but we had to move fast and there was broken glass on the floor. Your feet."

My feet? What the hell, someone just shot my dad and he's talking about my feet? "Hilary," she heard herself say.

He looked at her. The car was parked in a pool of shadow, taking advantage of two overgrown pine trees blocking the glow from the streetlight. Rowan couldn't remember how he had managed to get her into the vehicle. He'd carried her, cutting through the weak spot in the hedge between her back yard and the McClellans. She remembered the grasping feeling of the junipers grabbing at her hair. "I'm sorry," he said again.

Rowan let out a dry, barking sob.

A tiny thread of sound interrupted the tense silence inside the car. He flipped his cell phone open. "Delgado."

Whatever he heard must have been good news, because

he twisted the key in the ignition. The car purred into life. "Waiting for it," he said, and then, "Okay." He closed the phone, dropped it into his breast pocket. Then he put the car in gear and freed the emergency brake. "I promise I'll explain everything, Rowan. Right now I have to get you to a safe place, where you can have something to eat and warm up a bit. Half an hour, forty-five minutes at most. Can you do that?'

"Daddy," she whispered. "Hilary." It seemed all she could say.

He nodded as if she'd said something profound. "Don't be frightened, Rowan. I won't hurt you. I'm here to make sure you aren't forced into anything."

Don't be frightened. I won't hurt you. Memory lit up like a klieg light inside her head again. She fastened on it. It hurt less to think about last night that what had just happened. "It was you last night," she said again, numbly. "You're one of them, aren't you?"

"No. They'd probably take me down, Rowan, and try to drag me in for brainwashing. Look, I'll tell you everything soon. Right now I need to get us out of this, okay? I'm not going to hurt you, I swear it. I was trying to find a safe way to break the subject to you."

"My dad," she said. "Hilary. You could have helped them. Warned them. Why didn't you?"

The car drifted slowly past her house. Rowan's heart leapt into her throat. She stared at the black van, then at his profile. His dark eyes were on the road, his mouth drawn into a thin line. He had a gun under his left arm. She knew that because he had shot one of the men in black. Otherwise he was dressed normally—jeans, a navy-blue T-shirt, a hip-length black leather coat, a pair of Doc Martens. He looked normal…but maybe he wasn't. "My priority is you, Rowan," he said.

Why does he keep repeating my name? she wondered. Nurses did that at work to calm down an hysterical patient. Keep saying the name over and over, soothing the person. "Who *are* you?" she asked again.

"Delgado," he said grimly. He guided the car slowly around the corner onto Smyrna Avenue, flipping the headlights on. "Society operative attached to Henderson's unit. Specializing in covert operations and infiltration, interrogation and assassination. I measure a six-point-seven-five on the Matheson scale. You rate about an eleven, I'd guess. If not more."

"What are you talking about?"

The car accelerated. "The Matheson scale is a scale for the rating of psionic power. You're a psi, Rowan. Psionic."

"No I'm not," she whispered. *He knows. He knows what I am. God, please don't let him tell anyone, please don't let him hurt me.*

He shrugged. "The Society will help you, if you want. They'll teach you how to control it."

"No." Her throat was raw, she could barely speak. "You're one of them. You're *one* of *them.*"

"No. Did I try to snatch you in the parking lot? Did I shoot your father?" He shook his head. "If I had my way, I would have made contact and waited until you could trust me."

"No," she said, and buried her face against her knees. "I'm sorry, Rowan."

"Shut up," she said, her voice muffled by her knees.

He shut up. He turned left—Rowan peeked—onto Sigell Avenue, past the gas station Dad liked to visit because it was full-service.

Daddy. Daddy.

She sobbed, tears soaking into her jeans. He flipped the heater on. Welcome warmth stung her feet and hands. The man said nothing, just drove. Rowan knew she should be watching where he was going so she could get back home, but her eyes just wouldn't focus. She couldn't *think*, could barely even breathe.

When he slowed down for the last time, Rowan looked up in time to see an antique iron gate opening. As soon as he drove through the gate, she gasped. It was like sliding through a plastic film—and as soon as the film tore and the car was inside, it snapped closed. The air was suddenly curiously dead, as if she was inside a bell jar. The little prickles of electricity running over her skin intensified. "Where is this?" she asked.

"A Society clean house, shielded from the outside. Feels good, huh?"

It didn't feel good. It felt like she was suddenly, utterly naked. Rowan shuddered. "You're crazy," she said. "They killed my father. What about Hilary?"

"I'm sorry." His mouth was a thin line again. "I didn't know Sigma would move in so quickly. It's my fault."

"No," Rowan said dully. "I'm a freak. I've always been a freak."

"Not a freak, Rowan. A psion. There are more than you think." He pulled up a long graveled driveway to a slowly opening garage door. "Don't worry right now. We'll get you something to eat and—"

"I want to go home."

He pulled into the garage. Rowan looked over and saw a neat row of cars, all dark-colored, and two black vans with heavy privacy tinting. And a shabby blue van parked at the very end that looked vaguely familiar.

She was too tired to think about it. Her entire body hurt. Her head pounded, an agonizing dry pain. *Daddy.*

"If you go home, Sigma will scoop you up and fill you full of Zed. That's a bad thing, in case you're wondering. I'd hate to have to come and collect you."

"I don't believe—" she began.

He shut the car off, set the parking brake, and looked over at her, his dark eyes glittering. "I would come and get you, Rowan. I've seen psionics that get taken by the Sigs. Mind-shattered hulks, most of them, and the rest just like dogs on a leash. You don't deserve that. I'm sorry, and I'll watch over you. Okay?"

Rowan buried her face against her knees again.

He finally got out of the car. The ticking sounds of cooling metal echoed inside Rowan's head.

He opened her door. "Come on. You can rest soon."

"I want to go home," she repeated dully, staring at the dashboard.

"It's not safe, Rowan. Just trust me a little longer, okay?"

What else can I do? she thought, and the numbness rose again. *Daddy. They shot my daddy.*

He said nothing else, just offered his hand.

Rowan finally uncurled enough to slide her legs out of the car. The concrete floor was cold. She swayed. He shut the car door and took her elbow, his hand strangely gentle. "This way."

He led her through the garage and up one step, through a door, and into a small wood-floored room that held a rack of coats, with boots in a neat row underneath, and an incongruous washer, dryer, and laundry sink. The floor was warmer, and she swayed again. He steadied her.

Footsteps resounded. Rowan flinched.

"Steady," he said. "It's my boss. You'll be all right." His tone was kind, just a low murmur. Rowan looked up at his face and saw that his eyes were flat and dark. He looked worried, a vertical line between his dark eyebrows. "Don't worry. You're not in any trouble."

"Dammit, Delgado, you disobeyed a direct goddamn order!" The man was tall, with bushy iron-gray hair and steely eyes, wearing a long black coat that whispered as he moved. The light glinted off his metal-rimmed glasses. He walked stiffly, and as he rounded the corner his coat flapped open. Rowan saw a gun in a holster under his left arm.

"General," Delgado said, "may I present Rowan Price? She just saw her father and best friend murdered by Sigs."

Rowan took a deep breath. She saw the taller man blink just before she started to scream.

* * *

The only thing that calmed her down was a sedative patch. Delgado didn't want to do it, but she wouldn't stop screaming even when her voice broke. It took the patch a few minutes to work, and he spent the time trying to calmly talk to her, keeping his voice pitched low and soothing, especially when Henderson called Cath in and the Mohawked girl had burst into the room, skidding to a stop and frightening Rowan even more.

When the drug hit, she slumped all at once. He caught her and carried her to the bed. The safe room was done in green and blue, no windows but a gas insert fireplace. She hadn't tried to escape. She'd just kept screaming, backing away from him, and struggling against his hands. Getting the patch on her had been problematic, too. He'd had to invade her comfort zone and slip the clear plasilica square on her wrist while she struggled to get away from his hand, which was closed around her upper arm. She'd been so busy trying to get away she hadn't even noticed the patch. And he'd avoided touching her skin, even though he'd wanted very badly to just take her in his arms and let her scream herself out.

Catherine let out a long breath from the doorway. Henderson had apparently thought that another woman might soothe her, but the Mohawked girl had been of little help. She stood next to the old man, her arms folded, the silver hoops in her ears brushing her cheeks.

Henderson sighed. "That was not pleasant," he said dryly. "Explain yourself, Delgado."

"The Sigs moved in and did a full-scale penetration on her house," he said. "Killed her father and her friend. I got her out

58   Lilith Saintcrow

of there and called for a distraction so I could finish the
extraction. They must want her *really* badly." He laid her down
on the bed and pulled the quilt up over her. Her hair tangled
over the pillow.

"It's not surprising," Cath said. "Want to know her index?"

Henderson ignored her. He looked at the woman lying on
the bed. "How fragile is she?"

"Very," Delgado answered. "We have to get her out of the
city."

"Oh, wow." Catherine grinned, her earrings swinging as
she moved. "Delgado's got a girlfriend."

"Catherine, if you don't have anything useful to add, can
you please be quiet?" Henderson said mildly.

Cath shut up. The chain on her belt jingled as she fidgeted.

Henderson studied Delgado for a long moment. "All right.
We'll get her out of the city. I don't want you to disobey another
order, Del. Okay? I need you."

Delgado nodded. "Sorry, General."

Henderson shrugged. The dim lamplight was kind to his
ravaged face. "It couldn't be helped. If the Sigs got her we'd
be fighting her in a month or two. This way's better. Good
instincts, Del. We'll tear it apart in briefing later. For right
now, I'll take you off active and make you her mentor."

Delgado shook his head. "She won't respond well to me.
They never do. I've never had a neophyte before."

"Then it's high time you learned." Henderson unfolded
his arms and straightened. "It's either that or a full-scale court-
martial. I need you too much to do that. So from now on,
you're responsible for getting her trained."

Delgado shut his mouth and nodded.

Henderson waited another few moments, as if gauging his
silence. "Well," he said, "if she's that fragile, the Sigs would
have broken her in less than a day. Probably best this way,
though we still have faulty telem rigs. Goddammit. We'll leave
in twenty-four hours. Have her ready to go by then."

Delgado nodded again. "Thank you, sir."

Cath sniggered. Del looked at her steadily, and after a
moment she shut up and looked away, the chains on her leather
pants clicking as she shifted uneasily.

The General swept for the door. Halfway there, he paused.
"Delgado?"

"Yessir?"

"Good work. I had no idea you were so patient."

Left alone with Rowan, he paced to the side of the bed. It took a moment to peel the plasilica off her wrist, but the sedation meant she couldn't feel him. It also meant he couldn't feel *her*, but that was a good thing. He paused, looking down at her sleeping face. She looked as if she was barely breathing. When she woke up, she was likely to be disoriented from the drug and shock, not to mention mistrustful of him.

"I'm sorry," he said to her weary, sleeping face. "I'm sorry. I'll take care of you."

Twelve

"Good morning," he said quietly.

Rowan blinked. She had been dreaming of something very important—a green hill? No, something else.

"There's breakfast. And coffee." He ran his hand back through his short dark hair. The light was brighter and showed a scar on his chin, white against his dark-stubbled skin.

Rowan jerked up to a sitting position, bracing her hands on the mattress. The quilt slid off her shoulders. Her mouth tasted dry and odd, and her head felt fuzzy. Her throat ached, and her arm too.

Rowan hitched in a breath, feeling as if she would scream again.

Delgado held out a coffee cup. The familiar electric prickles ran over her skin. He was looking at her. Really looking at her. "Here, have some. It will help you feel better."

That made her laugh, a dry, awful sound. Her throat was on fire.

The room was small, and the curious dead quality to the air told her she was in the same place he'd brought her to last night. Wood paneling, a bed, two chairs, a small table, and a rug—no plants, no bookcases, not even a painting on the walls. Rowan took this in, and then she looked at the fireplace, which was merrily burning a cement log. *Gas*. It was a gas fireplace. The place was like a tomb.

"It feels funny in here," she said huskily, and took the coffee cup with trembling hands. Her bruised arm twinged.

"That's the dampers and the shielding. Keeps us safe from the Sigs and also blocks out all the noise of so many people thinking." He hadn't shaved, but he was wearing a fresh T-shirt and a pair of dark jeans. His coat was gone, and so was the gun.

Daddy, she thought automatically, and the memory of her father's heavy body, the last chilling gurgle as he died in her arms, rose again.

She stared down into the coffee cup, her hands trembling even more. The terrible feeling of nakedness was still there, too. "I don't feel good," she whispered. "I want to go home."

"It takes a little while to get used to the dampers," he told her. "And if I could take you home I would. I don't like this. But if you went home, or back to your job, or even stayed in this city for very long, Sigma would pick you up. They use people like you as weapons."

"People...like me?" She managed a scalding gulp of coffee. Even though it burned her throat, it did help her feel a little better. *Daddy's dead,* she thought, and the rising wave of unreality swamped her. "But I'm not anything special."

"You're a psionic, Rowan. We don't know what you can do yet, but you're so powerful Sigma probably doesn't care." He picked up another cup of coffee. The mugs were blue lacquer, and very pretty. He carefully settled down in one of the chairs. "The bathroom's through there, if you need it. Want some breakfast?"

"Who *are* you?" she asked. "You've been following me."

"I was trying to find a good way to make contact with you. Then the Sigs moved in. I'm sorry."

She watched him over the rim of the cup. "So you *spied* on me."

"Would you have preferred me abducting you in a parking lot? Or shooting your family? I didn't want to frighten you. I still don't." His eyes were narrow and flat. The electricity humming over Rowan's skin had settled into a steady, prickling buzz. Why was he looking at her like that?

"Who do you work for?" she demanded, wincing as her throat reminded her she'd been screaming last night.

"The Society," he answered patiently. "We won't force you. You can work with us if you want, but you don't have to. I'm going to be your mentor. Teach you how to control what you do."

He sounded so matter-of-fact Rowan was almost convinced. "You mean other people...You mean it's *real*?"

"Of course it's real."

"So you're saying you're psychic. Can you read my mind?"

"If I wanted to, probably," he said quietly. "But it hurts. My talent's not gentle, Rowan. The people I use it on usually die or go mad."

It wasn't his words that convinced her. It was his quiet tone of finality. She believed him. She looked back down into her coffee cup, the thick black liquid reflecting a shimmer of light. "I can't go home?" Even to herself, she sounded wistful.

"We can't stop you," he said. "But *listen*, Rowan. If you go back to that house, Sigma will waste no time scooping you up."

"What about my f-f-father? And Hilary? A f-f-funeral—" *I sound like an idiot,* Rowan thought grimly, and took a deep breath.

This is crazy. This is absolutely crazy.

"We'll do what we can," he said practically. "For right now, though, you should have some breakfast. We're getting ready to leave the house, and you might want to meet some of the others. They're probably very curious about you, too."

"You mean you've done this to *other* people too?" She vaguely remembered an older man and a punk-rock girl from last night, but she hadn't looked at either of them. Last night was a confused patchwork of terror, screaming and cold—and this man's flat, dark eyes.

"I was recruited by Henderson. You'll meet him. Cath and Zeke were rescued—kind of like you—from holding tanks in a Sigma installation. Yoshi and Brew were recruited right out from under Sigma about two years ago—they were part of another team until recently. You'll see." He seemed utterly calm, sitting in the chair, sipping his coffee. He wore boots, and he stretched his legs out as if he wasn't used to sitting for very long.

"You were recruited?" Rowan took a scalding gulp of coffee. The hot liquid burned all the way down into her stomach. "What do you mean, recruited?"

"Henderson found me and told me about the Society. I decided to join up, haven't looked back since." His eyes narrowed. She got the idea there was more to that story.

Rowan started to shiver. The prickles intensified, running down her arms, and she had to close her eyes to shut him out. *I could reach out and touch him,* she thought, *just like I do with the patients.* "You say other people can do…these things?"

"Probably not to the same extent that you can. You work at Santiago County, don't you?"

"So?" Plenty of people worked at the mental hospital. It proved nothing. She kept her eyes closed, the warmth of the coffee cup sinking into her hands. She was beginning to feel as if she might be alive.

Why do I feel so numb?

"Did you know that your hospital has statistically less violence than any other mental hospital in the country? Especially your ward? *Despite* the fact that some of the most violent offenders in the western half of the U.S. are housed there?"

She could tell he was looking at her. Staring at her.

He knows, she thought miserably. *He knows what I can do, that I'm a freak. Dear God.*

"We have state of the art techniques for—" she began.

"Ninety percent," he said. "*Ninety* percent, Rowan. And that started the exact month you began working there. Think about it. If you can pacify an entire hospital of mentally ill patients, think of what you could do with a Super Bowl crowd. You could incite riots, or stop them. You could start revolutions."

"Is that what you want me to do?" Her throat threatened to close with panic.

"No," he said. "The Society wants you to do what *you* want with your gifts. We'll help teach you to control it, so it will work *for* you instead of screwing up your life and crippling you with fear."

She took a deep breath and opened her eyes. "How do I know you're telling the truth?"

"You know I am." He set his cup down on the table.

"How long have you been spying on me?"

"Two days," he answered promptly. "Since you blew the circuits on our security perimeter at the house that night."

"I did *what?*"

"You shorted out all the security equipment," he said patiently. "Henderson thought you were an excellent candidate for recruitment. I was supposed to watch over you and make sure the Sigs didn't snatch you."

"How would they know where to find me?" she challenged him.

"Because of us. I'm sorry, Rowan." He even sounded faintly sorry.

"They killed my father. Did you know they would do that?"

"No, I thought they'd try to kidnap you again. If I had known they were that desperate…I thought they were just sloppy the first time. If I'd known, I would have tried to save your father."

His eyes met hers. Rowan's back roughened with goose flesh. His gaze was dark, level, and utterly focused. She wasn't used to people really *looking* at her. Most people's eyes just slid past her, judging her as pretty but brainless. It wasn't bad. She preferred being ignored and concentrated daily on making herself invisible.

"I defied direct orders to stay with you and keep you safe," he said softly. "Henderson ordered me to get out of there. I didn't want to. I wanted to stay and make sure you were all right. I won't let anyone force you into anything."

"Why?" She glared at him, lifting her chin. *This is insane. This guy is telling me the government's chasing me because I'm psychic? And that he's part of this secret society that wants to "save" me? Good God.*

He shrugged, then stretched, the stretch turning into a graceful movement that brought him to his feet. She noticed abruptly how smoothly he moved—no wasted motion, every gesture economic and efficient.

She took another deep, jagged breath and finished the coffee in two hot gulps. "Justin?" she said, tentatively. "That's your name, right?"

He went absolutely still, looking at her. "They call me Delgado here."

"Okay," she said. "Delgado. Those…those men in black. The ones that killed my father. They were in the kitchen. How did we get past them?"

His jaw set and his eyes glittered. "I killed them both," he informed her bluntly. "Look, I'm going to go find you some clean clothes. The bathroom's in there, and there's breakfast on the tray. I'll be back." He swung around and stalked across the room to a big, heavy wooden door.

She sat there, stunned, while he opened the door. He vanished, but he didn't close the door behind him. He left it open, and she heard his footsteps going down the hall.

It was that single thing—the open door—that suddenly convinced her he was telling the absolute truth. If they wanted to keep her captive, he would have locked the door, wouldn't he?

But then again, maybe she couldn't escape the house. And if what he said was true, where would she go?

His voice echoed in the air. *I killed them both.* He said it like it was no big deal. Like he did it every day. For all she knew, he did.

Rowan dropped the empty cup onto the bed. *Jesus.* It was as if the entire world had twisted off its axis, all because she'd been curious about lights in the windows of the Taylor house. *I thought there were a bunch of teenagers messing around in there,* she thought. *If I would have just left it alone, maybe Dad and Hilary would be…alive.*

She buried her face in her hands. Her father was dead. Hilary was dead.

And her? She might as well be dead too.

Thirteen

When Delgado came back, he heard the shower running. She'd made the bed, but she hadn't touched any of the pastries on the tray. He laid the clothes on the bed and poured himself another cup of coffee from the thermal carafe before it occurred to him that she might not want to walk out into the room naked.

He walked to the bathroom door. It was slightly open, and steam drifted out. "Rowan?" he called, knocking twice.

A listening silence descended on the bathroom. "Yes?" she finally said cautiously, her ruined voice echoing on tile.

"I have some clothes here. Some of them might fit you. Can I put them on the counter?"

Another long silence. "Sure," she said, and he could tell she'd been crying again.

I'm so sorry, he thought. *This should never have happened.* Del clenched his teeth against the words and shoved them down.

He laid the stack of clothing on the counter, not even daring to glance at the glassed-in shower. The bathroom was clean, lit with brilliant incandescent bulbs and tiled in dark blue. It was a far cry from her neat, cozy home. There wasn't even a potted plant in the entire clean house. Nobody had the time to take care of them.

He retreated to the bedroom and settled down with his cup of coffee, vaguely surprised she was still here. He'd left the door open deliberately so she wouldn't feel any more trapped than was absolutely necessary. If she wanted to, she could probably get a fair ways through the house before he caught up with her.

The shower shut off after a short while, and he listened intently, hearing her move. He'd given her two sweaters, a pair of jeans too small for Catherine, a pair of sweatpants, and socks—he hadn't found any undergarments. They would have something at Headquarters, if she consented to going.

When she finally emerged, chafing at her wet hair with a towel, he found his mouth dry and his throat blocked. Her eyes were red, and her cheeks blotched. She was absolutely lovely. She'd chosen the red cashmere V-neck sweater, probably because it was too big for her. It was one of his, one of the few brightly-colored pieces he had. Seeing her in an article of his clothing literally robbed him of breath.

Oh, no, he thought, seeing her stop dead and stare at him, her eyes huge and rimmed with red. *I am in so much trouble.*

"There wasn't...I mean..." She pushed the too-long sleeves up, her slim wrists lost in the cuffs. The jeans were rolled up and a little too loose. She was smaller than Cath.

"I couldn't find everything," he said lamely, around the lump in his throat. "We're traveling light. But I...you know, I just..." *I sound like a total fucking idiot. You'd think over a decade of military operations would have prepared me for something like this.*

If she'd been any other subject, he would have been smoothly moving himself through the stages of trust, minimizing her resistance, capitalizing on her vulnerability. The trouble was, she wasn't just any other subject. He didn't want to see her hurt. And he had almost no idea of how to shield her from the pain. *It's not that I promised not to hurt her,* he realized suddenly. *It's not the promise at all. It's that I meant it.*

"It's okay," she said finally. "I don't suppose it matters much. If I can't go home, I probably can't use my bank card or my driver's license either. Not that I have either of them. They were in the house. I don't have anything."

"It's hard in the beginning," he said. "But I promise, it gets easier. We'll get you a new identity, and you can draw off the Society accounts, and—"

"I don't want another identity," she interrupted. "I want *my* identity."

He shrugged. There was nothing to say.

She watched him for a few moments, evidently gauging how far she could go. "You spied on me," she said, finally. "You lied to me. You told me you were a student at a university."

"A lot of the research we do benefits the universities," he broke in. "And we investigate parapsychological phenomena. I couldn't tell you that I was a Society member pursued by a black-sector government collection of psychos, could I?" He didn't raise his voice; she didn't deserve that. But he was perilously close.

She stared at him, the blue towel swaying in her shaking hand. "I never wanted—" she began.

"But it's *happened,*" he told her, trying to keep his voice low. "I'm sorry I couldn't stop it, Rowan. I tried. But it's happened, and you'll get a lot farther if you just accept that it's happened and *listen* to me. I'm trying to help you."

Then he could have slapped himself. *Way to go, Delgado. She's really going to trust you now.*

Amazingly, she smiled. It was a weak, watery smile, but a smile nonetheless. "You're right," she said quietly, hoarsely.

"I'm sorry, Rowan." He had the uncomfortable feeling that he was going to be repeating that phrase a lot.

She nodded, her long hair, dark with water, lying against her shoulders in tangled strands. "Me too," she said. "Me too."

After a long crackling silence, she retreated back into the bathroom, and Delgado let out a soft, tense breath. That had gone well. Almost too well to be believed.

He closed his eyes, thinking. *She's remarkably resilient,* he thought, trying to analyze the situation. Unfortunately, it defied easy analysis.

A cold appraisal of the situation would tell him to maneuver her as quickly as possible into a dependence on him, to ensure she didn't bolt. If she ran from the Society, she'd be scooped up by the Sigs in no time. The thought of her in a Sigma white-room, a needle dropping Zed into her veins and her head shaved, made him shiver.

And nobody had ever made Delgado shiver before.

When she came out again, she was fiercely dry-eyed. "Okay," she said, quietly. "What's next?"

"I suggest some breakfast," he said, watching her carefully. She didn't look like she was going to bolt. "You need to eat. Then I'll take you to meet the General."

"The General?"

"Henderson. He was in the military for a long time."

"Were you?"

He nodded. "Marines," he said. "Semper Fi." *At least until Sigma got my transfer and started in on me.*

"So Dad was right." She crossed her arms over her chest.

"He was. Good observation." He couldn't tear his eyes away from her face. She'd combed her hair and pushed it back. Her eyes seemed far greener now, rimmed in red. The insistent prickle of her gift pushed at him, ran over his skin in rivers. It would be interesting to find out if the others reacted to her the way he did.

Red anger surged through him at the thought of anyone else touching her. Even *looking* at her. He took a deep breath and pushed the rage down.

She stared at him. *She's sensitive, so she probably felt that. Goddammit, use some of that goddamn control you're famous for.* He clamped down on himself. Pointed at the tray. "More coffee?"

She approached him cautiously. "I guess," she said, and looked at the pastries. Her face changed slightly. He tried to read it, failed. "You look angry." She finally settled down in the chair across from his, perching unsteadily.

"I wish I could have saved your father, that's all."

She studied his face intently for a long time. "I believe you," she said finally. "Let's get this over with, okay?"

Fourteen

The coffee boiled uneasily in Rowan's stomach as she followed Delgado down the hall. The house was pretty, she supposed, furnished in a kind of impersonal pseudo-Victorian style. There were some silk plants, but nothing living, and the entire place felt cold and unlived in despite the overstuffed chairs and attempts at softening with artful drapes and dim light.

In the middle of this, he was the only halfway familiar thing, and oddly enough, it was comforting to have him stalking down the hall in front of her, his broad shoulders held absolutely straight and his dark hair precise and neat. Rowan took a deep breath and tried to square her own shoulders.

She was barefoot, her arm hurt, and even though she had probably slept for hours she was still exhausted. She lagged behind him until he looked back over his shoulder and stopped. "Sorry," he said. "I forgot, you must be tired."

"I feel like I'm walking through syrup." She caught up with him and paused to catch her breath. "This is so strange."

"It takes a while to get used to," he said. "When I got to my first Society clean house, I couldn't grasp the freedom bit. I thought I had to ask permission to do anything. It took me a long time to figure out I could do what I wanted and I wouldn't be sent in for punishment."

"Punishment?" she asked.

"They don't do that here," he answered. His jaw set and his eyes glittered.

"Where were you before?" She took a deep breath and looked up at him. He wasn't looking at her. Instead, he was examining some spot over her shoulder with a great deal of interest. She glanced back. There was nothing there but a blank piece of paneled wall. When she looked back at him, he was looking at the floor, his eyes hidden. His mouth was still drawn into a tight line. *Hilary would like him,* she thought. *She has a thing for bad boys.*

Then, with a terrible jolt, she remembered Hilary was dead. Her mind returned to that fact, picking at it like a scab. In the confusion of last night, she hadn't even seen Hilary. A lump rose in her throat, tears pricking hotly behind her eyes.

"I was a Sig," he said quietly. "So I know. They got me

from the Marines and hooked me on Zed. Then they trained me."

"Zed?"

"A drug. It doesn't interfere with psionic ability, but it's extremely addictive and breaks down resistance to electroshock conditioning."

"Electroshock?" Her jaw dropped. "But that's—"

"They used a combination of Zed and electroshock as well as physical torture on me," he said. "I was resistant, and they wanted what I could do." He was pale. Was he sweating?

"What can you do?" Fascinated, Rowan moved closer. The hallway was deserted, the air dead and quiet. A scarred marble bust of Octavius in a niche looked over his shoulder.

"A variant of touch telepathy. I can crack a mind like a bank vault and take what I need." He shrugged. "Useful for intelligence-gathering, especially after Sigma trained me to use it effectively."

"So why did you leave?" Rowan crossed her arms, cupping her elbows in her hands. The look on his face, flat and unemotional, and the absence of inflection in his voice all screamed *trauma* to her professional senses.

"Every time they sent me out, I lost a little of my soul." He stared at the floor. "My handler—they mostly pair psionics with a handler, sort of like a baby-sitter—was a sadistic son of a bitch, played me like a fiddle. He went too far one day."

"What did he do?" Rowan pitched her voice low, but it was the wrong question. He slanted her an indecipherable look, some life coming back into his face. But he was still pale, and sweat dampened his forehead.

"I'd rather not talk about it. I'll walk a little slower." But he didn't move and looked down at her. "So I know all about Sigma," he added finally. "Personal experience. I hate the thought of them getting their filthy hands on you."

"They sound pretty bad," Rowan agreed. "They killed my father. Why?"

"I suppose they thought he would be in the way. A psionic with your power...If you had any family left alive, you might have tried to escape to rejoin them, or he might have caused problems by looking for you. Killing your father would neutralize both scenarios. Your friend Hilary was incidental damage—they couldn't leave any witnesses." He shrugged, muscle moving under the T-shirt. For a moment she was vaguely afraid of how much taller he was—her arm twinged again, reminding her. She suspected this man could hurt her worse than the man in the parking lot had—probably far worse and quicker.

"Because they didn't get me in the Shop'N'Save parking lot?" she asked.

He was so still she wanted to check him for pulse and respiration. "Maybe," he said. "Almost certainly. I'm sorry."

"If they'd kidnapped me then, would my father still be alive?"

"Unless he made trouble," Delgado replied.

Rowan absorbed this.

"Rowan—" He was about to apologize again, she could tell.

"No," she said. "Don't. It's not your fault." She took a deep breath and then reached up and touched her fingertips to his shoulder.

If she'd thought he was still before, he was absolutely motionless now. He stared at her from under half-lowered eyelids, his dark eyes no longer flat and shuttered but raw and open, begging to be *touched*. Soothed, just like the patients at the hospital.

But if she did that, they would know she was a freak. And they would…what?

What would they do?

He was telling the truth. She *knew* he was telling the truth, that deep, undeniable knowledge rising from that calm instinctive place that had never let her down. And he was in pain. Just like the patients she worked with. "Justin." She licked her lips, nervous. "What else did they do to you?"

"We should go find Henderson," he said, stepping away so her hand slid from his shoulder. "We're leaving here in less than twelve hours, so there's probably chaos down in the comm room. Just stick close to me, okay?"

Rowan nodded. "Okay." *He doesn't want to be helped,* she thought. *Just like Benny.*

The thought of her patients made her heart hurt even more. If he was right, she would never see them again. And she'd been so close to helping Siegfried.

I can't go home. I can't go to work. I can't do anything. Rowan's throat closed. "Justin?"

He froze again, looking down the hall instead of at her.

"Thank you," she said. "For saving me."

That earned her a genuine, if somewhat shocked, smile. The smile transformed his face from a harsh mystery into...Well, she found herself smiling back. The expression felt odd on her face, her cheeks aching from crying so much.

"Anytime, Rowan," he said. "Let's go. I want you to meet the others. Maybe you'll find out we're not all so scary."

"I don't think you're scary," she said, following him down the hall again. He walked a little more slowly, frequently glancing back to see if she was still there.

"Well, then," he said, and nothing else.

Fifteen

The comm room was, as Delgado had predicted, in chaos. Henderson leaned over Yoshitsugu Yoshio's shoulder. The thin bespectacled Japanese man hunched over his keyboard, fingers flying. "See? Right here, the flux turns into a recognizable pattern."

Zeke crossed the room, trailing a sheaf of paper printout. "Comin' through!" he said, and deposited the paper on Brew's worktable. Brew himself, a muscled man who looked carved out of ebony, checked the action on a 9mm. "The ballistics are out, Brew. Got the packing done?"

"Almost," Brew said absently, pushing sunglasses to the top of his bald head. "If you want to help, there's plenty of work."

"Don't you go stealing my slave labor," Cath snapped. She wore an acid-green T-shirt and ripped jeans today. Her feet were encased in clodhopping boots. She was packing another computer in Styrofoam and a cardboard box.

They were all armed, except for Delgado—he hadn't wanted to frighten Rowan—and they were a little too busy to pay attention. But Rowan's entry into the room made Henderson straighten and glance around, and Catherine jerked, her eyes widening.

She feels like a thunderstorm, Delgado thought, by now used to the prickling of Rowan's power touching his skin. He wondered if it felt the same for any of them.

"Everyone," he said into the thick silence, "this is Rowan Price. She's had a rough couple of days, so play nice. Rowan, the tall one over there with the white patch on his head is Daniel Henderson. The one on the computer is Yoshitsugu Yoshio, Yoshi for short. Miss Punk is Catherine White, that's Deacon Brewster, and the human Mack truck is Ezekial Summers, goes by Zeke. There would be more of us, but we're shorthanded right now." He stole a quick look at her face. She was so pale.

"Hello," Rowan said, in her tear-ravaged husky voice. "Nice to meet you."

Henderson crossed the room. He wore a casually elegant gray Armani suit, and his shoes were mirror-shined. "Miss Price," he said. "Daniel Henderson." He offered his hand, and

Rowan took it. Delgado watched carefully. "I suspect you must have many questions, all of which will be answered. For right now, let me say I am exceedingly sorry about your father. None of us wanted this to happen."

Rowan took this in. Her luminous eyes rested on Henderson for a long moment, and her shoulders relaxed. "Thank you, sir," she said, and Delgado heard the echo of a military father in her voice. "I'm glad to be here, I suppose. From what I hear, the alternative is..." She glanced at Delgado. "Very unpleasant," she finished.

Henderson nodded sharply. "Is there anything I can do to help smooth this out for you?" he said, taking his hand back and standing in what Delgado recognized was parade rest. "Delgado has agreed to be your mentor, unless you have an objection."

"No," she said, looking at Delgado again. Was she looking to him for reassurance? *Good God,* he thought, and his heart began to pound. *She is. Damn.* "No objections. He saved my life."

Catherine made a small, choked sound. Her violet eyes were sparkling. She was trying not to laugh. "Welcome to the Psion Parade, Price," she said, setting the box on the table with a grunt. The front of her green Mohawk bobbed, and six silver hoops decked each ear. Her nose was pierced once on either side, and she had a tongue-stud too. "I hear you're off the charts."

Rowan flinched slightly. Brewster wiped his hands clean on a rag and approached cautiously, offering his hand too. "It's very nice to meet you," he said, his British accent turning the words into softly precise syllables. His teeth were very white against the carved ebony of his face. "Don't pay any attention to Catherine. She has a constitutional inability to be nice. I'm Deacon Brewster. Nice to meet you. I'm a precog—I can sense danger. Just like Spiderman."

Delgado didn't think her eyes could get any rounder. "You just say it out loud?" she asked, looking dazed. "Just like that?"

"Why not?" he replied. "We're all psionic here, Miss Price. You're probably the most powerful of all of us. No bloody fundies or deadheads here."

"Fundies?" she asked, letting go of his hand. "Deadheads?"

"Fundies are fundamentalists—all those 'don't suffer a witch to live' types. I had real trouble with those. Deadheads are people without psi. It's just lingo." Deke gave her a wide, white grin, and Delgado watched Rowan smile back tentatively. Brew could engage just about anybody with his easy smile and calm voice.

"Deadheads," she repeated, and his grin widened.

"That's right," he said. "You just stick with us, Miss. We'll teach you."

"All right," she said, shyly, and gave him another one of those precious smiles. Delgado watched this while leaning against the door, his arms crossed.

"Hi." Zeke stuck out his massive hand. Rowan flinched slightly away from his size, but covered it well. Zeke was used to it and didn't say anything. "Ezekiel Keaton Summers, ma'am. Pleased ta meetcha. Call me Zeke. I'm the Tank."

"The tank?" Her hand was lost in his.

"Zeke's impervious to psionic attack," Delgado supplied. "The punk over there—Catherine—is telekinetic. Can move things with her mind."

"I hate to interrupt," Yoshi said, "but we might want to think about moving."

"Sigs?" Henderson asked, turning on his heel. Zeke took his hand back and stepped away with a glance at Delgado.

"Absolutely. They're setting up search grids. We've got maybe four hours at most." Yoshi, light from the monitors reflecting off his wire-rim glasses, shook his thick, straight black hair back.

"That's Yoshi," Delgado said again. "He's our tech guy. All business while we're on a job."

"All right, people, let's *move!*" Henderson barked. Rowan flinched. He swung back to her.

"Miss Price," he said, seriously, "we have a situation. Some very bad people are looking for us, and we need to get out of this house and to a safe location. Are you capable of taking orders?"

Rowan's chin lifted. "I am," she said quietly. "At least, when the orders are reasonable."

Good girl. Del felt suddenly, absurdly proud of her.

"Good," Henderson said crisply. "Then I'm going to ask you to go with Delgado. Listen to what he says, and we'll meet you in two days at a safer location." He waited for her assent, then turned his laser-like gaze on Delgado. "Del, find her some shoes. Take whatever car you need and take a few thousand from the petty and get her *out* of the city and to Headquarters. It's imperative to get her away from Sigma. She's overloading the entire damping system. Got it?"

"Yes, sir. Did you get the telem rigs working?" Delgado straightened, his arms dropping to his sides.

"Yeah, we found the problem, but we've brought the whole damn house of cards down on us." Henderson sighed. "It was the capacitors, of course. We finally had to cut the power in half, go node-by-node, and get it done that way—"

"General! Call from Central! It's Kate." Yoshi broke in. "Nice to meet you, Rowan," he threw over his shoulder.

"Th-thank you." Rowan's eyes were wide. "Likewise."

Henderson sighed. "Oh, Christ. Get going, Delgado. And take care of her. You hear that, Miss Price? Del will take care of you."

She nodded, a few strands of her rapidly-drying hair falling into her face. "Yes, sir," she whispered.

Delgado sketched a lazy salute. "Headquarters it is, two days or less. Meet you there. Let's find you some shoes, Rowan."

He ushered her out the door and looked back over his shoulder. Henderson, his steel-colored eyes cold, nodded. He heaved a silent sigh of relief. The General had weighed Rowan and implicitly accepted her as part of the team—a novice, to be sure, but still part of the team. The reaction of the others had been favorable—even Catherine, who was the prickliest member of Henderson's Brigade.

Rowan was rubbing at her arm. "Hurts?" he asked her.

"Yes." She pushed the too-big sweater sleeve halfway up her upper arm. Delgado whistled out through his teeth when he saw the bruise. It was deep and nasty, clearly a handprint. "This—the man in the parking lot. At least you haven't done anything like this to me." She said it quietly, then fell silent. He wondered if her throat hurt. It was painful to hear her talk.

Delgado caught her wrist, his fingers closing on soft flesh. The shock of touching her lanced through him, but he pushed her sleeve up with his other hand and examined the bruise. "You've been carrying this around and haven't said anything?" His eyes met hers. The feel of her skin under his fingers did something strange to his head, made his heart thud behind his ribs, shortened his breath.

She stared at him, eyes round and dark. A flush crept up

her pale cheeks.

He let go of her sleeve, his fingers seeming welded to her skin. He had to try twice to make his fingers loosen. "Sorry," he said, his voice sounding strange even to himself.

"It's okay." She sounded breathless. "They all call you Del."

If she was trying to change the subject, it only barely worked. Her wrist slid out of his fingers, and the strange drowning feeling went away. "Short for Delgado," he said.

"Oh. Okay." She nodded. "Are all of them...like you?"

"Like me? Psionic?" He started to move down the hall, and she came, walking next to him now. "Yeah. In one way or another."

She thought this over, biting her lip. "And you think I am."

"I don't think. I *know*. It's science, Rowan. We're not table-tippers or crystal-crawlers. We *know*. We have empirical proof. You're no more a freak than an Olympic athlete. You have lots of talent, and with training, you'll be able to use that talent effectively."

She was silent for a long time then, as he piloted them through the house. He finally swept a door open—his room—and she stepped inside.

I have her in my bedroom, he thought, and had to take a deep breath. "I've got to pack a few things," he said. "The rest will go with them. Have a look around; make yourself at home."

She nodded and came delicately into the room like a stray cat, looking at everything. His was the least decorated room, as usual. He couldn't stand all the frilly stuff.

She came to a halt near a low dresser and looked down at the white cloth on its top. Four guns, six knives, and various other implements lay in a neat range across the surface. "Are all these..."

"I was trained that way." His black messenger bag lay on the bed, a dimple of darkness. He left it there, slung a duffel bag down next to it. A few pairs of clothes, his kill book, a few toiletries. His practice of keeping a bag mostly-packed for emergencies had always stood him in good stead. "What size shoes do you wear?"

"Six," she said. "You really carry all these around?"

"Necessary sometimes. You know, be prepared and all that." *Is she going to be frightened now? Please, don't.* "I don't ever hurt anyone who doesn't deserve it, Rowan. Like those

Sigs. Look, Cath's shoes are going to be too big for you—she wears a nine. Do you mind wearing a pair of Yoshi's sandals until we can get you some clothes and some shoes that fit?"

"N-no." When he looked back, she was touching the hilt of a knife with one finger.

It was uncomfortably like her fingers touching *him,* and he froze, staring at her. She touched another knife's sheath, trailing her fingers down the supple leather. Delgado waited, his breath hitching.

"Do you use all of these?" she asked, haltingly.

"Yeah," he answered.

Her eyes swung over to him. "Why?" Then she grimaced and rubbed at her throat. It must hurt her to talk.

"Because the other side has worse," he said. "Much worse. And I like to be prepared."

She nodded, crossing her arms and cupping her elbows in her hands. It was a defensive gesture, he realized, closing herself off from the world. She retreated a few steps from the dresser, then glanced at him. Reassurance, again. She was looking to him for reassurance.

Why? All I've done is destroy her life. He stared at her. Against the velvet and burnished wood, she seemed to glow.

Then he shook it off. He had to get her out of here. Sigma was infiltrating the city, setting up search grids. *Focus, Delgado,* he reminded himself, with a sharp mental slap. *Focus.*

His hands hadn't even paused in packing the bag. He carried it to the dresser, extracting a leather harness from the drawer underneath it. He shrugged the harness on, then started holstering his guns. His hands moved smoothly, automatically. The knives came next, including the little hidden stilettos. She watched all this, her eyes growing wider and wider.

When he had the ammo cartridges locked into place on the harness and more ammo in the bag, he slid the bag over his head, the strap diagonally across his chest. "Next stop, Yoshi's room, then the petty cash," he said quietly. "Then we'll blow this joint and get you to safety. Just keep taking deep breaths, Rowan. I won't let anything happen to you."

"Don't people notice you're wearing that?" she blurted, as if unable to contain herself.

"It's part of shielding," he said before he could stop himself. "Deadheads can't see it—and if a psionic looks, I *know*."

She stared at him, her eyes huge as dinner plates. Delgado

froze. *Don't let her be scared of me, please, please.*
"I want to do something," she said. "Please."
"Okay," he said, without thinking about it. "Sure."
Jesus Christ. Did I just do that? What is wrong with me?
She blinked, apparently as shocked by his quick
acquiescence as he was.
Silence bloomed between them, a new and painful silence.
"I can do things," she said quietly. Her ruined voice made the
admission hoarse and painful. "It doesn't hurt, but it...I need
to..."
She's just tacitly admitted to being a psion, he thought,
and wondered why the thought should make him so uneasy.
"Go ahead," he said, and put his hands behind his back,
standing almost in parade rest. "Do what you have to do, but
we don't have much time."
She nodded, strands of pale hair falling into her face.
"I...I've never told anyone," she said. "Ever. Well, except my
parents."
A number of things suddenly fell into place. "Oh," he said.
She took a step closer to him, her eyes going dark. The
prickles of electricity running over his skin intensified. "So
you can't tell anyone," she said. "Please."
"Silent as the grave," he promised.
She took another step forward and looked up into his face.
Delgado discovered that he was shaking—and she looked as if
she was trembling too.
"I won't hurt you," she repeated, softly.
"It's all right," he told her. *Hurt me if you want to,* he
thought, and then shivered. *I don't care.*
She waited for a few excruciating seconds, then lifted her
hand and pressed her fingertips to his unshaven cheek.
Fire roared through his veins, coated his skin. He *felt* her,
slipping through the surface of his mind, but the feeling wasn't
like the agony of his own gift. Instead, it was as if every thought,
every sin, every bloodstained moment of his life was washed
clean. As if she had taken all the pain away, replacing it with
something suspiciously like calm.
When she pulled back, her fingers sliding from his skin, it
took every ounce of his control not to catch her wrist and clamp
her fingers back down on his face. She slipped out of his mind
like water slipping under sand, gone, but leaving something
changed and smooth, unruffled.

"You're not like any of them," she said, as if dazed. "And you're telling the truth."

He found himself unable to speak. Tried twice and failed, his throat closed. Then he took a deep breath. "I wouldn't lie to you," he managed.

"Everyone else, but not me?" Now one corner of her mouth quirked up slightly. He couldn't believe what was happening.

"I suppose so." He shook himself. *Got to get her out of here.*

Her eyes were still dark and depthless, her pupils dilated, the dark circles underneath them seeming almost bruised. "All right," she said. "I trust you. I'll go with you."

Sixteen

Delgado took the freeway going north. Rowan sank into the leather bucket seat and watched the miles slip by. He drove carefully, obeying the speed limit, and a sudden sense of absurdity swam over her. *Here I am,* she thought, *in a car with a man I don't even know, who has five thousand dollars in cash and a bunch of guns, being pursued by a government conspiracy. Because I'm a freak—only he calls it psionic. And Dad…and Hilary. How did I get here?*

She'd never used the *touch* on a normal person before. But then, he wasn't exactly…well, *normal*, was he? His mind was ordered, clean, not like the scattered wash of sensation and impression regular people gave off into the air or the screaming chaos of her patients' minds. *Is it because he's…like me?* she wondered, blinking in the late-morning sunlight. Two lattes stood steaming gently between them, in the cup holders. The car was new, a dark-blue Ford Taurus, without even an air-freshener. It was as bare and new as everything else these people seemed to have.

He glanced at her, checking. "You all right?"

The lunacy of the question taunted her. "No. I'm not. My family's dead and gone and all this…I'm not all right. I'm *not.*"

"I'm sorry," he said. "If I could have done this quietly—made contact with you, told you about the Society—I would have. I didn't want this."

That made a sharp acrid bite of guilt chew at her breastbone. She believed him. "I know."

"We need to get you some clothes," he said. "We'll probably stay in a hotel tonight, if that's all right with you. Just keep focusing on the next thing for right now, Rowan."

There it was again. He kept saying her name.

"Why do you keep saying my name?" she asked. "Are you trying to calm me down?"

"It's a pretty name," he said, and she stole another glance at him. He watched the road. She picked up her latte—nonfat, double hazelnut—and took a sip. It had cooled down considerably.

"My mother named me," she said, and her eyes filled with tears. She put the latte back in the cup holder and stared out the windshield.

His cell phone rang. Rowan almost flinched.

He fished in his jacket pocket and brought the phone out, flipped it open, glancing at the Caller ID. "Delgado."

Silence. Two tears tracked down Rowan's cheeks.

"Fuck," he said, and then glanced at her. "You're kidding. That's going to make it difficult."

Another long pause. *He sounds so calm,* she thought, and wiped away more tears. She'd promised herself she wouldn't cry again.

"No," he said. "I haven't yet. What do you suggest?"

Rowan could hear the faint sound of a male voice from the phone. Delgado laughed, but it was a short, bitter sound. "I'll get her there, General. Go ahead, don't worry about me. I *think* I can handle one extraction, even with—what?" There was a note of worry in his voice now, and that alarmed Rowan more than she would have thought possible. "Good Christ," he finally said. "Okay."

Then he shrugged, even though the person on the other end couldn't see him. "Okay. Be careful. Of *course* I'll get her there. I've been outwitting Sigs for years. I won't let them have her." Another bitter little laugh. "Okay. Be safe, old man."

Then he hung up.

"Henderson and the crew were surprised by a squad of Sigs at the house," he said, with no preamble.

Rowan gasped.

"Don't worry," he said, reaching into the back seat and snagging a box of tissues. "Here. Anyway, everything was already packed, they dealt with it and got out of there. Everyone's safe. They'll meet us at Headquarters, but it might take awhile for us to get there. We'll have to go a lot further and faster than I thought, because the Sigs have put out an APB on both of us through civilian channels. Someone must have identified me in the Shop'N'Save parking lot."

Rowan took the box and pulled out two tissues with numb fingers. She mopped at her cheeks and blew her nose. "What does that mean?" she whispered, stuffing the wadded tissue in the litter bag.

"It means they're really serious about acquiring you," he replied. "It also means they'll use anything—up to deadly force—to do so. And it means that they're kicking themselves for killing your father and friend and getting rid of valuable leverage. Last of all, it means we can't take a plane, so we'll have to drive. That'll take some time."

Leverage, she thought. *To do what?* "Leverage?"

"Leverage," he said grimly. "We'll drive for a few hours to get out of immediate danger and get you some lunch, and then we'll shop for some clothes."

Rowan felt her stomach somersault. "I don't think I can eat," she whispered.

"I need you to eat, Rowan. I need you strong. You're going to have to watch my back." He still watched the road ahead of them, but she had the strange idea that he was paying attention to her instead of his driving.

Rowan felt all the breath leave her. She actually gasped. "You don't *need* me," she said, sounding shocked even to herself.

"I do," he said. "Do you know what Henderson just told me? You're over thirteen on the Matheson scale. That means your talent's so huge we don't have the means to quantify it. I need you to look out for me. I'll teach you a couple of things while we're running, so—"

"I don't want to," she said immediately. "I *don't* want to. I'm a…a freak. You're telling me I'm too freakish even for your Society. And I did it—I brought those awful people—it was because of *me."*

He hit the turn signal, and before Rowan could protest, he had cut across two lanes and onto the shoulder. Gravel crunched and spun under the tires. A plume of dust went up, and he brought the car to a sudden halt.

Rowan's fingers curled around the handle on the door, hanging on. "What are you—"

"Who did it?" he asked, looking straight out the windshield. His knuckles were white on the steering wheel. "Huh? Who did that to you, Rowan?"

"What?" She could barely whisper, shocked.

"Who told you that you were a freak?" He stared straight ahead, his dark eyes fixed on some far-off point. "Who did it?"

"Nobody," she whispered. "I just know. Nobody else…nobody else knew what I knew. Saw what I saw."

"So you decided to keep it a secret," he said quietly. "You don't have to keep it from me. You're not a freak, Rowan. You're a normal person with some rare talents, that's all. Don't call yourself a freak. If you're a freak, I am too. You get it?"

"But—"

"No buts. You're not a freak, and you're not responsible for Sigma. They've been around since before you were *born*, Rowan. You're not responsible. Okay?"

Tears spilled down her cheeks again. "If I wasn't a freak my father would still be alive."

"That's my fault," he said. "I should have figured Sigma would try to acquire you without witnesses. Blame *me*, Rowan. Not yourself. Blame me."

If he squeezes the steering wheel any harder, he's going to break something, she thought, and reached out before she could stop herself. She touched the back of his hand with her fingertips. The prickling electricity slammed into her, submerging her in what he was feeling.

Rage. Red rage. Agony—a wounded animal, crouched low, blood on its muzzle, panting as it prepared to defend itself again.

She peeled her fingertips away, her stomach turning. Protective fury. And something else, something she couldn't decipher. It hurt him to think of her pain—hurt him viscerally. Why?

"Why?" she asked.

"Because I can take it," he said, turning to look at her again. His dark eyes were hot with something Rowan didn't want to name. "I can take it, Rowan. You shouldn't have to. Okay? You are *not* a freak. You're a psion. It's normal. Not freakish. End of story."

Rowan shrugged helplessly. He was her only way out of this situation, so she probably shouldn't make him angry.

But how do I know this Society isn't just using me? she thought. *If they think I'm so valuable?*

"I don't want to go to the Society," she said. "I want to go away. Far away where nobody can find me."

He stared at her, his mouth thinning. "You're sure?" he asked. "It'll mean that I have to get more hard cash to start us out, and some fake IDs. And—"

"No," she interrupted. "No, that's okay. It's fine. I might as well. I have no choice, do I?"

"You do," he said. "I'm trained for it. I could help you disappear, Rowan. Just…I don't want you hurt. Or scooped up by Sigma."

"What if I told you to fuck off?" Her voice broke instead of sounding bold, like Hilary's.

Oh, God. Hilary...

He shrugged. "I suppose I'd try to change your mind. I'm going to protect you, Rowan. It'll be easier with the Society behind us."

"Why?" Fresh tears trickled down her cheeks. "*Why*? Why are you doing this?" Her hands twisted, scrubbing at each other. Just like one of the patients, she realized. Now she knew why they did that.

"Because," he said, and then did something strange.

He reached over. His fingers closed around her left wrist. Her hands stopped scrubbing each other, and the prickles raced up her arm again, jolted her stomach. She hadn't touched very many people in her life, hating the overwhelming welter of sensations; none of them had felt like him. "Please," he said. "Trust me, okay? Just a little. Just a very little. I'll keep you alive, Rowan, and I won't let anyone force you to do anything you don't want to do. I promise."

He's serious, she thought, and heard Hilary's deep laughing voice. *Trust you to find a hero in a parking lot.*

Oh but it hurt to think of Hilary.

"All right," she whispered. "All right."

"Now I've *got* to get us out of here," he said quietly, his fingers shackling her wrist. "Okay?"

"Okay," she whispered.

"I promise," he repeated. Then he let go of her, checked over his shoulder, and eased the car forward again.

Rowan wiped at her cheeks with a fresh tissue. "Why?" she asked again as he cut the car to the left a little and pulled onto the freeway. Traffic was light, so he had no trouble.

He didn't answer.

Seventeen

Delgado stopped at an outlet mall a hundred miles from the city. Then he had the exotic experience of suggesting clothes to a mostly-silent woman who nodded and tried on whatever he suggested. He sent her into the lingerie store alone with a couple hundred, however. His heart wouldn't have been able to take it. Instead, he stood outside and waited, scanning the parking lot and holding three plastic bags full of clothes and assorted sundries. He had no idea what a woman would want beyond the usual extraction list, and did his best to guess.

The last stop was the shoe store. She chose a pair of boots and a pair of black sneakers, and he got a second pair of boots for her—stylish black ones, less functional than the combat boots but pretty.

Christ, he thought, seeing her scrub at her forehead with the heel of her hand, *I'm really playing house, aren't I?*

She took one longing look at a bookstore and then looked quickly down at the ground. He pressed a hundred-dollar bill into her palm. "I'm going to get a couple things. You get what you want from there. Stay in the store. I'll come get you in a bit, okay?"

She nodded. He slid his cell phone out of his pocket and slipped it into her hands. "There. Now you're ready for anything. Just get what you want, okay?"

She nodded again, a tendril of pale hair falling across her face. He had to forcibly repress the urge to brush it away. "Thanks," she said, and the rough honey of her voice reminded him of her screaming. "Are you sure?"

"We have time," he said firmly. "Go on."

She went, and he watched her hips move for a few moments as she walked away. *I am in so much trouble,* he thought.

He waited half an hour, putting the bags in the car and then drifting through the mall, buying a few odds and ends, a sharp eye out for anything out of the ordinary. Then he ducked into the bookstore and found her standing by the cash register, paying for an abridged copy of *The Decline and Fall of the Roman Empire*, a copy of *Leaves of Grass*, and a blank journal as well as a packet of pens. He waited by the door, his eyes moving over the entire store, marking two employees and a couple of other customers. No government presence.

Good.

She carried her bag up to the front door and tried to hand him the change, but he shook his head, only taking the cell phone back. "Come on. One last stop."

He'd taken a spin through the luggage store and got a few pieces to store her clothes and toiletries in, but he took her back there. "They don't have much," he said, "but I think you need a new purse."

She nodded and randomly picked out a small black number. He paid for it, and then shepherded her out to the car. "We can stop by a supermarket for anything else." He took her elbow as they crossed into the parking lot. "But we need food first. What do you want for lunch?"

"I don't think I could eat." She looked stunned, far too pale, her eyes far too dark. "Justin—" She caught herself. "Delgado."

"You can call me Justin." The name felt strange on his lips. Nobody had called him that in years. "It's okay."

"All right," she said. "Justin, where does all the money come from?"

"We have a couple psions who are really good with investments, and another couple that are really good with software," he said. "We own a couple companies."

That was a vast oversimplification, but he didn't want to discuss the funding. Especially some of the less than legal aspects of the funding—the initial capital for the Society investments had to have come from somewhere, right?

"Oh," she said.

"And every once in a while, someone goes to Vegas. Usually one of the telekinetics, but never the same one twice. There're all sorts of things." He checked the surroundings again. Nothing. Why was he nervous? "I think we should get out of here. Is fast food okay?"

She grimaced before she could stop herself, and then blinked at him. "I suppose. Look, I feel sick. I can't eat."

"You have to," he said gently, "or you'll get dizzy. You're in a kind of shock, Rowan. Eating will help. Will you at least try?"

She gave him one extraordinary green-eyed look. He'd seen the look before on interrogation subjects—the look that told him the subject was identifying with him, looking to him for guidance. "All right," she said quietly. "I'll try."

"Good," he said softly, and guided her to the car. He got the trunk open and dumped his few purchases in, ripped the tag off the purse with one efficient jerk, and emptied the paper padding from its insides. "There you go, ready to be filled up," he said. "Let's go."

She carried the purse and her bag from the bookstore around to her side, and he closed her in the car and scanned the mall again. He wasn't just uneasy—the back of his neck was prickling, and he knew what that meant. Danger.

He went around the car, got into his side, and twisted the key in the ignition. "Let's drive a bit and then do lunch," he said. "I'm a little nervous."

That made her eyes get even bigger. She stared at him, holding her seat belt in one slender hand. "Do you think they've followed us?" she whispered, and he regretted saying anything. She was fragile right now. Too fragile.

"Nah," he said. "Just better to be safe than sorry, you know. Look, don't worry, Rowan. I'll take care of you."

"You walked around that whole place with guns on," she said, buckling herself in. "Maybe they called the police."

"Nobody saw the guns, Rowan. They only saw a guy waiting for his girlfriend." He backed out of the parking space, dropped the car in drive, and started negotiating the maze that would get them back on the freeway. His neck was crawling and her nearness—and obvious trust in him—made his entire body prickle with electricity.

She blushed and looked down at the purse. "I keep thinking this is a nightmare," she said. "I'll wake up soon. And then I figure out it's not, and I won't."

"I'm sorry," he said again. *Get her talking about something else, you idiot.* Another question occurred to him—how had she showed up at the abandoned house, appearing out of nowhere? It wasn't the type of place he'd expect to find a psion. "Why were you at that house? I never asked."

"I thought a bunch of teenagers were playing in there. Then I saw a candle and wondered if someone was going to get hurt—a fire, or something. I was curious. I was going to call the police if it looked like some kids drinking."

That was close, he thought. If she hadn't stopped, he might not have marked her, and Sigma would have scooped her up in a heartbeat. He would never have known.

His entire body went cold for a moment. Thinking about what *could* have happened to her made him feel suddenly, terribly glad she had been curious. And who knew? Her curiosity might have been a kind of precognition. "I'm glad you were curious," he muttered, pulling out in front of a white Cutlass waiting at a stop sign. "If you weren't, they would have you by now."

She tucked the money he'd pressed in her hand into the wallet that came with the purse. *Got to give her more,* he thought, *maybe a third of what's left, just so she knows she can use it if she wants.* Then she stuffed the history book into the purse, the journal as well, and two of the pens. She left the Whitman and the rest of the pens in the plastic bag and reached back over the seat to put it in the back. She had to lean close to him to do so, and he took a deep breath, smelling her, the prickles of her talent running over his skin.

No wonder she feels like a lightning bolt, he thought. *Over a thirteen. God.*

She blows the equipment down without even realizing it, Henderson had told him. *She's over a thirteen, we can't even measure her. I think she didn't blow the dampers completely because of the sedation. We were goddamn lucky, Del. It was close.*

"Too close for comfort," he murmured.

"What?"

"Just thinking." He checked traffic and pulled onto the freeway on-ramp. "Look, Rowan—" It was a trick to extract his wallet while he was driving, but he did it. "Take what's in there and put it in your purse. Just in case."

"But what about—"

"I've got plenty, Rowan. That's for you." *Give her something to hold onto,* he thought, *even out the power pattern here.*

In a regular extraction, he wouldn't be evening out the power pattern. He would keep her dependant for another couple of days, just to make sure the relationship took. And for something like this, when he was playing not just for safety but for keeps, he should maneuver her into a bed to force the bonding.

What the hell am I thinking? I still might. But what would she do if she realized he was maneuvering her, even if it was to keep her safe?

She was just unpredictable enough, right now, to make him nervous when he thought about it.

He couldn't call Henderson to check in—they were radio silent, just in case. The next time he spoke to Henderson, it would be at Headquarters. Not like he needed advice on how to run an extraction, but he was beginning to think that maybe, just maybe, he and Rowan were being pursued.

And there was another problem. If he kept playing aboveboard with her, she might decide to try to escape him.

He had no choice.

I hate having no choice, he thought, and watched the traffic around them. It was light, easy to spot a tail in, but Delgado kept checking and rechecking. Something didn't smell right. His instincts were in a frazzle.

He glanced over and saw that Rowan had leaned back, her head tipped against the headrest and her eyes half-closed. She looked sleepy.

He didn't blame her.

"Go ahead and sleep," he said, quietly. "If you want, I'll wake you up for lunch."

She gave him a startled glance, and then her eyes drifted closed. After a long ten minutes, her breathing evened out, and the flush of sleep rose in her cheeks. The tingling along Delgado's skin intensified.

Are they tracking her? They couldn't be—nothing to get a pattern from. They never had a chance to scan her in a chair, so they couldn't...ah, shit.

He was assuming their technology was still the same, he realized. Even if Sigma wasn't scanning for her, he needed to trust his instincts. Maybe he was just afraid of fucking this one up.

He settled himself into driving. He had some thinking to do.

Eighteen

Rowan crawled. It took forever, the kitchen floor spreading away in all directions like a desert plain. Her hands smacked against linoleum, the copper smell of blood filled her nose, and she heard the awful chilling little gurgle—

"Rowan. Wake up."

She crawled on the kitchen floor. Daddy was bleeding, and Hilary screamed.

"Wake up, angel. Wake up."

Rowan leapt into full consciousness, her heart pounding. His hand was on her shoulder. The car had stopped.

She must have fallen asleep again after lunch, because it was dark now. Streetlights bathed a parking lot with a yellowing glare. She blinked, and looked up at Delgado. "Hotel," he explained. "I'll go get us a room. Stay in the car, okay? I'll be right back."

Rowan nodded. He looked like he might say more, but he just nodded and opened his door. She watched him walk across the parking lot and into the huge white hotel.

This looked like a city. The sky was orange with reflected light, and she'd smelled winter air and car exhaust when he'd opened his door. Rowan found she was clutching the purse he'd bought her, and she made her fingers loosen by the simple expedient of taking a deep breath.

How had this happened?

She could open up the car door and bolt, she supposed. There was a street with a bus shelter, and beyond that, another well-lit street where she could see cars going past, even at this hour. A 7-11 sign was just visible, not far away. She could call the police. She probably *should* call the police.

She unlocked the car door. He'd told her that the police were on *their* side, but of course he would tell her that.

He hasn't lied about anything yet, she thought, and her fingers played with the doorhandle. He'd left her alone out here—and left her alone in the bookstore, too. She could have asked to make a phone call. She could have dialed 911, faked an epileptic fit, done anything.

But the *touch* had told her he was serious. He wanted to keep her safe. He obviously thought the other people were a threat, and unless he was a sociopath or delusional, he wouldn't be able to fool her. He honestly believed she was in danger, and his actions made sense to her. Or at least, most of them did.

She sighed, frustrated, and moved in the car seat. *I want to run,* she thought longingly. She would never be able to go to the track again, never feel the weightlessness of an hour without worry ever again.

She wondered if anyone had found her father's body yet. Had the neighbors called the police? What about Hilary?

Another more awful thought struck her. Suppose the police thought *Rowan* had killed them?

That's ridiculous. The evidence wouldn't hold up in court.

But logic dictated that one of the simplest ways to catch her would be to have the police look for her, wouldn't it? And the easiest way to get the police to look for her would be to accuse her of murder.

Murdering her father and best friend.

Rowan flinched. Sometimes her brain worked too well. She settled back into the car seat, biting at a fingernail, trying to find a hole in her logic. A flaw in her reasoning.

None came to mind.

I'll bet he knows how to avoid police, she thought, and a warm flush of embarrassment crept to her cheeks. He seemed so competent, so endlessly efficient.

She was still brooding when Delgado came back and opened her car door. "I had to get us one room," he said, and offered his hand. "There's two beds, though."

She nodded, sliding her feet out of the car. It felt good to stretch, good to get out of the blasted car. Chill night air washed over her, and she suddenly wished for a coat. "It'll be warmer inside," he said. "Let's get you under cover, you can take a shower or something. Hot bath. We'll get room service. There's a Laundromat attached—see, over there—so we can get your clothes washed. How about that?"

"I just want to sleep," she murmured. Her throat hurt. The soda she'd had at lunchtime had stung as it went down.

"Okay." He guided her to the rear of the car and opened the trunk. She started to shiver. *Halloween's coming,* she thought, and it made tears rise to her eyes again. Dad had loved to feed trick-or-treaters. He stocked candy all year and gave it out by the double handful.

She blinked back the tears and swallowed them. Denied

them.

When Delgado opened the hotel room door, she saw deep maroon carpeting and a mirror. An awful tasteless painting of a mallard hung over the small table between the beds. "A security nightmare," he said. "But it's okay for now. Look, do you want to take a shower or something? A bath?"

She went to the bed farthest from the door, stripped back the covers and kicked off the sandals she was wearing. She dropped into the bed's embrace, then yanked the covers up and spent a few moments wriggling out of the borrowed jeans. Then she turned over, kicking the jeans out from under the covers, and picked up a pillow, jamming it over her head as she curled away from the light.

Delgado moved around for a while. "I'm turning the dampers on, Rowan. It'll feel a little strange." Something electric hummed into life, and Rowan felt the same awful feeling of nakedness that she'd felt at the Victorian house. He retreated into the bathroom and came out after a brief time. Plastic rustled—he was getting the new clothes out.

After another while of hearing him move, he sighed. "I'm going to put this stuff in the washer. It feels awful to wear clothes when they haven't been washed."

She didn't say anything.

He left the room, and Rowan curled even tighter around the hard knot of misery in her chest. Before she fell asleep, she had one more logical, terrifying thought.

If they're chasing us and they corner us, it might not be a bad idea for him to leave me on my own so he can escape. Or if there's a chance of them catching me, what's to say he won't kill me to keep me out of their hands? He could convince himself that's the best thing to do for me, and he's efficient enough to do it.

Ridiculous. They'd come this far, hadn't they?

Rowan fell into a thin troubled sleep before he came back.

Nineteen

The dampers were almost overloaded, even when she slept. Until she learned how to keep herself shielded, a tracker would have no problem latching onto her. Even a dowser might be able to find her.

How had she survived with no training, no shielding? And how had she escaped notice for this long?

Delgado crouched beside the bed, watching her face as she breathed deeply, her lips slightly parted, and her cheeks flushed. She still wore his sweater, one arm tucked underneath her pillow, the other flung out, her hand resting on the white sheet.

He rested his own fingers on the sheet, wondering if he dared to touch her. Would she wake up?

If she did...

His fingers hovered so close to hers that he could feel the heat of her skin.

She was exhausted. Shocked, numb. He didn't blame her. It must have been a kick to the gut to have her entire world yanked away in the space of twelve hours. Delgado was just lucky she hadn't decided he was the enemy. She might have tried to escape and been scooped up by the cops—and Sigma would extradite her, pretty as you please. She wouldn't even know she'd been caught until it was too late. And then he'd have to go into an installation and find her, probably, and that might kill him.

Just a little push, he thought. *Just to keep her here. What do you say, Del? Just a little push.*

If he did, and she realized...

No. He couldn't.

But the temptation was well-nigh irresistible.

He touched her.

Her skin was soft, and her breathing didn't alter. But the electric feel of her raced up his arm, down his chest, and wrapped his body in soft heat. His pulse pounded in his ears.

His callused fingertips rested against the back of her hand. He stroked her wrist once, marveling at the satiny texture of her skin. She was so fucking perfect, it made his entire chest go tight with something he had never even thought possible. She was *beautiful*.

"I'll take care of you," he promised, whispering so he didn't wake her. "Just trust me, Rowan. Okay?"

Of course she couldn't reply. She was asleep.

Think about something else, anything else.

The motel was a risk, but she needed sleep and comfort, and he needed a few hours of rest himself. Their clothes were washed and dry and folded, packed in the suitcases. He was hoping she'd wear the jeans and the pretty black boots tomorrow. He was betting her legs would look even longer.

That was the wrong thing to think. He took a deep breath. Rest. He needed rest, and it was late already. He'd set up a perimeter. If anyone from Sig came close, he'd know. It had taken concentration and energy, two things he would have less of if he didn't get some sleep.

In a few minutes, maybe. Once he got enough of the feel of her skin under his.

He crouched there, watching her sleep for another half-hour. Then her eyelids fluttered in REM, and she made a soft sound of distress. She moved, and Delgado froze.

She turned away from him onto her back, her chin tipped up, her pale hair unraveling over the pillow. He had a sudden flash of wrapping his fingers in that hair and had to close his eyes.

I'm not doing this right, he thought. *Who the hell do I think I am, some kind of nice guy? They'll kill her if they take her—leave her a Zed-shattered hulk of psion with a handler who might...might...*

He didn't want to think about the handlers. He didn't ever want to think about the handlers again.

So what am I going to do?

He didn't have a choice. He kept turning the problem over and over inside his head, but the answer was always the same. He didn't have a fucking choice.

The good thing was, the situation was perfect. She'd just been traumatized, and she would cling to him before long. He would have plenty of time afterward to help her heal. But for right now, the closer he could get to Rowan Price, the safer she would be from Sigma.

But the closer he got to Rowan, the higher the risk she would find out he was manipulating her. And he didn't think she'd take kindly to that.

Not kindly at all.

It wouldn't be a problem if he wasn't so goddamn fascinated with her. He'd be able to keep a corner of himself reserved, evaluating, watching, moving from square to square in the game. The trouble was, he *wanted* her—badly. He didn't want to hide anything. If she turned those huge eyes on him and bit her lower lip in that absolutely charming way, he had the uncomfortable feeling he would be…well, helpless. And if she ever let him into her life, *really* into her life, he would never want to leave. What would happen once they reached Headquarters and she found out he was a monster?

Cross that bridge when we come to it, he thought. *For right now, get some goddamn sleep, Delgado. Quit second-guessing yourself. Play it by the book and keep her right next to you for as long as you can.*

It was another ten minutes or so before he could tear himself away. He dropped down gratefully onto the other bed. Hearing her breathe quietly in the silence of a motel room, he fell into deep sleep, one corner of his mind monitoring the security perimeter. But right before he fell asleep it occurred to him that he was actually happy she was with him, and that she had nobody else to turn to.

And that proved he was not a very nice guy.

Twenty

"Rowan," he said, shaking her again. "Get up, angel. We've got to go."

She made a sleepy sound of inquiry, then her eyes flew open. "What?" Her voice was a harsh croak.

"It's okay. They haven't found us yet. But we have to go *now*. Here—" He gave her a fistful of cloth. "Clean clothes. Get dressed, use the bathroom. We've got to hurry."

She was about to protest, but the back of her neck prickled. The instinctive feeling of danger approaching hit her, and she bolted out of the bed so quickly he actually stepped back. "Something's wrong," she whispered, and grabbed the clothes. Her throat was on fire.

"I know," he whispered back. "Get dressed, angel. If anything happens, hit the ground and stay there. I'll come get you."

She didn't bother to say anything, just ran for the bathroom. The room was dark, and she almost tripped over something laying on the floor. As soon as she reached the bathroom, sour heat rose in her throat, and she had to fight down nausea.

She dressed quickly, splashed some water on her face, and wished she had a toothbrush. A moment's quick thought made her use the toilet too.

When she finally came out, carrying the red sweater she'd been wearing, feeling a little bit more like herself with new clothes and underwear on, Delgado was standing by the window, watching the parking lot through the curtains. A single suitcase lay at his feet. "All ready?" he said.

"I think so," she replied, and the unreality of the situation walloped her. Her nape prickled, just as it had right before the men in black—he called them Sigs—had burst into her house and killed her father.

I'm taking all this as a matter of course, aren't I? she thought, and nausea rose again.

"Stay close to me," Delgado said quietly. "And, Rowan, no matter what happens, I *will* find you and take care of you. All right?"

She found her dry throat would barely work. "All right," she husked. "But what if—"

"But nothing," he said. "If Sigma manages to get their hands on you, you just hold tight and wait for me. I'll come for you. Okay?"

"Let's go," she said. The tingling, prickling feeling of danger now ran down her back in waves. "I don't feel so good."

"I'm not surprised. Here, your purse."

She took it with numb fingers. He took the red sweater, bending down to stuff it in the suitcase at his feet. "Justin?"

"Hmm?" He took one last look out into the parking lot and then picked up the suitcase, straightening. "Just stay close to me, that's all." He sounded as if he was reminding himself, not her.

Why are you doing this? she wanted to ask, but she knew why. She was valuable to their Society because of the freakish things she could do. Valuable to these other people too. Sigma. The people who shot and kidnapped and killed.

What does Sigma stand for? she wondered. "What does Sigma stand for?"

"Standard Integrative Intelligence Growth and Management Agency," he said. "Go figure, right? You ready? Let's go."

She followed him out the door and down an indifferently-carpeted hall. The elevators were to the right, but he chose the stairs instead. "Harder to get caught," he murmured, as if reading her mind. "Stairs you can get off at any floor. An elevator—well, they can just pull a wire and have you trapped between floors."

Rowan's mouth was desert-dry. "How can you think of all these things?"

"Training. Wait a second." He stopped short, and Rowan froze.

Prickles ran up and down her back. She felt a headache beginning at the base of her skull, tightness turning into pain. "It hurts," she said.

"You're getting more sensitive. It happens. Just take a deep breath."

Rowan reached out and grabbed his free hand. The electric prickles of his touch raced through her, up her back, chasing away the nausea and pain and replacing both with a strange light sensation—her heart hammering and her head spinning instead of hurting.

He started again, pulling her down the stairs, his feet soundless. She tried to stumble along quietly behind him, failing miserably. The electric feel of his skin against hers intensified.

She could tell he was concentrating on something.

"What are you doing?"

"Trying to keep us hidden," he whispered back. "You're like a magnet, Rowan. A big one."

"I'm sorry."

"Don't worry. It's okay." He squeezed her fingers slightly, ran his thumb over the inside of her wrist. "It's easier with you touching me. Just be calm, angel."

Irritation rasped at her. "You keep calling me that," she accused him.

"I do," he confirmed, as they reached the ground floor. "Hang on."

She waited, looking at his broad back as he peered out the small window set in the metal door between the stairwell and the lobby.

He cursed in a whisper, his fingers tightening on hers again. "Stay still. Breathe deep. Pretend you're invisible. Can you do that?"

Rowan shut her eyes. *I've been doing that since I was four years old,* she thought, and concentrated.

She dimly heard him let out a sharp breath.

I'm not here, she thought. *Ignore me. Your eyes slide right by me.*

There was a subliminal *snap*, as if something had broken under her temples, in the very center of her brain.

Rowan?

I'm here, she answered Justin's silent whisper.

Good work. Let's go. He tugged on her hand again. *She's so powerful. God, how did she learn how to—*

The blast of thought made her whimper, driving her teeth into her lower lip. She had gone too far, inadvertently *touching* him, sliding below the surface of his psyche to where the dark things in every human brain lived. In him it was something hard, cold, and fierce as an animal, but without an animal's unconscious harmlessness.

The car door opened. "Let go," he whispered. "You have to let go of my hand, angel. We can't stay here all night."

Rowan blinked. Cold air touched her cheeks. She was perched in the passenger side of the car, Justin's fingers still tangled with hers. She made her hand uncurl, sliding free of the borders of his mind. Her head pounded.

What did I just do? she thought.

"You linked with me," he said softly, and brushed a strand of hair back from her face. "Get your legs in the car. We've got to go. They're sweeping the hotel. We just missed them."

Was that disbelief in his voice? Rowan numbly pulled her legs inside the car, and he shut the door, managing not to make much noise. In short order he was in the driver's seat, and she wondered what he'd done with the suitcase.

The car's engine roused with a swift soft purr. He pulled out of the parking space, and within fifteen minutes they were cruising smoothly on the freeway. Rowan rested her head against the seatback and wondered why her hands were shaking.

"What was that?" she whispered, and he gave her a single dark-eyed glance.

"That was two full Sigma teams," he said. "They've got a tracker or something. *Damn.*"

"I'm sorry," Rowan offered, inadequately.

"Don't," he said shortly, his eyes on the road, flicking up to the rearview mirror. "It's all right."

Oddly enough, that made her feel better. If he said it was all right, she had no choice but to believe him.

Something dropped on her hand. Rowan looked down. It was a tear.

She scrubbed at her cheek with the back of her left hand. *Stop it,* she thought. *Stop crying.*

He handed her the tissues again. "It's normal to cry, angel," he said quietly. "Sometimes I wish I still could."

"It felt horrible," she whispered. "Whatever it was, it felt *horrible.* Something awful."

"Definitely a tracker," he replied. "They take remote-viewers and locators, and brainwipe them with Zed. Then they—"

"I don't want to know." Rowan's breath hitched on a sob. "Please. I don't want to know any more."

"Sorry." He watched the road, the rearview mirror. "I'm sorry, Rowan."

"It's n-n-not your f-f-fault," she whispered. "It's mine."

"I already told you—" he began, but broke as lurid light drenched the inside of the car. "Oh, *fuck.* Rowan, I have to pull over. There's a cop behind us. Stay calm, okay?"

"Oh, God." Rowan balled the tissue up in her fist. "What if he recognizes me?"

"I can handle this, Rowan," he said, "but I need you to be

calm, all right?"

"All right." Her throat ached with unshed tears and her ruined voice.

He pulled over, slowing, and the cop whizzed past them in the left lane. Delgado let out a long, harsh breath. "Isn't that a piece of luck," he said. "Good job back there, angel."

"I didn't do anything," Rowan said. "I'm useless."

"Hardly. You threw them off the scent with that little invisible trick. You're a pro."

A thread of pride bloomed in Rowan's chest. "You think so?"

"I think so," he replied. "Try to get some sleep, angel. I'm going to get us out of range. You did good work. I think we'll get out of this yet."

Twenty-One

I told her that to comfort her, Delgado thought grimly. *They're tracking us. I don't know how, and I've got to figure out how to lock her down.*

She was like a beacon, apparently, especially without the dampers. If he hadn't set up countermeasures they would have been caught in the hotel room, and he didn't like the idea of fighting free of two full teams and a net. He wouldn't get out of that without shedding blood—his *and* theirs.

Don't think about that, he thought as he drove. Dawn had broken, and Rowan had finally fallen asleep. What was he supposed to do? He'd never run an extraction with a psionic who couldn't be dampered before.

I've either got to teach her something, or drug her until we get to Headquarters, he thought.

He saw a blue Rest Area sign and decided to chance it. They had made good time.

Rowan woke with a violent start as soon as he slowed down and took the exit. "What is it?" she gasped.

"Easy there." He applied the brakes, and they were soon neatly pulled into a parking spot. "Need a break. You should probably stretch your legs too."

"I guess so." She looked out the window at the trees and green grass, pulling at the collar of the white dress shirt. He'd given her a pair of jeans and the dress boots too. "I always wanted to come out this way. North."

"We're actually northwest, but it's the same thing," he said. "We'll double back east for a while after we get far enough north, and then hook down."

She shook her head. "It might be best if you don't tell me," she said dully. "If they catch us—"

"Don't even worry about that." She shouldn't be thinking about that; it was his job. "If they catch you, you tell them whatever they want to know. They might hold off on the Zed if you're compliant. You just wait for me to come get you."

"What if you can't?" Her green eyes were dull. She tucked a strand of pale hair behind her ear and regarded him steadily.

She definitely shouldn't be thinking about that, either. "Unless you see them decapitate me," he told her evenly, "you can be sure I'll come and get you, Rowan. They trained me well. Maybe too well."

"What did they do to you?" The colorless tone in her voice hurt even more than the dull lifelessness in her eyes.

"Nothing I couldn't handle," he lied, and unlocked his door. "Let me worry about Sigma, Rowan. That's my job. I promised Henderson I'd bring you in safely, and I promised you I'd take care of you. I don't promise things I don't do." He raked stiff fingers back through his short hair.

"I'm tired," she said. "I don't want to do this."

"Neither do I," he replied. "I want to be back at Headquarters, with you safe and sound and learning whatever you want to learn to keep that talent of yours in check. That's what I want. Don't *worry*, Rowan. I'll take care of it."

"I don't even know you," she whispered, and that cut him all the way down to the bone.

"You don't," he agreed. "But you have to trust me, Rowan. I'll keep you safe, I promise."

That earned him a bitter little laugh. "Oh, yes," she said, "but safe from *who*?"

Oh, shit, he thought. *I've said the wrong thing.* He decided to play a get-out-of-jail card. "I didn't tell anyone about your talent, Rowan, even though you used it on me. So you can probably trust me. And who gives you the willies more, me or Sigma?"

She shrugged slightly, her breasts moving underneath the white cotton. He tried not to think about that, or about the dress boots and how they would make her legs look even longer. Or about the fact that he'd handled the bra she was probably wearing.

That was the wrong thought to have, too, but her face eased a little as he studied her.

"I suppose *them*," she said. "Every time they get near, my head starts to hurt."

Understanding hit him, right between the eyes. *They might be using a scanlock on a migmeter. Of course. She's high enough on the scale that they can do it. Christ, why didn't I think of that?*

"Oh," he said. "I might be able to fix the problem, then. Come on, let's take a break and then figure out where to find some decent coffee, all right?"

She nodded, a little color coming back into her cheeks. "I'm sorry," she said abruptly. "I know you're not like them. I'm just tired."

That made him smile, unfamiliar amusement tilting up the corners of his mouth. "It's okay, Rowan. We're both tired. I'd be surprised if you didn't distrust me."

She reached for her door handle, and he grabbed her wrist without thinking. Electricity poured down his spine. "Wait for me," he said softly. "Okay?"

She shrugged, pulling her wrist free of his fingers. He let her go reluctantly, then opened his own door. Crisp, cold morning air poured into the car.

She did wait for him to come around and open her door. But when she got out, she didn't look up at him. Instead, she set off for the low stone building that served as the rest area.

Delgado let her go.

He followed her up the slight hill and used the men's room, then came out and waited for her, leaning against the hood of the car. Metal popped and pinged, cooling. He would have to get gas soon, and coffee, and figure out how to extract himself from the mess of things he'd made with her.

When she finally came out of the women's restroom, she picked her way down the walkway on the hill with deerlike grace. He'd been right—the dress boots suited her very well. Her pale hair caught fire in the morning light, and she swept it back over her shoulder as she scanned the deserted parking lot, looking worried and exhausted—and incredibly lovely. Delgado's heart bolted inside his ribs. She saw him, and the sigh of relief she gave was audible even to him

Oh, man. I am in so much trouble.

He was involved. It was the one thing that should have never happened to him—he was too damaged once Sigma finished with him. He shouldn't have been able to feel a goddamn thing. But there it was.

"Ready to go?" he asked. "I need to look at the map and figure a few things out."

She nodded. "I want something to tie my hair back with." But she smiled at him, too, and that weary smile made something funny happen inside his chest. Not to mention his head.

"I put everything in the trunk," was his lame reply. "Standard procedure, you know—just carry one bag with you. Makes it easier."

She nodded, then looked at him expectantly. After a moment, he realized she was patiently waiting for him to open up the trunk so she could find a rubber band or something. "Oh," he managed. "Sorry. Here." He peeled himself up from leaning on the hood, and she followed him around to the back. "We'll be okay, Rowan.

I figured out how they're tracking us, and a few minutes with my kit and some copper wire will fix it." *Shut up, you fool.*

"Copper wire?"

"You get a headache when they get close, right? Means they're probably using a migmeter—a Matheson electronic signature reader linked to a computer chip. It doesn't work outside of a certain radius, but inside that radius it's pretty effective—and untraceable unless the subject has telepathic ability."

She looked down at the suitcases. "Which one has an elastic?"

"Try the blue duffel, it's got bathroom stuff in it. Anyway, a little copper wire and a little concentration will throw off the—"

"I don't want to know," she said, digging in the blue duffel. "Please."

He took a deep breath. "I've got to teach you something, Rowan. Either we have to get you buttoned down or—"

"Or what?" She reached up, gathering her hair behind her head. He had to look down at the pavement.

"Or if you wanted, we could sedate you until we get to Headquarters. I don't want to do that."

"Sedate me with what?"

"A form of Demerol usually works."

"Do you have any?"

"Some."

"Fine." She made a ponytail with a few quick, efficient movements. "I think I need it. I don't want to do this, Justin. I think I'm in shock."

"I think you are too." He closed the trunk with a sharp sound. "Are you sure, Rowan?"

"Can we get in the car and get this over with?" The dull listless tone was back in her voice. His chest ached. She was hurting too badly to feel any fresh pain. It was a defense mechanism—one he understood and had suffered himself—but it made his guts twist to think of her going through this.

"Rowan—"

"Please." Now she looked up at him, her eyes brimming with tears, and he found himself swallowing roughly.

"Okay," he said, and privately cursed himself. He should have listened to the voice of efficiency instead of his fucking conscience. If he'd done what he wanted to do she would have been emotionally attached to him by now, instead of deep in listless shock. "Whatever you need, angel. Let's go."

Twenty-Two

Rowan took the pill he gave her, and twenty minutes later reality retreated into dim fuzz. She curled into herself and watched the world slip by, uninterested.

She didn't know where he got the pills from. She didn't care. She only cared that he gave them to her without demur. He stopped for food at restaurants and supermarkets, told her when to go to the bathroom and stood guard outside the door while she did. She didn't know or care how he was taking care of himself during that time. All she cared about was the warm blanket of chemical numbness wrapping around her.

She didn't know how long it was, that zigzagging cross-country journey. She only remembered dim fragments—leaning against Justin's shoulder while he talked to her in a low voice, telling her something important that she couldn't quite remember. His fingers laced through hers, leading her up a flight of stairs. A warm touch on her forehead while she lay, her eyes firmly shut, in yet another hotel bed.

There were other flashes—him swearing as the car bucked and shuddered, her own thin breathless scream. A dim intimation of danger as they slipped out the back of a Chinese restaurant, Justin saying something over his shoulder as they vanished into the night.

Then there was a long time of nothing, not even flashes.

A single image etched itself into Rowan's memory. Justin, blood sliding down his face, holding the knife. *Don't move, Rowan.* Justin whirling, his hand coming up, a roaring sound—and the constriction on her arm eased. She didn't look, just closed her eyes, and heard him swearing. *Goddamn it, Rowan, talk to me.*

Another long time of no flashes. She simply abdicated control.

"What the hell happened to *you?*" A vaguely familiar voice, sharp and crisply authoritative.

"I just ran a goddamn Sig gauntlet." Justin sounded exhausted. Rowan leaned against his shoulder, her eyes drifting closed, and the world turned into meaningless colored blurs. "They had the whole damn western half of the country in an uproar. I saw Andrews. He says hello."

"Jesus. What's wrong with her?" Now the voice held an

edge. "Delgado?"

"Nothing, she's just sedated. Asked for it. Look, General, I've got to tell you—"

"Save it. Get her in a room and get your ass up to Four East. I need you. You're late."

"I told you, I just dragged through every fucking Sig you've ever heard of. They want her *bad*."

"How well trained is she by now?"

"Just some basic shit. You know you can't do much when they're sedated. What crawled up your ass and died?"

"I just had to live for three weeks without my right hand, that's all. What the hell's wrong with you?"

"Don't push me, General. I'm in a mood. I've got news for you. Give me a few minutes and you can have my full attention."

Slight pause. Sound of a hand meeting shoulder, a male greeting. "Good to have you back."

Darkness closed over Rowan. She felt Justin catch her as she swayed.

Rowan came back to herself slowly, lying in a bed. She stared up at a plain white ceiling for a long time before realizing she wasn't alone in the room, and also realizing that the strange naked sensation was back, but oddly muted this time.

Dampers. He'd said something about dampers. And his voice inside her head, teaching her. Showing her things. How to shield herself, how to keep herself separate from the world around her—and also how to keep *them* from seeing her, how to redirect people's attention away from her more efficiently than pretending to be invisible.

Rowan blinked, pushing her hair back from her forehead with a limp hand. She was bone-tired. "Justin?" she whispered.

"I'm here," he said, softly. The room was dark, the ceiling softly glowing in the dimness. He was a shadow with a glimmering pair of eyes. "Just take it easy. You're groggy from the sedation. It'll wear off. I gave you a system flush to get it out of you, so you probably feel tired."

"Are we safe?" she asked, trying to clear her head. He was wearing dark clothing. She could see a paleness glimmering on his left arm.

"Of course," he said. "We're at Headquarters. They're working on the dampers now, but it's no problem. You're safe, angel."

"Why is it so dark?"

"It's three in the morning. Close your eyes, and I'll turn on the light."

She obediently closed her eyes, wondering if she would fall asleep again. Light bloomed painfully against her eyelids, she was glad he'd warned her. She felt emptied, swept out. Strangely clean.

Finally, blinking her watering eyes, she managed to prop herself up on her elbows and look at him.

He had a white bandage tied around his left arm, and a row of stitches along his forehead. "God," she said. "What happened to you?"

"Just a little mix-up with an old friend." One corner of his mouth quirked up. His face looked oddly familiar—*of course,* she thought. *How long have I been with him?*

"How long—"

"Two and a half weeks. It took a little time." He shrugged, leaning against the wall.

Is he using the wall to hold himself up? "Are you all right?"

The question seemed to surprise him. At least, he seemed to consider it carefully before his flat eyes returned to hers. "I think I'll make it," he said quietly. "It was a bit touchy there for a while. I almost thought they'd manage to get us both."

That piece of news made Rowan's heart thunder against her ribs. Her mouth went dry. "Sigma?"

"Sigma." He shrugged again and winced slightly as if the movement hurt him.

"You look like hell," she informed him.

"I probably do. I think I should get some rest."

"I'm sorry," she began, but he shook his head.

"You kept me on my feet, Rowan. *I'm* sorry, for not taking better care of you. But it's over, and we're at Headquarters, and we're safe for now. So I'm going to catch some sleep."

Rowan sighed, forcing herself to sit up all the way. She was wearing a T-shirt and sweats, her hair was tangled, and she felt crusty-eyed and dry-mouthed. "What should I do?" she asked, and hated the way that sounded—as if she was too stupid to figure it out.

"You can just roam around, however you like," was his reply. "I've keyed the door to you, so it'll open for either of us. Anyone you meet will be able to help you if you get lost. I'm sorry, Rowan, but I've got to get some sleep."

Shame gnawed at her. "Oh. Okay." Abruptly she wished for more pills to make all this uncertainty go away. "Justin?"

He dropped into a big, shabby orange armchair set next to a rickety round table holding a dark-blue glass lamp. "Hm?"

"Thank you," she said quietly. She didn't really have the words to thank him for what he'd done.

"No problem, angel. Anytime." And just like that, he tipped his head back against the back of the plush chair and seemed to fall instantly asleep. He was freshly-shaved, but he looked gaunt, and there were huge dark circles under his eyes.

I wonder if he slept at all during that entire time, Rowan thought. *Two and a half weeks? Did I hear that right?* She glanced around, taking in the room.

Long heavy drapes were closed over what could have been a French door. There was also a draped window. The floor was hardwood. Other than the bed she was occupying and the armchair and table, the room was bare except for a steel bookshelf in one corner and their suitcases piled near the door. *I don't think much of their decorating,* she thought, and stretched, yawning. She felt tired, true, but also clear-headed for the first time since the attack in the parking lot.

Her father had still been alive then.

Rowan's heart clenched inside her chest. She studied Justin's weary face in the light from the lamp.

What am I going to do now? she thought. *What would Daddy do?*

She shivered. The room was just slightly chilly, and the naked feeling from what they called dampers was pressing against her skin. And the electric prickles that told her she was near him.

Justin. He was either asleep or faking it so well she couldn't tell.

Rowan slid her feet out of the bed. *First things first,* she thought. *I've got to take a shower. Then I should find something to eat.*

PART TWO

Twenty-Three

Delgado woke all at once, snapping painfully into full consciousness. The chair squeaked as he bolted to his feet, the knife hilt in his hand.

The long, trailing psychic scream came again, loaded with despair and pain. Someone in the infirmary was having another nightmare.

Rowan was already up out of bed, and by the look on her face, still half asleep but moving. She hit the door at a run, bare feet shushing over the hardwood; he was right behind her. He was so close that a long strand of her hair brushed his cheek before he matched his pace to hers. She ran down the hall and took a sharp right, having been here long enough to find her way even in her sleep. He had time to admire the clean economy of her stride before she took another sharp right and bolted into the infirmary, slowing only slightly.

The young boy sitting on the bed was blank-eyed and white-faced, his mouth open. He inhaled to scream again, and Rowan skidded to a stop right next to his bedside. Two other patients were beginning to sit up and reach for their bedside tables, and another two lay sedated and sleeping soundly.

Rowan grabbed the boy's hand. His inhale stopped, and for one long breathless second Delgado waited, ready to move if the boy exploded into motion. The kid was only eleven, but he was wiry and terror would give him strength. Last time he'd had a nightmare like this he'd almost clocked Rowan a good one; would have, if Del hadn't grabbed his arm.

Then the child exhaled, his eyelids drooping. "Rowan?" he slurred.

"It's me," she replied. There was no trace of sleep or impatience in her voice. There never was, when she was working with the wounded. "Just relax, Bobby. I'm here."

"It's so *dark*," the boy whimpered, his face crumpling. Delgado scanned the infirmary. He was glad his room was so close to this ward, used for the most critical cases. It was the only place Rowan actually seemed content.

"It's Rowan," a thin woman with a bandaged head whispered to the other conscious patient, a stocky man with incredible sideburns who was hooked up to an IV. "Go back to sleep."

"Hard to sleep with all the ruckus," the man growled back.

"Hey, Del."

"How's it going, Boomer?" Delgado answered. Boomer had been shot in the gut by a Sigma team in Las Vegas.

"Shitty," Boomer replied promptly.

"Watch your language," Eleanor said sharply. "There're kids here."

"It's all right," Rowan said softly, almost crooning. "I'm here, Bobby. Tell me about it. What happened?" As usual, she showed no trace of impatience. Del supposed she'd had a lot of practice dealing with terror at the mental hospital.

"They've heard worse," Boomer said.

"Let her work, Boomer," Eleanor chided him.

"It's so d-dark," Bobby said. "There's a spider hanging from a helicopter. The helicopter looks funny. Then they're inside the house, and it's dark."

The tension in Delgado's shoulders eased slightly. He scanned the infirmary one more time and decided nobody was lurking between the beds. He was dragging up a chair for Rowan when the night nurse Emily arrived, holding a mug of coffee. She saw them and stopped, her mouth rounding into a soft "O" of surprise.

"We heard him," Del told her. "It's all right. Everyone's okay." *Where the hell were you, you dilettante? You're always off doing something else when you should be paying attention on your shift. Wish we had more medical personnel so we could put you on the kitchen roster. You deserve it.*

"I just went for coffee," she whispered. "Everyone was sleeping."

"It's okay," Del said again. *Coffee my ass. Were you playing grabsies with that lanky guy from Eric's team again? You should have been in here at your post.*

"Christ, I'd need coffee too," Boomer growled. Eleanor shushed him. The Sigs had captured her team and had almost washed her with Zed before another team could get to her. Following a short, vicious firefight, Eleanor had been the only one of her team left alive.

"Bobby," Rowan said, "I'd like to help you, the way I did before. Can I?"

The little boy, shivering, gazed up at Rowan's face with

open adoration.

Delgado knew the feeling. *You wouldn't know that he saw his family murdered right in front of him, barely escaped the Sigs, got caught again, and then got scooped up by us during transport. It's a wonder he doesn't have more nightmares,* he thought, and a cool finger touched his nape. Rowan didn't take the chair he dragged up to the bedside, but she might later.

"Oh, sure," Bobby said. "Like you did when I got here?"

"Just like that, kiddo. Feels like it was years ago, doesn't it?" Rowan eased herself down so she was sitting on the bed, still holding Bobby's hand. The boy curled down against his pillows, nestling into the covers. The IV taped to the back of his other hand would dispense another shot of antibiotic in twenty minutes or so, dealing with the infection from his weeks of wandering through city streets. His broken arm was still sealed in a cast. "I'll tell you a story, too, if you're awake afterward."

"Okay, Rowan." Bobby grinned at her. He didn't even look at Delgado.

Del watched Rowan's profile as she smoothed the boy's fingers, then held his small hand in both of hers. Kids and adults alike, anyone in pain welcomed her attention. "Let's see," she said, and a slight smile touched her lips. "Did you like the horse?"

"The red one? Oh, yeah. That was neat."

"Neat, huh? How about we turn it into a rocket ship this time?"

Delgado's skin began to prickle faintly. Rowan's eyes seemed luminous in the dim light. Eleanor and Boomer watched, and Emily took a sip of her coffee, her own eyes round as plates.

Bobby's eyes closed. Delgado's entire body tightened. He knew what it felt like—all the pain and the guilt washed away, leaving calmness behind.

And there was another thing about Rowan's talent that nobody had expected: she could *heal.*

Bobby's broken arm was mending much faster than it should, and so was Boomer's bullet wound. Delgado himself had felt the effects of hanging around Rowan while she learned to use her talent—his stitches had come out early, and the knife wound in his left arm had healed completely in a matter of days. Jilssen called it a sort of focused bioenergetic field and went around muttering about "cell mutations" and "frequencies."

Ten minutes later, Bobby was breathing deeply. Rowan looked back over her shoulder and her eyes met Delgado's. He felt a sharp spike of pride that she would look to him for reassurance, and wondered what would happen when she didn't need to.

"He'll be all right," she said quietly. "Another nightmare."

"I'm not surprised," Delgado replied, just as quietly. "You okay?"

"I don't even remember getting out of bed," she said, gently freeing her fingers from the boy's and easing off the bed. Delgado stepped up to her side and took her elbow, steadying her. "Maybe I should just sleep in here."

"If you want," he said automatically. *I wouldn't bet on it, angel,* he thought. *You need your privacy. You've got your nightmares, too.*

"You're a godsend, Rowan," Emily said, her cooling coffee still held in one hand. "I'm so sorry."

"Oh, patients always call just when you get a cup of coffee," Rowan replied, tucking a strand of hair behind her ear. "I know that. How's he doing, Emily?"

"Better than me," Boomer snorted. "Can I go back to sleep?"

"You're a crotchety old man," Eleanor told him, settling back in her bed and closing her eyes. "Shut up. Good work, Rowan. The boy's much easier now. He even laughed yesterday."

"Old witch," Boomer said, just softly enough.

"Shut *up*," Eleanor returned.

Emily was trying in vain not to grin.

Rowan smiled, shaking her head. "I suppose I should inquire about my other patients," she said. "Including a rather crotchety old man."

"Just fine," Boomer muttered. "Can't a man get any sleep around here?"

Rowan cast an amused glance at Delgado. His mouth went dry. She brushed her tangled hair back and crossed to Boomer's bedside. When she reached down and took his wrist to check his pulse, the stocky man peeked out from under his eyelashes at her. Then his face eased, and in a few moments, he was asleep too. "There," Rowan said softly. "Don't dream. Just sleep until morning."

"Good riddance," Eleanor said. When Rowan took a step toward her, she added, "No, none for me, Miss Price. I'm fine. Thanks anyway."

Rowan nodded, then looked to Delgado again, tucking her pale hair back behind her ear. "I'm sorry," she said, but Delgado shook his head and offered his hand. She took it, the electric jolt of her skin against his making him glad the lighting was so dim. How could a woman in a torn sweatshirt and shorts make his pulse race?

"Thank you, Rowan," Emily said seriously. "I don't know how we got along without you."

"I'm just glad to be useful," Rowan replied, and Delgado ushered her through the infirmary's swinging doors, his arm carefully over her shoulder.

Out in the hall she sighed, her shoulders sagging. "God," she said quietly. "Does it ever end?"

"Not really," he answered. "They want psionics, and they'll do what they have to do to get them."

"But he's just a little boy." Rowan didn't shake away from his arm. If he was careful and casual, helping her through the halls when she was too tired to notice, she let him stay near her.

"A little boy who can start fires just by staring at things," Delgado reminded her. "They can use that."

Rowan shuddered. He gently stroked her shoulder with his thumb, a soothing touch.

The first few weeks of her stay at Society Headquarters had been touch-and-go. She hadn't eaten much and had almost invariably refused to leave Delgado's room. She had slept eighteen hours out of twenty-four, and then she'd spent the rest of the time staring blankly at the ceiling, no matter how Delgado cajoled or pleaded with her.

It had been Henderson who had found the solution. On one of his frequent visits, he had mentioned Boomer's nightmares and sighed heavily. *He needs help,* Henderson had said, *but nobody knows what to do for him.* And he had left soon after that, winking at a mystified Delgado.

That day, Rowan had prowled his room restlessly, and finally—hallelujah—asked where the infirmary was.

Since then, things had been much easier. For two months

now she had slowly been exploring Headquarters and learning about the new place she found herself in. And if she didn't seem to notice that Delgado was sleeping in an armchair, if she didn't notice that he was building on the foundation he'd laid while she was sedated, teaching her how to control her gifts, if she didn't notice that he was always there when she woke shuddering and sweat-soaked from another nightmare— well, he was happy. What she didn't notice, she couldn't tell him to stop doing.

Henderson had begun to spend an hour a day with her, too, teaching her some basic psionic theory. It was excruciatingly slow, but Delgado had time. As long as she let him stay close to her, he had time.

"Why doesn't someone stop them?" she asked.

He felt a quick swell of pride in her. It usually took most new recruits, especially the shell-shocked ones, at least eight months to ask that question. "They're government, Rowan. They believe they're fighting the good fight. Each psionic they get hooked on Zed and obedient is one more psionic to make America strong. And since they're black sector, they have the funding they need as long with no Congressional oversight as long as they produce results. And they've been producing results for a good forty-seven years now."

Rowan sighed as they turned the corner. "It just seems so wrong," she said.

You have no idea, angel, he thought. "It's making certain people very rich," he pointed out. "Very powerful people."

"But the newspapers....the media..." She sighed again.

"Some of the media magnates are the ones getting rich," he pointed out. His door slid open as they approached. "It's a dirty thing, Rowan. A really dirty thing. We do what we can."

He scanned the room before letting go of her shoulders and locking the door with a touch on the handpad set in the wall. Nobody here, of course. He paused, struck by a novel thought. *It looks different in here.*

Books were piled on a new nightstand of pale blond wood, and two new bookshelves of the same unfinished type flanked his old metal shelving. Rowan had found a length of green chiffon somewhere and draped it over the top of the curtain rod. She sometimes remarked that she wanted to sleep with the French door ajar when it wasn't so chilly anymore. A rubber tree in a terra cotta pot stood on a wrought-iron plant rack by the window, and he'd put up ceiling hooks so she could hang airplane plants and one plant with pretty, trailing purplish leaves. A fern she'd rescued from a neglected corner was now green and healthy, perched atop one of the bookshelves, and she'd thrown a blue and green shawl over the plain white bedspread. Rowan dropped down on the bed and yawned, her shoulders slumping. She would probably sleep in tomorrow.

Well, she's moved in and made herself at home, he thought, and the flush of heat that went through him wasn't unpleasant at all. She'd made a wistful remark about a CD player yesterday, and he reminded himself to requisition one for her. Nobody said anything directly to Delgado, of course, and nobody asked her why she was staying in his room instead of requesting a suite of her own.

She stopped yawning and looked up at him. "Justin," she said quietly, "is this your room?"

He shrugged. How could he explain to her that no place was home? He just slept wherever he could find a moment to close his eyes. He hadn't had a place to call his own since Sigma had trained him. "I like what you've done with it," he said cautiously.

"You mean I've kicked you out of your own bed for *months* and you haven't said a word about it?"

He shrugged again. "It's not a big deal, Rowan."

"I thought you were just worried about them coming after me again," she said, and shivered slightly.

"They would have to spend a lot of money and man-hours to crack Headquarters," he said immediately. "That is, if they could *find* it, which they can't. We have defenses in place, Rowan. They can't attack us any more than we can attack them."

She looked down into her lap, her fingers twisting together. "This is really happening, isn't it," she said, dully.

Christ, just when we were doing so well, he thought, and crossed to the window and peered out. It was habit, and he barely paid attention, only noting the frozen garden below and the field beyond lying under a scrim of moonlight. "I wish you'd talk to one of the counselors. They're qualified; I'm not. I'm just an operative."

"They're all frightened of you," she observed, mildly enough.

He let it go. He knew her well enough not to push. "Are

you?"

"I don't think so. Should I be?"

"Maybe. Probably not." His neck was beginning to hurt.

"You're trying to teach me, aren't you?"

"Just what you want to know, that's all."

"I've been wondering if there are...classes. Psychic classes."

"There are. You can attend if you want." *They're required classes if you want to be an operative, angel. But you need time. They won't push you.* The thought of anyone trying to force her into something as simple as a meditation seminar made a bubble of anger rise inside his spine.

"If I do..." She worried at her lower lip with her pearly teeth.

God, please don't let her say what I think she's going to say.

"...what will you do?"

Relief welled up inside him. "I'm officially your mentor. I'll be with you."

She nodded and her hands relaxed. *I doubt she even knows how tense she is,* he thought. *I should have forced the issue with her when I had the chance. It would give me an excuse to try some old-fashioned therapy on us both right now.* "Okay," she said. "Can I talk to you about something?"

He leaned against the closed door. "Sure."

She pulled her legs up on the bed, sitting Indian-style, fully awake. "About...about my father."

Delgado sighed inwardly and stuck his hands in his pockets. He'd been sleeping in his clothes for months now, not that he minded. "Your father."

"Did they cover it up? How did they explain it? How can I...I mean..."

We just keep going from one dangerous subject to the next, he thought, and winced. One question leading to another and another, and before he knew it, he'd be telling her everything. "There's been total media silence, but there's a warrant out for your arrest as a material witness. Your father was buried at the VA. Hilary had insurance, and her boss—some guy named Vernon—made the arrangements for the memorial service. She's buried at Mount Hope."

Hope sprang up on her face, but it was swiftly smothered. "I can't even go to their graves, can I."

Christ, she's too smart. "Rowan…" *What can I tell her?* "Look, it's dangerous. But if you have to go, tell me. We can find some way to get you there."

She stared at him, an expression of such patent surprise on her face that he was tempted to laugh. Did she think he would tell her she couldn't visit her own father's grave after seeing him die violently right in front of her? *You haven't even gotten out of the numb stage of grieving yet, angel. And when you do…* "You'd really do that?" she asked.

"Of course." *I want you happy, Rowan. I want you safe, and I want you happy. You won't ever understand.*

"Justin?"

He surfaced from mulling over the dilemma to find her examining him. Her eyebrows were drawn together, and her lovely eyes were shadowed with something he was uncomfortably familiar with.

Anger.

"These…these Sigma people." She took a deep breath. "I want to stop them."

Delgado blinked, shoving his hands even further into his pockets.

"Are you listening to me? I want them *stopped.* They killed my father. I want them in court. I want them to go to prison."

Delgado stared at her. Whatever he'd expected, it hadn't been this.

She was waiting for him to reply, something suspiciously like trust shining in her luminous eyes, and faint color brushing her cheeks. Why hadn't he *pushed* her when he'd had the chance? He could be on the bed next to her right now, and he could distract her from this conversation.

He cleared his throat. "Ah, Rowan." *How am I going to tell you this?* "The justice system won't help us. Believe me, we've tried. Witnesses disappear, papers get destroyed, all of a sudden people get alibis or can't be found, and the whole thing's swept under the rug. They have carte blanche to do what they like. The cops and the judges and the media won't stop them. Hell, in some cases they *are* the cops and the judges and the media. We've tried taking them down before, and all we've accomplished is losing a lot of good people."

She stared at him like he was speaking a foreign language. He tried again. "Look, Rowan. Sigma's *government.* They have the weight of the government behind them, and the work they do for the intelligence agencies makes them golden. FBI, CIA, ATF, NSA—*nobody* can touch them. If we gave proof of their activities to media outlets, all we'd have would be a bunch of dead journalists and missing pieces of proof. And it would be heart attacks and car accidents instead of surgical seek-and-capture teams, angel."

"There's got to be *something*—" she started.

"There is," he interrupted. "We recruit who we can, and we save kids like Bobby and train them. We fight where we can, we stay alive, and we wait. Someday we'll have the odds in our favor, Ro. When we do, we'll erase the motherfu...ah, we'll strike where it hurts 'em most. Sooner or later they won't have enough psionics to do any work, if we just quietly keep stealing them. That way we don't have a lot of dead bodies."

"Except my father," she said, her eyes glittering. "And Hilary."

"What do you want me to do? We've tried before. We can't do it. They have too much help from the big boys in politics, angel. It goes all the way to the top."

"Why doesn't anyone *talk* about this?" she almost yelled.

That's a good question, angel. "Sometimes they do," he said quietly. "They end up in mental wards. Or with their lives destroyed, branded as nutcases. Or they have a heart attack or a car accident or they vanish and the cops say, 'Maybe they just went to Reno, people vanish all the time.' People do vanish all the time, Rowan, and if it isn't reported on the six o'clock spot, who will ever put the pieces together? And most people don't want to know..." He trailed off, seeing the fury on her face. Her hands were back to scrubbing at each other.

"You told me I'm a thirteen," she said suddenly. "On this Morris scale."

"Matheson," he corrected automatically.

"Matheson. You told me I could incite riots." Her eyes glittered, deadly sharp.

Oh, Christ. Don't, Rowan. Don't do this. "You could," he agreed cautiously. "You've got the talent."

"All right," she said. "I want to take classes. I want to know how to...how to use whatever this thing is. This psychic thing."

That's a relief. Whatever it takes to drive her through getting some control. I can always talk her out of it later, can't I? But Delgado wasn't sure he could talk Rowan Price out of anything, especially when all he could think of was how soft the fragile curve of her throat looked; how her eyes were full of depth and shading even now, when she was furious. "Of course," he said. "We'll teach you everything we can. *I'll* teach you everything I can."

"And then I'm going to do whatever I have to," she said. "Will you help me?"

Oh, Jesus. "Rowan—"

"Will you?" She was merciless. Those eyes bored into his, and the prickling intensity of her ran over his skin. He was almost used to it now, the way his body responded. This wasn't reasonable or rational or logical. He was in deep trouble. "Please? I can't trust anyone else, Justin. You know I can't."

That was exactly where he was most vulnerable, whether she knew it or not. He knew she didn't think of him as anything other than a defense against the violent turn her life had taken.

"All right," he said, his heart sinking. "But if you want to take on Sigma, you'll need some hard training. You probably won't like it."

His last-ditch attempt failed. "I don't mind hard work." Her hands turned into fists. Delgado couldn't help himself. He crossed the room, dropping onto the bed next to her with a weary sigh. He reached over, took one of her hands, and pried at her fingers until they uncurled.

"You've got to relax," he said quietly. "If you go working yourself up, you'll affect the patients. There are a lot of sensitives in here, Rowan, and you're powerful. You could make them very nervous. I've already told you I'll help you. Just take a deep breath, okay?"

She stared at him for a few moments, her face unreadable. Then she shut her eyes and inhaled deeply.

Delgado watched her face. She took another deep breath, and another. The angry flush in her cheeks faded.

The prickling heat that ran through him from the touch of her skin did not.

No wonder they think I'm crazy, he thought, examining the curve of her cheekbone, the soft vulnerable space beneath her lower lip.

"Sorry," she said finally, without opening her eyes. "You're right. I shouldn't get carried away." A long pause, silence ticking through the room. "Should I get a room of my own, Justin?"

"Only if you want to," he answered unthinkingly.

Hey eyes opened, caught him unawares. "You're a nice guy," she said, as if surprised.

No, I'm not, he thought. *You just haven't seen me yet, angel.* He had to concentrate before he could open his hand and let her fingers slide out of his. "I like having you around," he admitted. "It's…soothing."

That's probably the best way to approach her, he realized cynically. *Use that soft heart of hers, Del. If you're determined, that is. If you've got the guts to try it.*

He knew what he didn't want. He didn't want to manipulate her, didn't want to move her through the game until he was where he wanted to be.

Too bad he was going to have to. If she planned on taking down Sigma, she would need him.

I'm insane, he thought. *I've gone mad.*

She grinned, the shadows in her eyes easing for a moment, and Delgado's heart made a funny twisting movement. "Nobody's ever called me soothing before," she said, and patted his shoulder. "Why don't you take the bed tonight, and I'll sleep in the chair?"

He shrugged, standing slowly. *If I don't get out of here I'm going to push her, and she'll retreat again.* "No, I should go check in at Central anyway. You go ahead and get some sleep. I'll be back in a little while."

"All work and no play," she said, but shook her head and motioned him away. "Go on, I'll be fine. Thank you, Justin."

What the hell is she thanking me for? Doesn't she know why I'm doing this?

"No problem, angel. Anytime."

The trouble isn't that I say that, he thought grimly, shutting her in his room after making sure the hall was clear. *The trouble is I mean it. I've gone domestic. God, what a mess.*

He sighed, squared his shoulders, and set off down the hall.

Twenty-Four

Rowan turned over, pulling the sheet up. Then she yawned and opened her eyes.

Delgado sat on that awful, battered orange armchair, his head in his hands and his elbows on his knees. He looked tired, and he was wearing the same clothes he'd worn yesterday—jeans, a black T-shirt, and a pair of boots. *Does he always sleep in his clothes?* Rowan wondered.

She pushed herself up on her elbows, watching him, sudden guilt biting sharply under her breastbone. She hadn't even thought to inquire whose room this was; she'd thought it was a spare bedroom even though his clothes were in the closet and the chair was obviously his. She hadn't been thinking clearly at all.

Sunlight poured in through the French door leading to the balcony, poured in through the window as well. Rowan yawned again and ran her fingers back through her hair, wincing as she encountered tangles. "Morning," she said, and his shoulders hunched.

When he looked up, he didn't look any different. Same flat hazel eyes, same straight serious mouth. He was a little pale, that was all. "What's wrong?" Rowan asked immediately. "Did something happen?"

He shrugged, sitting up and stretching, the movement bringing him to his feet in one fluid motion. "How are you? Sleep well?"

"Don't put me off." She slid her legs out of bed. "What's wrong, Justin?"

Nobody else calls him that, she realized suddenly. *It's Delgado, or sir, or Del if they're feeling friendly. Nobody else calls him by his real name.* That made her frown, thinking about it. Had he told her his name, or had she picked it out of the air? She sometimes did that, and most people assumed they had just told her their names. She tried not to do that. Mom had always said it was rude to use someone's name without permission.

"We lost another operative," he said quietly. "One of Shelton's gang. It's just depressing, that's all. I hate losing good people." He watched her closely, she realized, without seeming to. *Why does he do that?*

"I'm sorry," she said immediately. It seemed like being one of the "operatives" was dangerous. This was the eighth one she'd heard about dying. "Why do they...I mean, what..."

"Sigma," he said, turning away. He crossed to the window and looked out. "Fucking Sigma. You want some coffee?"

"I should." She watched his broad back as he leaned against the wall, the sunlight bringing out chestnut highlights in his dark hair. She couldn't see any weapons, but she knew he was probably armed. Was it wrong to find that so comforting?

The hardwood floor was cool under her feet as she approached him cautiously. When she was close enough, she touched his shoulder. "I'm sorry," she repeated. "I know it...it affects you." Her fingers seemed to burn where they touched him, and her stomach fluttered.

He glanced at her, sunlight turning his skin coppery. Rowan was suddenly aware that she had just rolled out of bed. Her hair was tangled, and she was probably crusty from sleeping. She had morning breath, and she was wearing a ratty old sweatshirt and a pair of too-short shorts. Justin might look tired, but he never looked rumpled or imprecise.

"It does affect me," he said, looking back out at the garden. "I combat trained four or five of Shelton's kids. I keep thinking that if I'd trained them a little harder they'd still be alive."

"It's not your fault," she said, her hand moving almost of its own volition. She was rubbing his shoulder with her palm, trying to comfort him. "Really, it's not."

He shrugged. "I know it's not. But I just...I feel responsible."

Why do I want to hug him? she thought, and took her hand away. It was completely inappropriate, and he didn't know about the way her entire body seemed dipped in electric crackles when she touched him. She had noticed that he avoided touching anyone else, and they avoided touching him. Something to do with his talent, with something he could do.

Something Sigma had trained him to do.

He's lonely, she thought, and bit at her lower lip. "Justin—"

"I'll go get coffee," he said abruptly, turning away and brushing past her. There it was again—that sense of a wall going up, a door slamming shut. "You want breakfast here or in the caf? We're due at class at 0800."

"The cafeteria, probably, I want to stop by the infirmary

and...Justin, will you look at me? What did I do?"

He stopped, his shoulders coming up again. "You didn't do anything, Rowan. I'm just...upset, that's all."

"Justin—"

"It's not you," he said again, taking another step toward the door.

"Justin." Rowan used the same tone she would have on a balking patient refusing to take his medication—firm and clear. "What's wrong? You can tell me."

"I've just made a decision," he said, not turning to look at her.

What does that mean? she thought, and folded her arms. "Will you look at me, please?"

He turned, reluctantly. His eyes were dark and haunted, and Rowan's heart leapt into her throat. This was the most emotion she'd ever seen from him—except for when she'd *touched* him.

She took three quick steps, raising her hand, but he caught her wrist. Goose bumps slid down her back. "No."

"I want to help you," she said.

"I'm not injured." His eyes were, though—raw and open. Wells of pain. His mouth was drawn down too tightly, betraying nothing. He was taller than her, and muscle moved under his skin. She'd seen just how lethally quick he could be.

I should be afraid of him, she thought. *They're all afraid of him. But I just can't be.*

"Please," she said, softly. "Let me."

Something crossed his face swiftly, like a snarl. Rowan didn't move, didn't flinch—she was used to this. He wasn't going to hurt her. "It's okay, Rowan. Save it for the patients, I'll be fine."

"But—"

He looked at her hand, her wrist caught in his fingers, as if he was trying to figure out how it got there. "I'll be *fine*. Don't worry about me. I just decided what I'm going to do, that's all."

Rowan's heart began to pound. "What does that mean?"

"Just relax, okay?" He let go of her wrist, and her hand dropped uselessly down to her side. "I'll be back in a minute with some coffee. If you want to go to class, you should get ready. There's a trip into town scheduled for tomorrow, too, if you want to go with Cath."

"I have to get—"

He was gone out the door before she could finish the sentence.

Well, that was weird. No weirder than anything else, lately, I suppose...but still. Why did he touch me like that? Like he was trying not to hurt me. She rubbed at her wrist, even though he hadn't hurt her. He'd been exquisitely gentle, the way he always was whenever he touched her.

Rowan's hand flew to her mouth.

No. It wasn't possible. But...

You just stop that silliness, she told herself. *Go take a shower and get ready for these classes. You've got work to do, and the sooner the better.*

But all through her morning ritual, even though she scolded herself, dropped the shampoo and nearly killed herself slipping on some soap, she felt his fingers on her wrist and smelled his after-shave. And oddly enough, that made her heart race every time. Even when she started yanking the tangles free of her hair and banged her hip into the sink when she heard a slight noise and thought perhaps he'd come back.

Twenty-Five

"Headquarters" was a complex of brownstone buildings, and the cafeteria was in another building. Rowan could have used the underground transport system to get there, but she liked being out in the open. It was a sunny day, even if the wind was knife-edged with the promise of snow. So she walked across the landscaped quad and into the east building, shivering and carrying the folder Justin had suggested she bring. In it were blank pieces of paper, two pens, and a sharpened No. 2 pencil.

Rowan still didn't know a quarter of the huge place. On the surface it looked just like a college campus—brownstone buildings, gardens, paths going here or there. The real bulk of the place was underground. She'd seen at least two hangers big enough for aircraft, then there was Four East, where Henderson had his command center. She still wasn't sure exactly what Henderson did, but he seemed to be a leader here, and Justin was his second in command.

Justin had even taken her into the great nerve center of Central Op. Banks of computers and funny things that looked right out of futuristic movies. They had technology here that wouldn't be available to the general public for at least a decade.

The cafeteria was underground, and Rowan was hungry. She had no choice. Justin hadn't come back with coffee, and that was unusual. He was usually so punctual. The cafeteria's fluorescent lights shone on a linoleum floor, and the place looked like every other communal eating place she'd ever seen—a sort of orderly chaos, groups of people clustered at their regular tables. Every "neophyte" had a "mentor," someone to show them the ropes and steer them around the complex.

"Rowan! Hey, Rowan!" Catherine waved her arm frantically, silver bracelets flashing. She was at their usual table. Beside her, Zeke hunched over his tray, shoveling in a small mountain of grits loaded with cheese.

Rowan made it to the table, tucking wet hair behind her ears. She should have dried it; she was still chilled. "Hey, guys," she greeted.

"'Bout time," was Catherine's idea of a pleasant hello. She seemed incapable of being polite, sometimes going out of her way to be abrasive.

Yoshi looked up from a thick technical manual. Light glinted off his wire-framed glasses. "Miss Rowan," he said, and smiled. "You look magnificent."

Rowan had to laugh. Yoshi was calm, and cool, and professional without being dry. He also had a wickedly ironic sense of humor.

"I got you a tray," Brewster said. "No bacon, right?" Rowan made a face, laughing. "You know I like bacon. Justin was supposed to bring some coffee, but I guess he got hung up. I start class today." She eased herself down next to Brewster, glancing at her tray. "How did you know I like grapefruit?"

"I'm bloody well psychic, remember?" He grinned, his white teeth shining. "So you're taking operative classes? How'd you talk Del into that?"

"Good morning, everyone," Henderson said, and there was a general scramble. Zeke and Brewster would have made it to their feet to salute, but Henderson waved them back down.

"Hey, General," Catherine greeted him. "Our star girl's going to class today. Looks like she'll be a full op before long, whaddaya say?"

"I say that's her business and not yours, young lady. Good morning to you, by the way." Henderson lowered himself into the seat opposite Rowan's. "Good morning, Rowan."

"Morning, sir," she said, taking a sip of orange juice. Brew had loaded her plate with extra bacon, and she was hungry. She set to it with a will.

Someone across the room laughed, the sound sharp and clear above the crowd-noise. Rowan glanced around. Until now, she had always felt uneasy in crowds, a soft press of emotion choking her on every side. Here it was different, a blessed relief. Everyone knew how to keep their emotions from drowning her. Justin called it shielding and had taught her how to do it, but Rowan couldn't quite remember how or when the lesson had taken place.

Justin's arm came over her shoulder, and he set a cup of coffee down on the table. A brief silence wrapped around the group. "Sorry I'm late," he said, his voice slicing the crowd-noise effortlessly. He lowered himself into the seat on Rowan's other side.

Sitting between Brewster and Justin meant that Rowan was effectively closed in from either side. She normally didn't like that feeling, but here it was comforting.

Justin settled himself, and then he looked at her as the conversation started again. Henderson asked about something called a flux-phase and Yoshi set his book aside.

"I got hung up, called to Central," Justin said quietly. "I'm sorry, Rowan."

"It's okay," she said around a mouthful of grapefruit. "I knew you'd be along."

He seemed pleased by that, smiling, and took a drink from his own coffee cup. "Nice to see you're getting along here."

"I like it," she said. "Everyone seems so…well, nice." It was still hard to believe they were all people who had freakish abilities like hers, but it was also kind of comforting. "Are you going with me this morning?"

"Of course. Hey, Brewster, did you finish that mock-up?"

"I did," Brew said. "I wondered when you'd ask. Listen, I'm not sure about the third sequence. It's too hard to tell."

"I can guess at it, I think. I just needed the second to figure out what the beginning of the third looked like. Any news from Blake's team yet?"

"None yet. It's beginning to look grim. Soren's wearing his red bandanna again." Brew took a long drink of apple juice and grimaced as if it was bitter.

"Any luck with dowsers?" Justin looked quiet and calm, as usual, but Rowan could feel tension vibrating from him.

"Nope, they were operating standard-silent. If we had another 5RV we could probably track them down, but as it is we have to wait until they break cover."

Rowan wondered if she'd ever been discussed at this table. Had she been a "subject under watch?"

And what had Sigma been saying about her? Had she been measured, plans drawn up, risk assessments done?

It was an uncomfortable line of thought. Rowan finished half her breakfast and stared into her coffee cup. Her stomach had closed itself, as it did so frequently nowadays.

"You should eat," Justin said quietly.

She looked up to find him watching her. How long had he been watching her?

"I can't." She finished the rest of her coffee in one scalding gulp. "Is it time?"

"We've got a little while. I'd like to show you something."

"All right." She eased herself to her feet, chair scraping

on the linoleum. Henderson glanced at her, Brewster nodded, and Cath gifted her with a rare, beneficent smile. "See ya round, Price," the blue-Mohawked girl said. "Glad you're signing on."

What choice do I have? Rowan thought. "Thank you, Cath. Thanks for getting my tray, Brew."

"Just leave it, love. I'll carry it up," he replied, wearing his trademark wide white grin. "See you this afternoon!"

Now what does he mean by that? Rowan settled for nodding and letting Justin draw her away.

"He'll have basic meditation with you this afternoon," he said in her ear as they negotiated the maze of tables. "I'm sorry I was late, Rowan."

"It's all right." She slid her arm through his and felt his surprise. It was odd. He was usually so closed-off she couldn't tell what he was feeling.

He led her through a faceless white hall with fluorescents and a stone floor, and then into a transport. "Second Level, Excel." His voice didn't change, but Rowan's cheeks suddenly felt hot. The coffee rose uneasily in her throat. "Are you all right?" he asked

"I just hate being underground. Justin?"

"Hm?"

"Did you mean it? About…about helping me?"

He went so still she wanted to check to see if he was breathing. "Of course," he said. "I wish it wasn't like this, Rowan. I wish I could have stopped them from hurting you."

I wish you could have too. "Why didn't you tell me?"

"Would you have believed me?"

She knew he was right, but it didn't stop the nausea or the lump in her throat. Or the sudden tears filling her eyes. *He did everything he could,* she told herself. *Don't blame him.*

But there was nobody else, was there? She had nobody else left in the world. Dad was dead, and Hilary was dead, and Rowan was alone.

Except for Justin Delgado.

The transport slowed. Rowan, without meaning to, tightened her grip on Justin's arm. He said nothing.

When the doors finally opened, he led her out, and she gasped.

"It's a track," he said. "Quarter mile. In the middle there's free weights and a practice ground."

The track was covered in rubberized black stuff, perfect

for runners. The lighting was as close to sunlight as you could get, and cool air raised goose bumps on her arms. It was as close to perfect as possible. How did they fit all this stuff underground? They lived like moles, barely surfacing, only the most claustrophobic living aboveground. Rowan was suddenly, intensely glad Justin had an aboveground room.

Ruin your knees, running like that, her father's voice floated up through her memory. A lump filled Rowan's throat.

In the middle, a group of people were doing t'ai chi— slow, even dancing movements. Rowan swallowed, hard. "Thank you," she said, right before something occurred to her. "How did you know I—"

"I would hate to be cooped up, and here you can feel safe. And you're in good shape, Rowan. It's obvious you exercise. You told me you liked to run."

Had she? She didn't remember telling him.

"Thank you," Rowan said, and impulsively went up on tiptoe. She kissed his cheek, pressing her lips against his shaven skin. He froze again, and she caught a flash of another feeling from him, gone too quickly to identify. *That's twice in a row. It's odd, he's normally so closed off.* "I mean it. Thank you. This is...it's wonderful."

"We'd better go," he said. "We'll be late."

Twenty-Six

The classes were not what she expected.

The room was bright and sunny, aboveground. Sheer curtains made the thin winter sunlight mellow; there were comfortable blue-upholstered couches scattered around. A merry fire crackled in a stone fireplace, a reproduction of van Gogh's "Starry Night" hung on one wall, and a watercolor of poppies in a wheat field hung on another. The room was full of plants—philodendrons trailing green, orchids in small terracotta pots, a small orange tree set in the sunlight near the window.

A woman stood in front of the window, her golden hair catching fire. Four other women were on the couches, one of them huddling next to a taller red-haired woman. Three teenage boys and one dark-haired man took some of the other seats.

"It's Rowan, isn't it?" Dr. Jilssen said, pumping her hand. His sticklike paw trembled with excitement, his soggy eyes behind their horn-rimmed glasses devouring her. "Come in, come in."

Rowan's stomach turned over and rose, choking her. She tried to free her hand from the doctor's but couldn't. Justin tensed next to her.

"Dr. Jilssen," the golden-haired woman said crisply, pushing her glasses up her sharp nose. Jilssen finally let go of Rowan's hand, leaving her pulse to thunder in her ears. *Sick, I'm going to be sick.* But the feeling passed away as soon as she thought it. "Leave the girl alone. You're an observer. Mr. Delgado, will you be participating today?"

"Of course," Justin said. "I'm her mentor."

"Good enough." She wasn't tall, but her posture made her seem that way. Her hair was pulled back in a chignon, a few stray strands escaping, but even those strands looked planned, intentional. She wore a blue peasant shirt and a pair of jeans, but the jeans were ironed, sharp creases standing out. Her eyes blazed green in the sunlight behind the lenses of her glasses, and a pair of long silver hoops glittered in her ears. "Will you please take a seat, then, and we'll begin. Edward, why don't you go first?"

Rowan lowered herself onto a blue velvet couch. Justin settled right next to her.

A teenage boy with faint ghosts of acne on his face stood up. "I, ah, I'm Eddie," he said to Rowan. "I'm borderline telepathic. I can make people go to sleep."

Rowan blinked. "Really?" She tried not to flinch. The boy was obviously painfully shy. *Do they just say it out loud like that?*

"Who wants to?" he said, and Dr. Jilssen raised one dry hand.

"You might as well try it on me, boy," he said, shifting his thin frame inside his lab coat. "Anything for research, you know."

The boy's dark, moist gaze swiveled around and met the doctor's. "*Noctis,*" he mumbled, and his eyes seemed to swell for a moment.

The doctor, who had been perched on a straight-backed chair, suddenly slumped.

"Edward," the woman said.

Rowan was suddenly fascinated. The teenage boy managed to catch the doctor as he almost fell off the chair. But what excited Rowan was that she could *see*, somehow, what Edward was doing, just like when she walked into the ward she could tell who was having trouble on a particular day, nurses as well as patients. She could see exactly where the boy had *pressed* to put the doctor to sleep. She could see how she could do it quicker and easier.

Justin was completely still next to her, but all of the people in the class were giving him funny little sidelong looks.

"Now," the woman said, "Edward's telepathy is sight-line, which is fairly usual. Amanda, why don't you see what you can do? Edward, try to retain control of the doctor's sleep pattern. Remember, I'm standing right here."

The girl, Amanda, was dressed in a red sweatshirt and a ragged pair of jeans. "I don't want to hurt him, Ms. Kate," she said, as she stood reluctantly. Her hair was a shock of carrot-top red, unsuccessfully slicked down with gel.

"Then don't," Ms. Kate said, but her tone had softened. "Remember, I'm here. There's no danger."

The girl nodded, biting her lip. "I'm Amanda," she said softly, not meeting Rowan's eyes. "I can make people do things, sometimes."

"A variant of telepathy and compulsion," Ms. Kate corrected primly. "Whenever you like, young lady."

Amanda approached Eddie cautiously. He sidled away from her, nervous, but when she stopped about four feet from him, a change came over her. "Don't be silly," she said, her voice suddenly deep with authority. "I won't hurt you. Why don't you come with me?"

Rowan found herself trembling. *She's pushing at him with her mind. Look at that. It's incredible—and I can see it. I could DO it. I never knew...*

"Sloppy, Amanda," Kate said. "Sharpen your focus."

Justin picked up Rowan's free hand. She was clutching her folder in her other fist, the stiff paper crumpling. The feeling of his skin on hers soothed her.

"Come with me," Amanda repeated, her face gone pale. "Leave him alone."

Eddie made a small sound, breath rushing out of him. Dr. Jilssen swayed in his arms.

"All right, that's enough," Kate said calmly, moving forward out of the bar of sunlight. "Let go, Amanda. You too, Eddie. Very good. Now, did everyone note that Eddie kept physical contact with the good Doctor while fighting off Amanda's pressure?"

The doctor woke with a start and grinned broadly at Eddie. He seemed not to mind being put to sleep or awakened.

And yet...there was a frightened, ratty little gleam in the doctor's eyes. It had come and gone so quickly she wasn't sure she'd seen it.

These people are like me, Rowan thought. *They can do what I can do. Dad would have loved this.*

"All receptive telepathy Talents are helped by physical contact, and *most* projective telepathy Talents are helped by physical contact," Kate continued as Eddie and Amanda took their seats again. "Can someone give me an example of a projective telepathy Talent that isn't helped by physical contact?"

Another teenage boy raised his hand. He had a smooth cap of sandy blond hair and blue eyes fringed with the thick eyelashes some boys were blessed with. "Some types of Pushing?" he ventured. "And the illusion-based talents, like Monica's?"

"Very good," Kate nodded. "The projective Talents that seem to utilize a form of autosuggestion are *not* generally helped by physical contact. In certain cases, like Mr. Delgado, aspects of 'the push', as it's called, aren't helped by physical contact because of the feedback from the pain endured by the subject. Certain 'magnification' types of telepathy also exhibit this trait to a lesser degree."

As Kate continued speaking, Rowan slipped her hand free of Justin's and began taking notes. This was fascinating, and if Henderson hadn't been spending so much time patiently coaching her, she would have been completely lost in the terminology.

"Do we get to see Del do something?" the third teenage boy said.

"No," Kate replied, with a freezing look. "Mr. Delgado's talent is not for public display."

"Is it true he was in Sigma?" the boy asked again.

Delgado didn't move. Kate glanced at him. "Ask him, Thomas. Now, if you don't mind, let's get back to class."

"What about her?" Thomas persisted. "What can she do?"

My God, he's talking about me, Rowan realized.

"Miss Price?" Kate asked. "Are you comfortable with speaking about your talent, for Thomas's edification? I'm sure the rest of us are curious, as well."

Justin turned to look at her.

Rowan gathered herself. "Oh," she said, her voice sounding strange even to herself. "I don't know what you'd call it. I…I help people feel better." She trailed off, appealed to Justin with a mute glance.

"Rowan's Talent is particularly interesting," he said. "With your permission, Miss Kate?"

"Of course." The teacher nodded, folding her arms.

Justin leaned forward. The entire group fixed their eyes on him. "Miss Price registers a 13 on the Matheson scale," he said, and everyone's eyes got a little rounder. "Her talents seem concentrated in telepathy and empathy, with a very interesting twist. Rowan helps people feel safer, calmer, almost like a tranquilizer. She calls it 'the touch', and it's particularly useful on developmentally-disabled people and the mentally ill."

"Those are the hardest kinds of people to Push," Amanda said. "Wow."

Rowan's cheeks were hot.

"She has a small but significant telekinetic talent that seems to affect living tissue, speeding the healing process; there is also a certain degree of precognition present." Justin had everyone's attention. "With proper training, most kinds of applied telepathy will probably be available to her."

"Very good, Mr. Delgado," Kate took up the thread. "Now, can anyone tell me what the drawback to mixed telepathy and empathy is?"

Rowan found that she was holding Justin's hand again. *Why do I do that?* she thought.

He squeezed back, and she had to swallow the lump in her throat. Her father would have loved this. He had always believed in unseen things.

She didn't know what she'd expected, but this quiet acceptance certainly wasn't it. Maybe it wasn't so bad being a freak.

As soon as she thought that, however, she saw her father's ghostly face and heard the chilling little gurgle as all the light in her father's body went out. *It is bad,* she reminded herself grimly. *It is bad. It killed Daddy, and it killed Hilary, and it—*

"Rowan? You okay?" Justin asked quietly, almost whispering.

"Fine," Rowan whispered back, and took a deep breath. *I can handle this. I can do this. I have to, if I want to get back at the people who killed Daddy.*

Then she looked up, and Dr. Jilssen hurriedly looked away, as if he'd been staring at her.

Twenty-Seven

Delgado handed her a bottle of mineral water. "Take a deep breath," he said. "It's okay."

She gasped out a curse that would have made him smile if his heart hadn't been pounding. "You'll learn," he continued. "You've just got to put some weight behind your punches, that's all."

Rowan took a long hit off the water bottle and looked up at him. "I've never...seen anyone...move that fast," she said. Her chest heaved.

"I've had a little more practice than you," he said. "Good thing I caught you. I didn't expect you to flinch. Sorry about that."

When he'd told her combat training was necessary for operatives, she'd seemed a little less than enthusiastic. Their third session was going much as he'd expected—Rowan had never even been taught to punch a man properly.

The big underground *dojo* was full of people, some practicing on heavy bags, Jack Morris taking four of his team through a *tae kwon do* lesson in one half of the hall, others performing *katas* or practicing with partners, one operative from Blake's old team going through some knife forms in a corner. Delgado scanned the room again and looked down at Rowan, who was struggling to get her breath back. His pulse thundered in his throat, but for an entirely different reason.

Christ, she's completely helpless, he thought, his heart sinking. *How am I going to do this?*

He'd taught plenty of green recruits, but never one that he wanted to protect so badly. "Wait until you're ready," he said. *Take your time. I'm not letting you go anywhere alone until I'm sure you can handle yourself, but that day might be a long time coming, angel.*

She had settled into a steady schedule of classes and shifts in the infirmary, training sessions with Ms. Kate and Henderson, and now workouts with Delgado. Jilssen was chomping at the bit to do some more tests, but Del had vetoed that. She hadn't reacted well to the first episode of being swabbed and measured, and the electrodes had turned her an interesting shade of white. He'd cut the session short over Jilssen's protests and gotten her out of there. No amount of scientific advancement was worth setting back all Justin's careful work with her.

Rowan took another pull off the water bottle. Sweat gleamed on her pale skin, her hair was yanked carelessly back in a ponytail, and the Spandex shorts and tank top clung to her. She seemed absolutely unconscious of the admiring looks she received from most of the men—and some of the women, too. Delgado didn't care. He was just happy she didn't notice. But he noted who watched her and for how long, and he noted as well those that looked hurriedly away when they saw him watching.

Rowan handed him the bottle. He took a pull, too, and then set it down. "Let's try something else," he said. "Make a fist and *mean* it. Right hook, right here." He held up his hand.

She balled up her fist and gave him a halfhearted punch, barely tapping his palm.

"You can do better. *Hit* me, Rowan!"

He startled her, his clipped yell slicing through the noise. She had drawn back her hand, and promptly jumped, punching him with hysterical strength. Then she stopped, as if horrified at herself. "Oh, God. I'm sor—"

"Do it again," he barked, and she stared at him as if he'd grown another head. "Come *on*, little girl, *hit* me!"

"Don't yell at me," Rowan started, but he grinned and moved in on her. She didn't like her personal space invaded and backed up involuntarily. He pressed forward, a spooky darting rush guaranteed to frighten her.

Rowan let out a half-yelp and punched at his hand. Another solid strike. Delgado stopped. "Good," he said, his tone softening. "Like that. See? Punch me like you mean it."

"I don't want to hurt you."

"Pretend I'm a Sig, Rowan. You won't hurt me." *Besides, if you did, I wouldn't mind.* He flashed her a smile calculated to unsettle her—the smile that his eyes didn't echo. He moved into her personal space again, backing her up toward the wall. "Come on, Rowan, hit me again. We've got to get you over this."

She wound up and hit him again, flinching right afterwards.

"Don't *flinch*, Rowan. Hit me."

"I can't—"

"It'll take time, but you've got to learn. You want to let Sigma get away with it? Huh? *Do* you?"

That seemed to make her angry. Her eyes glittered, her lips thinning, and he thought privately that if she ever truly looked at him like that, his heart might stop.

She punched his open hand, another good solid strike. Then something seemed to break inside her, and she hit him again, her lips peeling back from her teeth. Again, and again. She broke into a wild flurry of punches with both hands, tears blurring in her eyes. She made a low hurt noise as she punched, a noise Delgado recognized from the attack on her house.

Bingo.

Finally. Come on, angel, take it out on me, get rid of it.

Rowan uttered a low, hoarse scream, her fists almost blurring. Delgado blocked the strikes with little effort, and waited until she wound down.

She finally stopped after one last punch, her head down and her ribs heaving with deep ragged breaths. Delgado glanced around the room.

Everyone was studiously avoiding looking at them. It wasn't uncommon for people to go a little crazy during a sparring session, especially shell-shocked green recruits.

Delgado waited. Eventually Rowan's breath evened out. She still looked at the floor, tears dripping off her chin. It took everything he had to stay still, to wait until she moved. The next move *had* to be hers.

Finally, she looked up, her chin trembling and her eyes huge and vulnerable. "Justin?" She sounded as if she'd just awakened from a nightmare, thready, uncertain.

"Rowan," he answered. He couldn't put all the longing he felt into that word. Couldn't even begin. *Be gentle with her now, Del.* "Let's hit the showers and get something to eat, what do you say?"

"I…I'm sorry."

"It's my fault. I shouldn't have pushed you." That was a lie. She'd needed that, would need more of it in the weeks ahead. The shell of shock and calm she'd been in wasn't healthy anymore.

And she'd let her guard down with *him.* That thought warmed him clear through, even though it had been a foregone conclusion. He was the only emotional contact she had here. The only other person she might have conceivably broken down with was Henderson, and the old man had maintained a careful distance, waiting for Delgado's clearance.

"I—" Tears welled up again.

Delgado moved a little closer. He hadn't even broken a sweat, even though his heart was pounding wildly. He slid his arm cautiously over her shoulders. "Come on. Let's get you out of here."

She leaned into his body, her eyes dropping back down to the floor. Accepting his protection, even though everybody in the *dojo* was politely ignoring whatever was happening between Delgado and his neophyte. It wasn't so strange, after all—a society of psychic people were necessarily concerned with privacy.

He chose little-used hallways to get her back to his building, and they took the lift up to the third floor. Once inside the safe haven of his room, Rowan broke away from under his arm and bolted for the bathroom. The sound of running water from the shower did little to muffle her sobs.

It hurt him to keep his distance, standing at the window and listening to her cry. It was sheer torture, in fact, especially since he had been so careful, so gentle. She was stubborn, determined not to break down, staving off all her grief with fierce pride. The toughness she was so determined to display was one more thing to love about her.

Just use some of those interrogation techniques you're so proud of, Henderson's voice snorted in his memory. Delgado leaned his forehead against the window and looked down at the barren garden beneath its coat of winter gray. The weather had turned ugly. There were snowstorms coming. Some of the Society who had weather-sense were predicting heavy snows and an ice-storm, and everyone was uneasy. Part of that uneasiness was the recent upswing in casualties. Sigma was getting serious. It helped that Henderson had managed to get all the telem rigs fixed; the burr in the flux phasing had been responsible for a lot of Sigma's tracking them down. Things were holding steady, but everyone was still jittery.

And the other part of the uneasiness had to do with Rowan's quiet, numb misery. She was adjusting, true, but her grief was beginning to affect the whole complex. Henderson had finally quietly asked Del to do something about it. She refused point-blank to see any of the counselors; no amount of gentle cajoling or outright pleading would convince her. She only wanted to talk to him.

That was satisfying, but…

She turned the shower off, and he heard her moving around.
She hadn't mentioned him sleeping on the chair again. She
hadn't mentioned Sigma. But her nightmares were a twice-
nightly occurrence now, with her waking up, shaking and
sweating, and Delgado trying to calm her down, electric
prickles racing over his skin. It took a level of control he hadn't
been aware he possessed to keep himself at a distance. He'd
begun to pick up on her emotional state whenever she was in
the same building, let alone the same room, and she was
emitting high-level waves of distress that made even him tense.
She progressed quickly in her classes, but she was at a complete
standstill otherwise.

So I've got to, he thought as he watched the garden below.
I wanted to avoid this. That was a lie, too. He wanted her to
come to him of her own free will. He didn't want to manipulate
her.

But something had to be done. And he was responsible.

"Justin?"

He turned away from the window. His breath had fogged
a respectable patch of glass. "Hey." Now it was time to push
her a little, see how she reacted. "Better?"

"I'm sorry," she said, all in one rush. "I just—"

He found himself crossing the room. Rowan didn't back
up, but she drew herself up to her full height and bit her lower
lip. She wore his red sweater and a pair of jeans, and her feet
were bare.

Delgado stopped himself a bare few feet from her. "Don't
apologize," he said softly. "I kind of thought you needed that."

"I think I did," she agreed. Her pulse fluttered in her throat.
He tore his eyes away and found she was watching him, her
eyes wounded and defenseless. "Justin, I want to ask you
something."

"Anything." He didn't bother to try to hide the way his
voice caught on the single word.

Her eyes widened slightly, but she still didn't step back. "I
was talking to Catherine," she began, cautiously. "And she
said that you'd never...never trained anyone before. A
neophyte."

"That's right," he agreed. *Goddammit, Cath, if you've
screwed this up for me I'll tan your hide.*

"She also said that you disobeyed orders to rescue me.
That you should have gotten out of there and waited to see

what the...the Sigs would do." Her lip curled unconsciously. She was well on her way to hating Sigma.

"Henderson ordered me to get out of there," Delgado agreed. *I swear to God, Catherine White, if you've shot your big mouth off and made this harder I'll kick your little punk ass.*

"And you said you weren't leaving without me?"

"That's right." Now was the time to move another half-step closer and look down at her. She smelled fresh and clean, shampoo and soap and the cool fragrance of a woman, something pure he hadn't smelled in a long, long time. Like *forever.*

"Why?" she asked, tilting her head back to look at him. She was blushing.

Now was the time to tell her. "I couldn't stand the thought of them hurting you," he said quietly. "I had to get you out of there. Your father and Hilary too. I had to...I couldn't leave you behind."

"Oh," she said, and her eyes filled with tears again.

"Rowan—"

The sudden buzzing noise surprised them both. *Oh, fuck. The worst possible time.*

"It's from Central," he said, and fished the cell phone out of his pocket. *Dammit.*

Then he did the unthinkable. He turned off the phone.

Rowan gasped. She knew enough to tell he shouldn't do that—if Central was buzzing him instead of sending someone or just paging through the public areas, it was serious.

The moment was spoiled, but Delgado stepped close to her, looking down into her upturned face. "I don't want you hurt," he managed.

She blinked, as if he'd just spoken in a foreign language. "Hurt?" But she was reaching up, and when her hands slid around his neck and pulled his head down he didn't resist her.

Their mouths met. A jolt of spurred fire lanced through him. She was so soft, and the trickling, crackling sugar-glaze of her talent closed around him, drawing him close—and she *touched* him, too. The surface of his mind turned still and dark, that feeling of peace flooding him.

This is home, he realized. *This is where I belong.*

He barely realized that he had her against the wall, her hands locked at his nape, her slender body pressed against his.

He could barely remember where he was, *who* he was. The only thing that mattered was that *she* was there—and her mind opened to his, receptive as a flower.

For the first time, *ever*, it didn't hurt to use his talent. No feedback squeal of abused nerves and a brutally torn-open mind. Instead, he drowned in what she was feeling—a tidal wash of something clean and hot, his hands under her sweater, describing the shape of her, calluses scraping against her bare soft skin. He sank into her like a drowning man slipping under the surface of a placid lake, and blessed relief swamped him.

The doorbell and the sound of pounding alerted him. He surfaced reluctantly, breathing heavily, his forehead damp from sweat. Rowan blinked up at him, her eyes heavy-lidded and luminous. "Someone's at the door," she whispered, and he had to kiss her again, the corner of her mouth, her cheek, and would have taken her mouth again if she hadn't turned her head slightly. "Justin," she whispered, and his body twitched. He wanted her badly.

He wanted her *now*.

"Someone's at the door," she repeated breathlessly.

"Too bad," he whispered back. "They can wait."

She laughed, her fingers pressing into his nape, working a small, soothing tattoo into the flesh. "You can't do that," she said. "Your phone, too. You're on call."

"I don't care," he said, and would have buried his face in her neck if the pounding hadn't come again. "*Christ*," he growled, frustration rearing its ugly head.

"Shhh," she soothed him. "We have time."

He didn't have time. He was a dying man, and he wanted her. "Rowan…" It was all the pleading he could muster.

"Not right now. Let's find out what the emergency is. Later. I promise."

"Promise?" His mouth found the corner of hers again, teasing, tempting. She kissed him, and his mouth explored that wonder while her gift ran through him again, leaving a different sort of tension in its wake.

"You're so different," she said wonderingly, when he finally released her.

"Christ," he said, shaking, as whoever it was rang the doorbell again. "This had better be good."

Then the door-comm crackled. "Delgado! Get your ass out here!"

It was Henderson.

"Oh, Christ," Delgado groaned with feeling. "Just a minute. Let me get rid of him."

Rowan tried to straighten her clothing while Delgado ran his fingers back through his hair and stalked for the door. "Open," he said, and the door slid aside.

"About damn time," Henderson snapped. The old man was pale, the white patch over his temple glaring. "We need you. Get ready for jump-off ASAP. Is she coming?"

Something cracked inside Delgado's head. The switch flipped, and his shoulders relaxed. Nothing he could do about it now. "What's the brief?" he asked, his tone gone hard and cold. Rowan went still, her attention filling the room. He barely noticed, just marked where she was and scanned to make sure nothing dangerous was in the room.

Nothing except himself.

"They've found Morgan and Sheila. We need an extraction. Saddle up. Is she coming?"

Delgado didn't even think about it. "No. She's not ready."

"Hurry up. You've already wasted time." Henderson saluted Rowan briefly. "Miss Price. We need to go quickly; you'll be with Kenwood in Command. He's our liaison."

"Wait a minute," Rowan was suddenly at Delgado's shoulder. "I want to help."

"No," Delgado said. He crossed to the closet, took his harness down from the hook and buckled it on. Then he put his bag on over his head, tightening the strap across his body. He shrugged into his coat. He had his boots on already, thank God. "I suppose Brew has ammo?"

"Of course. Come on."

Rowan caught Delgado's arm. "Someone's in trouble, and you're all going somewhere. What do I do?"

"Wait and stay here. Kenwood will keep you up to date." He didn't have time. Every moment he delayed, Morgan or Sheila might be sitting in a blank room, looking at an IV while Zed dripped into their veins. "Be safe, Rowan. We're not finished."

"Ma'am," Henderson said, and then turned on his heel. He expected Delgado to follow.

"I'll be back," he said quietly. "We've got to talk."

She looked stunned. Her lips were flushed and ripe, almost bruised, and he'd mussed her damp beautiful hair. His entire body rose at the memory. He wanted to stay, he *needed* to stay.

He had to go.

"I'll be back," he repeated, then grabbed her shoulders.

It was a quick, hard kiss, and she still looked stunned when he let her go. "I promise," he said. "I'm coming back. Be safe."

Then he left before he could give in to the temptation to stay.

Twenty-Eight

I can't believe he left, Rowan thought, cupping her elbows in her hands and shivering slightly.

"You okay?" Mike Kenwood asked. He sat hunched over his console, a thin stoop-shouldered man whose talent of minor precognition made him valuable—or so Rowan had been told. "You should get some sleep."

Rowan ignored that. "How long has it been?" she asked again, picking up her coffee cup and taking a sip. It was cold, and she grimaced.

"Eighteen hours. Radio silence for two and a half. Don't worry—it'll be six hours before you should worry, Rowan. Why don't you go get some sleep?"

Rowan shifted uncomfortably on the hard-backed chair. *I couldn't sleep. Not with...not with Justin gone.* Her heart flipped over. She was going to miss her classes the next day, and the hour at the track she'd planned to get in. And her next scheduled sparring class. She was gong to miss *everything.*

It didn't matter. "So Morgan and Sheila were part of a team, and the team was caught by Sigma."

"Fucking bastards," Kenwood muttered, then cast her a blue-eyed glance. "Sorry, Rowan."

"It's okay. They *are* bastards." She stared at the screen he was hunched over. Green light touched his face, made them both ghosts.

There were other "home controls" hunched over other screens, and people went back and forth with paper printouts. Someone brought coffee every twenty minutes. There were six "active" missions going, and a couple of ones that hadn't "gone critical" yet.

Rowan mused that at least she was learning a whole new language.

The comm-unit crackled, and Kenwood sat straight up, knocking two sheets of paper to the floor.

"Kenwood." It was Henderson's voice over the comm. "Channel count."

"Delta five, two-zero-eight, stat," Kenwood replied. "Clear."

"We're under heavy fire. You've got the location?"

"I do. You need another team?"

"Nope, we've got Del. Del, come in."

"Just a minute." His voice made Rowan jump. He sounded cool, clinical. She "reached" out the way Kate had taught her but didn't feel him. He was a thousand miles away—the Sig installation was in the Midwest, far outside even her sensing range. Still, it was reflexive. And she seemed to catch a whisper of something if she strained herself. He was concentrating fiercely. "Got a little problem...There. What?"

"We're under fire. What can you do?"

"Hang on. Yoshi, give me the five-point on this due west here, I'm nervous about it."

Yoshi's voice said, "I'm in. Four guards. Del, be careful. They've got a net."

"Of course they've got a net. It's SOP. Knock 'em and give me a mark." Fizz of static.

"Mark." Yoshi didn't sound upset.

"Oh, *fuck*," Catherine suddenly snarled, "Zeke's hit. He's down. It's bad. Oh fuck—"

"Calm down," Delgado said. "I'm on my way."

"Zeke's hit." Catherine sounded breathless, and very young. "He's bleeding pretty bad."

"Just be cool. Yoshi, move with me, man."

"Right with you, Del. Watch your nine. There's a couple of Sigs hiding out with guns."

"I hear Andrews is in this complex," Delgado said.

"No way, dude. He hates the cornfields." Yoshi exhaled sharply. "Del, you're walking into crossfire."

"I know what I'm doing. Cath?"

"Goddamn," Catherine breathed. "Zeke's hit *bad*, Del. He's gonna need your girlfriend to patch him up—"

"Watch your motherfucking mouth, Cath." Now Del sounded irritated. "I've gotten to the cell block. General?"

"Catherine, stay put. Del, we're right behind you. Wish someone could shut those motherfucking sirens off."

"You want me to?" Yoshi said whimsically.

Delgado's bitter little laugh echoed through the electronics. "And stop all this fun? I've got Morgan. Fuck. Sheila's gone. Jesus. She's full of Zed and moaning. Bring her in or neutralize?"

Rowan's entire body went cold.

"Bring her in," Henderson said. "We leave no man behind."

"There you are." Justin sounded relieved.

Crackling static, Henderson's voice broke through. "Fuck you too. Give me that."

"Take 'em both. I'll go get Zeke and Cath."

Henderson exhaled, as if picking up a heavy weight. "Be careful."

"Can't be careful in a fire zone. Kenwood?" Now Justin sounded calm again, not relieved.

"Aye-aye-sir." Kenwood had gone pale.

"Sending Henderson and Brew out with our guys. Support them. Is Rowan there?"

"I'm here," Rowan whispered.

"She's here." Kenwood's fingers danced over the keyboard.

"Tell her I'm on my way." Delgado sounded cool and calm. "She okay?"

Kenwood glanced at Rowan, who sat bolt-upright, her hands locked together. "She's fine. A little tired, but fine."

"Tell her to go get some rest—*fuck*. Goddamn it. Catherine, get the fuck down."

"It's Zeke. He's *bleedin'*. Git'chor ass down here—" An accent had begun to wear through Catherine's voice. "Git'chor ass *here*, Delgado. What the fuck you good for?"

"Keep cool, Cath. Keep cool."

"Keep cool? Keep *cool?*"

Rowan inhaled sharply. "Give me a comm-link."

Kenwood tossed one to her, and then went back to clicking at his keyboard as he said, "Goddamn it. You guys have to get out of there. They're scrambling at the nearest base to get in the air and get to you. Move it along, guys."

Rowan's fingers fumbled at the comm-link. She finally managed to make it work. "Cath? It's Rowan. Take a deep breath."

"Shut up, girl! Zeke—*Zeke*—"

"Justin's coming, Catherine. He won't let anything happen to you." Rowan's teeth threatened to chatter. "Now stop yelling. You won't do Zeke any good by yelling."

Catherine swore under her breath. "Rowan, you tell your boyfriend to get here—oh. Oh my fucking God."

"Get him up. Zeke, on your fucking feet. *Now.*" Delgado now sounded strained. "*Now*, soldier!"

Rowan's skin roughened into goose flesh. "Catherine, Justin's there. He'll take care of you, but I want you to calm down and *help* him."

"'Kay...Zeke." Catherine sounded like she was crying.

"Thanks, Rowan," Henderson said. "Del?"

"I'm fine," Delgado said between gritted teeth. "Get up. Cath, hold him. He'll walk. That's a pressure bandage. Yoshi, give me another five-point here, okay? Shut down those goddamn lights. Giving me a headache."

"Shutting down the lights, on the mark...mark. Del, be careful, they're crawling toward you."

"I know. *Walk*, Zeke, you asshole. Come on! Catherine, drag him. Here—"

Confusion. Rowan bit her lip. "Justin," she whispered, too low for the comm-link to pick it up.

"Get him out of here," Delgado said harshly. "Wait *five minutes,* not a second more. You hear me, Yoshi?"

"Delgado, don't you fucking dare play hero," Henderson barked.

"I'm not playing hero, I'm getting my goddamn teammates out. Yoshi, *now!*"

"Right with you, Del," Yoshi said. They're in the red— move to your left, four feet. Oh fuck, there's a Sig at your six. *Drop,* goddammit...good. Move, move, move...okay, Henderson's out. Goddammit, *move,* Del. You can move faster than that. Get that motherfucker, Del."

"I got him. One less motherfucking Sig."

"Good, now *move it!"* Yoshi barked.

"Kenwood, is Rowan still there?"

Henderson again. "Don't worry about her, Del. Worry about getting out of there!"

"Of course I'll get out."

There was a noise like worlds colliding. Rowan winced at the burst of static and Kenwood cursed.

"Oh, *fuck.*" Justin sounded surprised, and Rowan's heart plummeted.

"Delgado?" Henderson didn't sound worried, but Rowan caught a note of worry nonetheless.

"I think I've been shot," Justin said slowly. Rowan's heart finished its drop by splashing into her stomach.

"We're out," Catherine said. "Thank God. Let's get the hell out of here."

"Del? *Delgado?*"

"I'm here, General. Get out of here, they're closing in."

"Not without you. We're clear, Morgan's good, Sheila's

under control. Dammit, Delgado, get the hell out of there."

"Justin? Get out of there." Rowan couldn't believe her own voice, authoritative, snapping like Hilary used to. "On your feet, soldier!"

"You...say...the...sweetest..." He stopped. There was a long ten seconds of silence.

"Get up, Delgado," Yoshi said harshly. It was the first note of panic Rowan had ever heard from him. "Rowan, talk to him, get him *up*."

"Justin, you have to get up," she said, motioning frantically and uselessly at Kenwood. His fingers danced over the keyboard. "Get up *now*."

"Rowan..." It was a long exhale. "Sweet..."

"Get *up!*" she shrilled.

"He's up," Yoshi said. "Down to your right, Del. Take the access hatch."

"Talk to me, Rowan," Delgado gasped. Her heart squeezed itself into a small black box in the middle of her chest. "Tell me something...anything."

Rowan saw Kenwood look up, his blue eyes swimming behind the wire-rimmed lenses. He shook his head slightly, and she didn't need to be psychic to understand it.

"Justin!" Her voice almost broke. "Move to your right! Now!"

"Good," Yoshi said clinically. "Fifty feet, straight ahead, will bring you to another access hatch. After that it's a straight shot to the open."

"Fifty feet straight ahead, Justin," she told him, her lips strangely numb. "Keep moving. Please. I don't know what I'd do if you didn't come back, we have to talk."

"That's right," he said, husky. "Talk to me, angel."

"He's in bad shape, Rowan," Yoshi said. "Keep him talking. Move him fifty feet straight ahead."

"Justin, keep walking. Keep walking, keep moving. Please. I want to talk to you. Please."

"Mad at me?" The vulnerable tone made her flinch. "Rowan, pretty Rowan..."

"Of course I'm not mad at you. You're my hero, remember? Just keep moving. Where are you hurt, Justin?"

"Don't ask him that," Yoshi said urgently. "Keep him moving, Rowan."

"Justin, keep going. One foot in front of the other."

"Chest. He got me in the chest. Christ."

"Just keep moving." Rowan's mouth was dry as sand. The vision of her father rose again—the little gurgle, Daddy's head tilted back, the light vanishing from his body. *If that happens to Justin...*

"Pretty...Rowan...mad at...me?"

"Of course not," she said sharply. "Keep moving."

"Okay," he said, obediently.

"Oh, shit. Rowan, get him to stop. Jesus." Yoshi sounded frantic.

"Justin, *stop!*"

"Okay." He sounded obedient. "Talk to me, angel. Talk to me..."

"When I was little, my mother told me I was special," she said, without any idea that she was going to say it. "She told me I should always do good, that God had blessed me. My father—"

Yoshi interrupted. "Have him start moving, Rowan. Straight ahead."

"Justin, I need you to move again. Straight ahead."

"Okay..."

"He's moving. Good work. Keep him moving."

"Beautiful. You're beautiful. Rowan—"

"Keep moving, Justin. I really need to talk to you."

"Mad at me?"

"Of course not. Don't be silly. Just hold on...keep moving."

"'Kay."

"Rowan, he's almost out. Access hatch on his nine. Tell him exactly that."

"Justin, there's an access hatch on your nine. Move."

"Moving..." He sounded dreamy again. A harsh, racking cough.

"He's out. Move down the hill. Rowan, move him down that goddamn hill. We're running out of time!"

"Justin, down the hill. Come on."

"'Kay." *He even sounds pale,* Rowan thought, her entire body cold. Waves of goose flesh spilled through her body. "Rowan.. *Rowan...*"

"I'm here. Keep moving."

"Lights—"

"We've got him, Rowan. Tell him not to fight us."

"Justin, don't fight them. Listen to me, *don't* fight them!"

"What if they're Sigma?" The dreamy tone began to frighten her. Rowan swallowed hot bile, wished she hadn't.

"They're not. Trust me, Justin. Trust me."

"All right." He coughed again, the sound sending static over the comm-unit.

"Jesus Christ," Henderson said. "Good work, Rowan. We've got him. Get us out of here, Yoshi."

"Ten-four. Lifting off. Good job, Rowan."

"Rowan?" Justin sounded faint, he coughed again. "Rowan?"

"I'm here," she said, numbly. "They have you, so relax. Just relax. You're coming home."

"He's passed out." Henderson sounded grim. "He took a few bullets. We'll do what we can. Get Med down as soon as we get there."

Rowan gasped. "Bullets?"

"Relax," Henderson snapped. "He isn't going anywhere. Get us out of here, Kenwood!"

"You got it," Kenwood said, and Rowan dropped the comm-link.

Justin, she thought, but there was no answer. None at all.

Twenty-Nine

Pain. A lot of it, but he was used to pain. His chest was on fire. Why couldn't he get up? Why couldn't he open his eyes?

"Rowan..." His own voice, quiet and breathless.

"Stay still," she said. His angel. The electricity of her nearness roared through him. *It's her,* he thought. *Where is she?*

"Still," he said. "Rowan..."

"I said, stay still." She sounded irritated, and his heart stuttered.

Thunder. *Don't you dare. Don't you dare leave me!* Now she was frantic, her breath coming high and harsh. *Justin!*

"Shock him. Stand back, Rowan!" Henderson, pulling her back. Delgado would have lashed out, stopped him, but something weighed his arms and legs down. "*Clear!*"

White light. Lightning, to go with the thunder. "Justin!" Rowan was screaming. "*Don't! Don't! Justin!*"

Darkness.

When he could think again, he struggled up through layers of blackness. *Rowan,* he thought fuzzily. *She was screaming.*

Had Sigma gotten her? No, she'd been safe at Headquarters. He'd heard her voice over the comm-link, cool and clear, even when everything else had faded to an indistinct gray pulsing of shock. He'd obeyed blindly, did what she told him.

Darkness took him again, but he seemed to hear Rowan's voice, quiet and listless. "He won't wake up."

"It's all right, Rowan." Brewster's crisp accent was hushed, strained. "He's tough. He'll pull through."

"I'm worried," she said.

"I know." Brew sounded soothing. "But he'll pull through. You did a good job."

"He carried me out of my house," she said. "After those men shot my father—and Hilary. He remembered I had bare feet and carried me."

"It's a miracle you got away from the Sigs."

"I guess so."

The curtain of darkness fell again.

When he woke the next time, he heard rain slapping against the window. He was in the aboveground infirmary. Why?

His eyes drifted open. Everything was dim and dark. To his left, the nurse's station was lit, but only a soft glow reached the rest of the room. A few of the beds were curtained off.

A sound. Someone moving, a footstep he knew.

Rowan glided through the infirmary, her white dress shirt seeming to float between the beds. She carried two coffee cups up to the nurse's station. Soft beeps told him that someone— or maybe a couple of someones—in here were being monitored very closely.

"Here you are," Rowan said softly. "Two sugars."

"Thanks," Emily replied. "You're a godsend."

"Any change?" Rowan leaned against the counter, an indistinct shape in the dimness. Delgado shut his eyes, opened them again.

She was still there.

"Yeah, for the better. Sheila's doing incredibly well. And Del…I think he might even be awake, but he hasn't made a peep. All his vitals are steady. Rowan, are you okay?"

"I'm all right. It's just a relief. Do you think he's going to be okay?"

"Well, he fought off the infection, and you're working your magic on him, so I'd think so." Emily sounded uncharacteristically gentle. "Why don't you go get some sleep?"

"I can't sleep."

"You haven't slept since they brought him in. You should get a little shut-eye or you won't be good for anything. Sheila will need another one of your treatments before long."

"I'll be fine." But she sounded pale, her words floaty and disconnected. "I'm going to go check on him."

"Okay…Rowan?"

She stopped, sweeping her hair behind her ear. "Hmm?"

"Can I ask you something?"

"What?" She sounded amused, and his heart leapt.

"Why him?"

"What?" Rowan took a sip from the cup in her hand.

"Why him? Why Delgado?"

"What are you talking about?" Now she cocked her head, as if puzzled.

"Nothing. Go check on him."

"Emily, what are you talking about?"

"It's just…well, you're pretty, and talented, and you could have pretty much any guy you wanted. Why *him*?"

Rowan laughed. It was a tired sound. "You mean why am I so worried about him? He needs it, I think."

"No, I mean why are you dating him?"

"We've never been on a date."

He recognized that tone in her voice—she didn't want to talk about something, was using humor to deflect Emily's interest.

"Rowan." Emily was having none of it.

"Oh, Emily. Really. It's just that...I like him. That's all."

"Stranger things have happened, I suppose." Emily sounded dubious.

"Was he really in Sigma?" Curious, wistful.

"He really was. Henderson got him out. They said he was insane from what they did to him. He roamed around Headquarters for a year like an animal. Hardly anyone saw him except the General. He kicked a Zed habit without any help, and that's unheard of. He knows everything about Sigma. They wouldn't give him clearance for a long time, because they thought maybe he was a Sig sleeper."

"Oh." Rowan said, thoughtfully. "Zed's the stuff Sheila's fighting?"

"I've never seen anyone pull through the Zed like that, Rowan. If you can figure out how to reverse it, it'd be...Well, we'd all be very happy."

"I'm working on it. I'm close." She sounded tired and thoughtful. "I'm going to sit with him for a while, Emily."

"'Kay. Thanks."

"No problem."

She approached the bed, lowered herself down in a seat on his left. He hadn't even seen the chair there.

He wasn't going to say anything. Let her think he was asleep.

"Rowan..." He couldn't help himself. His lips cracked over the word.

She set her coffee aside and leaned forward, her hand sliding under his. He felt the irritation—there was something stuck in the back of his hand. "Justin," she whispered. "It's all right, I'm here."

"Should be...sleeping." It was difficult to talk, his mouth seemed full of sand.

Rowan's fingers trailed over the back of his hand and touched his wrist. "I can't sleep," she said softly. "I have nightmares. Without you there they get worse."

"Sorry."

"Don't be sorry. How do you feel?"

"Tired." Even talking took too much of his limited energy; the darkness was closing in again. "Rowan."

"I'm here. Rest. You're going to be all right."

He fell into darkness again before he could tell her what he needed, wanted, to hear.

Thirty

Zeke grumbled but submitted to Rowan taking his pulse and blood pressure. Medical training was always in short supply around here, it seemed, and Rowan's gift for calming people made her even more useful. "You're going to be fine," she told him.

Catherine snorted. "He'd *better* be. You nearly fuckin' killed me, Zeke."

"On that note…" Rowan ducked out of the curtained enclosure, leaving the two to their bickering. The aboveground infirmary was almost full, and it was down the hall from Delgado's room, which meant it was where Rowan spent most of her time. Her attendance at the classes was spotty at best, but the General gave her homework and she was learning how to use her strange gift on sick, wounded, and traumatized people, just like at the mental hospital.

She checked on Sheila, who lay quietly sleeping, her lank brown hair lifeless against the pillow. The last battle with the drug Sigma had pumped into her had taken its toll on both Sheila and Rowan, but Rowan had won. She could almost taste, almost *see,* how to focus her gift to transmute the horrible physiological addiction back into normal health. Henderson was very pleased with that.

Pale, pearly winter sunlight washed the entire infirmary in shades of blue and white. Electronic beeps from monitors sang their usual song. Her boots squeaked slightly against the linoleum floor. The smells of disinfectant and sickness mixed with the sweetness of strawberry incense Catherine had lit, and the smell of ozone from the air purifiers. Her legs felt a little shaky from the punishing run she'd taken that morning, pounding on the track with only the sound of her own harsh breathing to keep her company. It was a blessing to find out she could still run—and that running made all the fear and worry go away.

Except for the worry about *him.*

She checked on Justin as she walked past, then stopped, her hands on her hips. "And just what do you think you're doing?"

"Isn't it obvious?" Justin flinched as he pulled his sweater over his head. Three white bandages glared against his torso, muscle rippling under his skin. The IVs were gone, but he was still wounded—three bullets. He was lucky none of them had hit bone. He was even more lucky that his heart and lungs hadn't been damaged, and further lucky that one of the two surgeons here could extract all three bullets without Justin coding on the table again. All in all, it was a miracle he was still alive. "I'm getting dressed. I can't take it anymore."

"Get back in that bed," she ordered, and he pulled the sweater down, smoothing it over his bandages. "You are the stubbornest man I know."

"Is that a compliment?" He gave her a lopsided smile, his hazel eyes warming for a brief second. Rowan approached him, hands still on hips.

"Get in that bed, Justin Delgado. Now."

He complied. She pulled the covers up, and his eyes moved over her face. "I hate bedrest," he complained. "I'm missing out on training. I'm going to get sloppy."

"You? Not likely. Now I'm going to take your blood pressure, and you're going to stay put like a good little boy. I'll come back and read to you, and you can take a short walk this afternoon, if you *really* want to."

"Of course I want to. I hate lying around." He looked up at her as she took his blood pressure. "How am I doing?"

"110 over 60," she said. "Good. You're relaxed."

"Not really." He caught her wrist, and a wave of heat slid up to her shoulder, dipped down her entire body. "Are you busy?" He let go of her wrist as she stepped closer.

"Not so busy I can't spare a few moments." Rowan dropped into the chair by the side of his bed, settling her stethoscope and folding up the blood-pressure cuff. "Is something wrong?"

"Just wanted to talk to you."

Her pulse sped up, pounding in her wrists and throat. "What about?"

"Kenwood tells me you spent the entire mission in Central listening." He examined her face.

She shrugged. "Do you need your pain meds?"

"No. Henderson tells me you didn't leave my bedside for the first four days except to go get more coffee and visit the bathroom. He was afraid you were going to collapse."

"I didn't."

"You didn't? Emily found you sleeping on the floor next to the bed."

"I was tired."

"Rowan."

"Justin." She met his gaze squarely. "What is it you want?"

"Just to say thank you." He picked at the blue ripcord bedspread. It was the first time she had ever seen him exhibit any nervousness. "You talked me through it."

"You'd have gotten out," she answered. *Of course you would have. You're Delgado. They think you can do just about anything, don't they? Nobody ever sees the human side of you.*

The more stunning thought that she had consciously used her talents on him and that he'd healed so quickly that even she was surprised, she pushed into the back of her mind. She didn't want to think that she'd been able to tell his body to heal itself. She'd spent hours staring at him as he slept, willing a trickle of energy into him, forcing her talent to its limits. *I shouldn't have done that. I've used my freak stuff on him. God alone knows what it'll do to him. But it's helping Sheila, and if I can find out how to break that awful drug, everyone will be happier.*

He shrugged at her comment, looking down. His eyes were flat again. Rowan examined his dark hair, a little longer now, and his broad shoulders under the black sweater. His flat, black bag was propped against one side of the bed within easy reach, she'd brought him a copy of Blake's poetry, and the only book he seemed to really read—a copy of Sun Tzu's *Art of War*, a glass of water, and nothing else. Zeke's bedside table was already full of magazines, a crumpled pack of cigarettes—Catherine's—bits of scratch paper, sketches, and various other minutiae.

Justin, however, had not even asked for the books until Rowan brought the Blake and announced she was going to read to him. He hadn't demurred, but she got the idea that he didn't really listen—he just watched her while she read. "I want out of this bed, Rowan," he said. "I've got work to do."

"Not until I'm sure you're all right," she said. "Dr. Jilssen—"

"Jilssen's an ass." His eyebrows drew together.

Rowan couldn't help herself. She chuckled. It felt good to laugh. She hadn't had much to smile about lately. "This is the part where I'm supposed to get afraid of you and let you do what you want?"

He actually frowned. "No. I don't want you afraid of me."

"Oh, good, because I'm not. You're staying in that bed for a few more days, Justin, and that's final. Clear?"

He mumbled something, then one corner of his mouth quirked up. "Did you just scold me?"

"I did." She reached out again and touched his wrist. The fiery prickles racing up her arm made her shiver a little. "For me? Please?"

"Fine," he said ungracefully. "For you. Don't tell anyone. You'll ruin my reputation."

"Silent as the grave," she promised, despite the chill that touched her back at the words. Then she took a deep breath, steeling herself. "Justin?"

"Yeah?"

"Do you mind that I'm still staying in your room?" Her voice came out a little funny, a little breathless, and she shifted on the hard plastic chair.

"Of course not." He glanced around the infirmary, and Rowan was suddenly aware of other people listening. "Stay as long as you want."

"All right." She let go of his wrist and gained her feet without any mishap. What was it that made her heart hammer and her mouth go dry when she saw him? "I'll be back in a little while to read to you."

"Rowan?"

"What?" She paused at the end of his bed, looking back over her shoulder.

"Thank you. Come back soon."

She nodded, then hurried away before she made a fool of herself.

Dr. Jilssen was poring over charts at the nurse's station. "Ah, Rowan! Just who I wanted to see!" He blinked behind his thick glasses, his thin face pricked with color high along his saw-like cheekbones. He set the charts down, one liver-spotted hand trembling slightly. "How is Delgado?"

"Feeling his oats, Doctor." Rowan forced a smile. Her skin crawled, like it always had since Justin had left and Jilssen had started actively pursuing her. *He doesn't mean any harm,* she thought. *He's just old, and he's one of those doctors that doesn't like messy human beings and has a horrific bedside manner.* "What can I do for you?"

"Oh, we haven't seen you in class or down in the Research Division for a week." Dr. Jilssen's eyes twinkled behind the

Coke-bottle lenses. There was a soup stain on his tie. It looked like tomato. Rowan's teeth set together tightly. "I know you've been busy working on Sheila, but I was wondering if you'd come down and test a telem rig for us."

"I don't know, doctor. I'm very busy with the patients."

"I'm sure someone else can look after them for a little while." The doctor reached out as if to pat Rowan's arm.

She skipped back, her elbow striking a vase of tiger lilies someone had brought in. It would have crashed to the floor, but she managed to catch it in time, water sloshing out and splashing the counter. Dr. Jilssen squeaked and whisked the charts out of the way. She managed to get the vase back up on the counter and stepped back nervously when Jilssen tried to touch her shoulder, maybe to reassure her.

"Sorry," Rowan said, not feeling very sorry at all. "Look, I have to go. I'm sorry."

With that, she backed down the central aisle, away from the nurse's station. "Rowan?" Dr. Jilssen peered at her, obviously perplexed.

Rowan's entire back started to crawl with chill goose flesh. She turned on her heel and began walking quickly away. *What's wrong with me? What's going on?*

She didn't even hear Justin say her name.

Thirty-One

It took a while before Delgado could get up out of the damn bed. Rowan fussed over him if he lifted anything heavier than a paperback. However, her talent must have been working overtime, because he only stayed down for two weeks before getting up and starting weak workouts again. He had a mountain of reports to catch up on and a debriefing to attend about the rescue mission.

He'd healed almost completely of three bullet wounds in record time. It was amazing. Jilssen kept poking around while Rowan was there, but she avoided him like the plague. Del wondered about that, of course. He wondered about Rowan's tight-lipped, pale scowl whenever Jilssen passed by Delgado's bed; and he wondered about her nervous laughter.

Something was going on with her.

The most truly amazing news was Sheila. She'd kicked the Zed in less than a week, and hadn't needed a detox kit for the last three days. Henderson had taken her to a bed and breakfast upstate and spread the rumor that she was in isolation, having a difficult detox. It was a lie, but a necessary one, since neither Del nor Henderson wanted news of this getting out.

Rowan had cured a case of Zed addiction, and that made her damn near worth her weight in gold. A psion who could cure Zed addiction wouldn't just be valuable to Sigma. They would go all-out to get her. So the fewer people who knew, the better, even within the Society. Henderson had even asked Del and Emily, who were the only people besides Sheila and Rowan who knew about it, to keep it quiet. Del was glad he hadn't had to convince Henderson of the value of silence.

It was a relief to finally move back into his own room, a relief to shut out the rest of the world. Rowan set his black bag down on the bed and started fussing at him to lie down. Instead, he sank down in the huge armchair and let out a sigh of relief. More plants had shown up—a miniature rosebush blooming red, some leafy green thing Delgado thought was maybe a datura, and another wrought-iron plant stand held four African violets, three of which were blooming vigorously. More books were scattered everywhere, and there was a pile of clothes by the bathroom door.

She descended on the clothes, scooping them up and stuffing them into the already overloaded laundry hamper. "I haven't had time," she said defensively, sweeping her hair back.

"I didn't say anything," he said. "You've been busy in the infirmary. Can I talk to you?"

Her green eyes widened, and he felt his heart skip a beat. "Of course," she said, stooping to scoop up two books from the floor. She started shelving the books, the crackling tension in the air following her like smoke. "Just let me do this."

"Calm down, Rowan." He knew what tone to use on her now, soothing and authoritative at the same time. "Calm down, sit down, and take a deep breath."

She dropped down on the bed, setting the books primly to one side, and glared at him.

He couldn't help himself. He began to laugh.

He laughed so hard tears blurred his eyes. His chest hurt, and curling his hands into fists, he sank into the chair's embrace and chuckled until he thought he would never catch his breath.

Rowan stared at him, perplexed at first, but then seeming to relax. A slight smile crept over her face. She relaxed and waited patiently for him to stop laughing.

When he finally did, she sighed and folded her arms. "Finished?" Her eyebrows rose slightly.

Good God, I don't think she knows how beautiful she is. "I guess," he answered, wiping his eyes. "God, Rowan. Don't look at me like that. You're dangerous."

"Dangerous?" She was back to perplexed. "What are you—"

"Why don't you like Jilssen?"

It was a little too abrupt. She paused, her eyes dropping. Weak icy-morning sunlight flooded in through the window, making her glow. She pushed up the sleeves of her blue sweater and kept staring at the floor.

"I don't know," she said finally. "I...I just don't want him to touch me."

Delgado felt his eyes narrow. "He tried to touch you?" His tone abruptly dropped, became serious.

"When you left. I don't know. I just...He always seemed to be watching. I'm just nervous." Her shoulders eased.

"Don't worry about Jilssen. I'll keep him away from you." *He'd better not try to touch you, Rowan.* Del had to take a deep breath, invoking control.

"He wants me in a telem rig," she whispered. "You know about those?"

"Oh, yeah. We've been working on those for a while. They just amplify a psi's talents, Rowan, but some of the telepaths don't like them very much. It's hard to shield." He settled himself more comfortably. He shouldn't have been so tired after just a weak workout and the walk back to his room, but he was. It was damn near a miracle that he was still alive, even if Rowan had performed the impossible and healed him. *That's not the only miracle she's worked,* he thought, watching her tuck a strand of pale hair behind her ear. *If Sigma ever gets wind of the fact she can cure Zed addictions, we'll have a lot more trouble on our hands than even I can handle.*

"I don't like the way he looks when he asks me, Justin. I'd prefer it if you were there if I ever use one of those things."

That warmed him clear through. "No problem. Nobody here is going to hurt you, Rowan."

She shrugged, looking down again. "I've got a bad feeling," she said, as if she expected him to laugh again.

"What kind of bad feeling?" His attention sharpened.

"Just...I'm uneasy. Really uneasy. The nightmares. When I can sleep, that is, and—" She bit her lip, stopping as suddenly as she'd started. "What if Sigma can still track me?"

"They would have scooped you up before now." *While I was bringing you in. And that was bloody well close, as Brew would say. Andrews nearly had us both.*

"But this is the Society's Headquarters," she pointed out. "They can't just walk in and try to grab me. They have to go a little more carefully, don't they?"

Justin shrugged. Her face fell, and he cursed himself. "I'll take a look, Rowan. I know most, if not all, of Sigma's procedures. I'll ask a few questions. And if anything seems off, we'll go to Henderson. All right?"

"You believe me?"

"Of course I believe you." He made his tone flat and matter-of-fact. "If you told me the moon was made of green cheese, I'd get out crackers, angel."

The smile that broke over her face made his chest ache with an entirely unphysical pain. "I'm glad you're here," she said. "Really glad."

"Good. I promise I'll keep Jilssen away from you." Delgado felt something prick at him uneasily. "Anything else?"

She shrugged, her fingers playing with the bedspread. "Nothing, I suppose." But her eyes were dark. Something else, then.

"Are you sure?" He didn't want to press—it wasn't the time. But she looked so uneasy.

"Nothing. Just...before you left."

Ah. He had to squelch a flare of comprehension—and satisfaction. *That's right, angel. You and I have unfinished business.* "Before I left," he echoed, finding enough energy to lean forward from the chair's embrace.

"You...um, I...I mean, I..." It was such a novel experience to watch her flounder that Delgado allowed himself a few more moments of it, watching as she picked at the white bedspread.

"About that," Delgado said, and her gaze flew to his face, the color draining from her cheeks. He didn't have the heart to play with her, not when he wanted her this badly. "I meant every word, Rowan."

The color rushed back into her cheeks, she dropped her eyes again. *What do you know?* he thought. *I have an effect on her.*

It was unexpectedly sweet. He wanted to savor it.

"It's just...I...I mean, I..." She coughed, uneasily. "You just...I mean..."

What exactly do you mean? He searched through every scenario he'd planned for and couldn't quite figure out where this one fit. "It's all right," he said, trying not to look as if he was enjoying himself. "If it makes you uncomfortable, I'll—"

"You said we had to talk."

"We do."

"What about?" Her hands twisted together.

"Us," he said, and watched her eyes fly up to meet his.

"Why are you doing this?" she asked. "Everything?"

"I want to," he said. *Wait a minute, what are we talking about?*

"I really like you," she said, her eyes fixed on the floor, her cheeks crimson. "I really do."

"I'm sorry this happened," he said finally. "If I could have stopped it, I would have. I'd give anything to have your father back, and Hilary. For your sake."

I should be talking to her about how dangerous it is to have everyone know what kind of magic she worked on Sheila, he thought, and then the thought went clean out of his head when she looked up, a tear-track showing on her pale cheek.

"Thank you."

It was one of the few times in his life Delgado was speechless. Silence stretched between them, a not-quite-uncomfortable silence. Finally, Rowan sighed and pushed herself up from the bed. "Henderson wants you for a briefing after lunch. And I want to check on—"

"Screw him." Delgado sighed, raking his fingers back through his hair. "Look, Rowan, I—"

She smiled at him. It literally took his breath away, made his chest feel tight. Outside the window, winter sunlight bounced off a hard frost and the light blanket of snow covering the fields, the sky a depthless gray promising the storm the weather-sensitives had been muttering about. The light was good for her. *Hell, any light's good for her. She'd even look good dipped in mud.* "He's been tearing his hair out without you." She swept a long tendril of her hair back. "How about I bring you some lunch?"

"Hey." He caught her wrist as she moved past him. Immediately, his skin prickled with an even sharper awareness of her. "I don't want to talk to Henderson. I want to talk to you."

She went still, her extraordinary eyes wide and fixed on him. "Justin." Just the one word. Then she blinked. "Did you tell me your name?"

He shrugged. *I don't care, angel.* "Call me what you like." He made sure his fingers were gentle, controlled the impulse to pull on her arm and tumble her onto his lap. *I've been a fucking saint. I deserve it. What do you say, God? I deserve something, don't I?*

The instant he thought it, he wanted to curse. He didn't deserve a goddamn thing.

Rowan sank down slowly until she was crouched next to his chair, her wrist in his hand. "What's wrong?" she asked, the shiny tear-track on her cheek mocking him.

"Nothing." He lifted her hand and used his other fingers to trace a line in her palm. His calluses scraped against her softer skin. He touched her sensitive fingertips, the hollow of her palm. Her eyes half-lidded, she took a deep shuddering breath. "Forgive me?" he asked.

She looked stunned. "For what?"

"I didn't guess the Sigs would move so fast," he said. "I should have guessed." He let out a long breath. *I didn't even know I was going to say that.*

"It's all right," she said, but her mouth drew down bitterly at the corners. "I forgive you."

Slowly, deliberately, he slid his fingers through hers. Let go of her wrist and held her hand. "Okay."

It wasn't exactly what he wanted, but she stayed with him, holding his hand for a few moments before glancing at the clock and announcing, "I'm hungry. We need some lunch before you meet Henderson."

Minx. I didn't agree to that. "All right, sweetheart. Whatever you say."

"Henderson's the boss." Now Rowan smiled slightly. That weak, tremulous smile made Delgado's heart start to pound. "When he's done with you, I'll bring you back and tuck you into bed. We'll have a nice long chat."

"I'm a wounded man, missy."

The smile turned into a full-fledged grin. "I'm a medical

professional, sir. Are you objecting to my diagnosis?"

"Of course not," he said, his own mouth curling up to echo her smile. "I'd love to have a nice long talk with you. As long as you like." *How does she do that, make me feel human again?* He knew that when Henderson finished with him he'd be exhausted, and Rowan would too. She was spreading herself too thin in the infirmary. They wouldn't talk tonight.

But soon. Very soon.

"Great." She took her hand back, but slowly, her fingers sliding against his. The intensity of her talent had become a warm blanket wrapping around him. Her pulse had quickened. He could feel it even across the space separating them. "Thank you, Justin."

What is she thanking me for? I destroyed her life. "What did you say Henderson wanted me for?"

"Paperwork," she said, rising slowly. *How does she do that? How does she move like that, like silk?*

"Oh, Christ," he moaned. "No."

"You'd better believe it," she said. "We've got just enough time to get something to eat. And the sooner you finish it, the sooner we can come back here."

"You've got a way of putting these things," he admitted. "All right. Point me at the papers. Where do I sign?"

Thirty-Two

Three weeks later, she looked up from the files she was sorting as Henderson said her name.

"Can you run these to Central for me?" he asked, handing Rowan a sheaf of folders. He wore a pair of steel-rimmed glasses, darts of light striking off the frames; the gun he wore had become normal. Guns made Rowan nervous, but the people around here were starting to look strange if they were unarmed. "Catherine's crunching some numbers, and Brew—"

"It's all right." Rowan laughed, taking the armful. "Tell Justin I'll be back in a few moments, all right?"

He nodded absently, shoving his hand through his hair and turning back to the computer screen. Holding the folders, Rowan watched him for a moment. His back was iron-straight and his sharp, kindly gaze reminded her of her father's. The white patch at his temple glared in fluorescent light.

Four East was an underground room, a huge circular dome like Central Op. Only here, Henderson's Brigade had hung Halloween decorations—Catherine's—and a huge print of Monet's water lilies—Brewster's—and a poster of a wet cat clinging to a branch with the caption *Just Hold On*—Zeke's. Rowan's contribution was a salvaged airplane plant, sending out long tendrils with balls of whippy green leaves at the end.

"I don't know what you did to get Del on his feet so quickly," Henderson said suddenly, still staring at the computer screen, his fingers flicking over a keyboard. A perpetual-motion thingie—four steel balls hung from thin filaments, clicking back and forth—stood next to his computer. Henderson's command chair was an ergonomically correct black-mesh-and-cushion deal, and he leaned back and took a swallow from a silver hip flask while she stood there, the files balanced in her arms. "But it's a miracle, and I'm grateful. He's working the best he has since he got here. I've never seen him so happy."

Happy? I don't think I've ever seen him looking really happy. "I'm glad." She took a deep breath. "Sir?" she asked carefully, gathering her courage.

"What?" He didn't sound angry or even impatient, he hit the "enter" key twice, reached over and grabbed another manila folder and flipped it open.

"When will I be able to…do what the rest of you do?" Her heart hammered, coppery dryness in her throat. *I know I'm practically useless, but I don't ever want to be here alone again and listening to Justin get shot at.*

"You mean be an operative? You've been here for months, but you've been missing classes and Del hasn't cleared you through combat training. Brew will need you in weapons, too. We can't take you on operations until we're sure you won't get yourself or one of us killed. I really need those files run down to Control, Miss Price."

"Yes sir." Rowan turned sharply and strode for the door. *Well, that went as well as could be expected, didn't it?*

The passageway outside was lit by yet more fluorescents, and Rowan hummed to herself as she stopped in front of the transport door. The files were heavy. She was lucky to be allowed into Central, especially after being here for so short a time.

Short? It feels like forever….Justin's back to normal; he's been putting in fourteen-hour days and we haven't talked about anything. She sighed. Those nightmarish days of holding him to life, willing him to survive, were like a sore spot inside her head. She didn't want to speculate what sort of emotional muscles she'd pulled. The thought of losing Justin—of him dying like her father—made her entire body go cold.

And the thought of her father made the familiar black ball of grief and anger rise up in her throat, like a lump of tears with sharp spikes.

I should check in at the infirmary. Annika's team came back all beat up. Rowan shifted her weight from side to side, feeling her calves protest from the punishing run she'd taken that morning. Annika, a short, gymnast-muscled woman with long dark hair and empty flat blue eyes, had brought everyone back safely, but she'd lost half her spleen and now boasted a long scar down the side of her face. It was yet another thing to hate Sigma for, and Rowan found that hating the faceless monolith didn't make her uncomfortable at all.

And yet sometimes, she wondered.

The transport door opened, and Dr. Jilssen's blue eyes peered out from behind their thick lenses.

Rowan's stomach did its best to rise in revolt. She tasted bile, and her skin prickled.

"Rowan!" As usual, the old man sounded delighted. He jammed the button that kept the transport door open, his rumpled lab coat rustling. "Just the person I wanted to see! Where are you going?"

She clutched the files to her chest like a schoolgirl, hitching in a breath. "Central," she said, unable to lie. *Why do I feel so sick every time I'm around him?* she wondered, and the prickling intensified right on her nape.

Danger.

He's not dangerous, she told herself, and moved forward as if to step into the transport. She stopped.

Her body literally wouldn't step onto the transport. She struggled with herself, not wanting to be impolite.

"Good! I'll go with you." He was beaming, his hands trembling slightly, like usual. But today there seemed something predatory about his face, lean and leathery instead of just old and fragile. His tie was blue, stained with something darker, and his right loafer was untied.

"I…I left something," she stammered, backing away. This wasn't like her. Rowan Price didn't lie, and she didn't give into irrational fear.

What if it's not irrational? I felt this way before that man tried to drag me off in the parking lot. But that was because they were Sigma, wasn't it?

"Rowan?" Now Jilssen stepped out of the transport, his face the picture of concern. But was there something else beneath that concern? Something…almost hungry?

"I have to go," she began breathlessly, backing up two steps, then whirling—and almost running into Justin, the breath slamming out of her chest as she halted. He seemed to just appear sometimes without the benefit of moving through space like a normal human, and since starting his regular workouts again, his shoulders seemed impossibly broad.

He caught her, one hand curling around her shoulder, and the other catching her upper arm and setting her back on her feet. "There you are." His dark eyes, flat and ironic, flicked over her, probably taking in her scarlet cheeks and set jaw. Then he turned to Jilssen, who had retreated back into the transport. "Henderson says he needs one of those back. Afternoon, Doctor."

Jilssen put on a jaunty smile. Was it Rowan's imagination, or was he *sweating?* She stared at him, feeling her forehead wrinkle. "Well, maybe next time, Rowan. Remember, I've got my eye on you!"

The transport doors closed. There was a slight whoosh.

He was gone.

Rowan let out a shaky breath. Justin used two fingers to tip her chin up so he could examine her face. His mouth was a straight line, his cheeks dark with afternoon stubble. The tingling from his touch washed through her, almost but not quite dispelling the sick sense of fear and dread. "Christ," he said. "He really upsets you, doesn't he?"

"I don't know why," she answered, leaning into his touch. "It's probably nothing. I just..."

"Just what?" he looked interested, of course, but his eyes had fastened on her mouth.

"I get that sort of storm feeling, I guess, and my head aches. And my stomach. It's..." She hesitated, plunged on. "It's how I felt when that man tried to kidnap me."

Justin's eyes met hers. Rowan's breath left her in one swift gasp.

His eyes had gone even more flat, cold and dark, and his jaw set. But it was as if a switch had flipped, turning him from Justin into Delgado, the cool machine of a man the rest of them saw. There was something else, too. Something she'd only seen once or twice, a kind of thoughtlessness in his face that seemed to be the scary, static-laden last breath before an explosion of violence.

His fingertips were still under her chin. He trailed a soft

touch along her jaw, then up her cheek. Rowan's entire body flushed.

"Listen to me," he said quietly, as if taking it for granted she would. And she did—she froze, her complete attention focused on him. "Don't *ever* doubt that feeling, angel. Ever. It will keep you alive. From now on, don't go anywhere without me, all right? I'll make some more inquiries."

"What do you think is going on?" she whispered. *Is he saying it's not safe here?* The bottom dropped out of her stomach as if she was on a roller coaster; not a fun amusement ride but a scary, rickety, dangerous plunging toward the ground.

"I don't know yet." He caressed her cheek. It was vaguely jarring, the contrast between that empty emotionless face and the gentleness of his touch. And the fierce emotion pouring out of him, wrapping around her, not drowning her like other people's feelings, but...cradling her. "But I'll find out. Until I do, don't go anywhere without me. All right?"

She wanted to nod, but that might dislodge his fingers. "All right," she whispered, and his gaze dropped down and fastened on her mouth again.

"You going to Central?" he asked.

"Um-hmmm," she managed. *If he leans down just a little...*The memory of that other kiss burned through her. "Did Henderson want one of these back?"

He kissed her cheek, just a gentle press of lips. Rowan's breath became shallow, and her pulse raced. It was a sweet fear, better than the clinging, painful panic of facing Jilssen.

"No. I lied. You all right?" he asked.

"I guess." She sounded whispery, couldn't quite make her voice work. *He lied? Why? Because I looked upset, or...Oh, God, could Jilssen tell what I was feeling? No, he's normal. A deadhead, Brew would say.*

"Let's go to Central. Then I'm free for the rest of the evening. Have dinner with me?"

It sounded unexpectedly intimate, though they usually both stole the same meal and coffee breaks during the day. "Of course," she said, and smiled. She'd spent more time with him than anyone except her father, and it felt just as natural.

He smiled back. For a fleeting moment, his eyes weren't flat—they were warm and deep. Then his face closed with an almost audible snap. "I'll find out what's going on, Rowan. I promise." His fingers trailed down her cheek, and he slowly, reluctantly, peeled his fingertips away.

"I know you will," she said, struggling for a normal voice. "I just...I wonder if I'm jumping at shadows. A person can only handle so much trauma before they start to unwind."

"Don't worry, you're perfectly rational." He punched the button for the transport, moving with that quick, eerie grace. "And you're stronger than you think."

It took a few moments for his words to sink in, and Rowan didn't answer him. *That's what I'm afraid of,* she thought, and then tried to shove the idea away.

Thirty-Three

The sound of her moving around in the bathroom was familiar by now, so familiar Justin dismissed it. He sat cross-legged on the floor, his spine straight and his attention centered and focused. He needed it badly.

What exactly are you thinking?

He didn't know. He only knew Rowan didn't like Jilssen.

Had exactly the same reaction to Jilssen as she did to Sigs. She'd been paper-pale, her eyes huge; the same look she'd worn during that distant time he brought her in. Vibrating with terror, hanging on by a thread.

The urge to hold her had been overwhelming. And the thought that perhaps the Society had been infiltrated was chilling.

Nothing like that is possible, he told himself. *She's just high-strung, that's all. Time for you to quit screwing around, Delgado.*

He sought stillness, the calm center of himself that had never been broken. It was there, all right. It was always there.

The trouble was, Rowan was there too, even in the spaces of his meditation. The room was dark, he hadn't bothered to turn the light on and dusk had already crept through the corners.

Use your logic, Del. Rowan doesn't like Jilssen, associates him with the same feeling as the Sigs. That doesn't mean he's anything other than a nasty old man who wants to shove her in a telem rig and take samples so he can figure her out.

But if that was the case, why on earth would Rowan feel so terrified? And *terrified* was the only word that applied. She'd even been unusually quiet during dinner, but that could have been because Cath and Zeke had descended on them, and Cath's chattering damn near filled the air. Then Yoshi had shown up, and Del had been absorbed in turning over the problem of Jilssen and the sequences Yoshi had brought him. A nice leisurely dinner with Rowan shot all to hell.

He heard her humming, tried to place the tune and couldn't. The sound was too muffled.

He would start prowling around and making little inquiries. He'd have to be careful—if anyone suspected he was researching Jilssen, word might get to the doctor and spook him. Besides, it wouldn't look good if Henderson's right hand started nosing around the doctor that had been with the Society almost from the beginning. It would make trouble for the General, and trouble for

Rowan as well. If Del got called onto the carpet for it, Rowan might be left unprotected.

She opened the bathroom door, flicking the light out. He sighed, opening his eyes. There was nothing but a bunch of suppositions. But those suppositions were based on Rowan's talent and instinct—something he had a healthy respect for.

"You sound happy," he said, surprising himself.

She paused, the hand with the hairbrush poised over a long fall of pale hair. Oddly enough, she didn't bother to turn the overhead light on, just stood there in the gathering darkness. The pose literally robbed him of breath. "I didn't guess you were trying to concentrate," she said.

He unfolded himself from the floor, wincing a little as a bruise on his left quad reminded him of his last sparring session with Henderson. The old man didn't pull any strikes, that was for sure. "I like hearing you," he told her, and watched her flush visibly even in the dimness.

Quit fucking around, the deep, cold voice told him. *She's in danger. You know she is. That feeling's never let you down.*

And that was the crux of it right there. He was uneasy too. Something wasn't right—some deep premonition of danger was beating like a drum inside his head. He should have moved to the next stage with her a long time ago.

He wondered if she would forgive him, if she'd ever guess what he was up to.

He crossed the room, intent on her, stalking noiselessly. Her eyes fixed on him, extraordinary almost-glowing green depths. Eyes he could drown in.

That actually doesn't sound so bad, he thought. *If I drowned in her, would I forget everything else?*

An unfamiliar smile tugged at his face. How long would it take for a smile to feel normal again? "I'll brush your hair, angel. Want to turn the light on?"

She studied him for a long moment, thoughts moving behind her eyes, and the tingling wash of her talent spilling down his back. The others felt her like a pressure against their minds, but he felt her all along his skin—and all the way down to his bones. Whether it was because of his own ability to *push* or simply because he was emotionally involved with her, he didn't know.

Didn't care either.

"I don't think so," she said finally, dropping the brush. It clattered against the hardwood floor.

He didn't have any time to react. Rowan stepped close, that prickling feeling running over his skin, the smell of her hair closing around him. He froze.

She ran her hand up his arm, her palm sliding over his sweater, past his shoulder. She had to reach up to cup her hand around the back of his neck. "We have to talk," she breathed. "Right?"

Oh, my God, he thought through a sudden haze, *she's seducing me.*

His throat was desert-dry. "Um," he managed, staring at her eyes. *She doesn't have any idea. Of course not. She can't be serious.*

"You know what your problem is, Justin? You're too serious. You think too goddamn much."

"Must be genetic." *Don't joke with her, you idiot. She might decide not to touch you.*

Her smile widened briefly. Then she pulled his head down.

He hadn't expected this. Hoped, wished, prayed—but not expected.

Her mouth met his. Liquid fire slid down his spine. She kissed him thoroughly, taking her time. His hands moved around her waist, spread against her back, and he did his best to pull her into him.

It seemed to last forever. Her slenderness against him, the cleanness of her mind swallowing his. He disappeared into her, her mouth warm and forgiving.

She finally took pity on him and broke free, but only halfway. Delgado kissed the corner of her mouth, her cheek, her temple under the mat of silken hair, buried his face in her hair and inhaled deeply, shuddering.

"We definitely have to talk," she said, breathlessly.

"Talk later." His hands found their way under her sweater. Her skin was cool and smooth under his fingers. "*Much* later."

She pushed him toward the bed. He was only too happy to comply, pulling at the sweater. Her hands were fiddling with his jeans, he was surprised into a bitter laugh. "I suppose you're not thinking about—" she began.

"Later," he muttered into her hair, finally getting the damn sweater up over her head. She wasn't wearing a bra, and he had to suppress a groan. The bed hit his calves, and they went down in a tangle of arms and legs, her elbow smacking a fresh bruise. He inhaled sharply and she gasped a helpless apology that he trapped with his mouth, kissing her as if he was dying. In a way he was.

"No." She sounded frightened. "Justin—*no.*"

He froze, tangled with her, her hair webbed over his face. Her breathing shuddered under his hand, ribs heaving, the delicate architecture of bones rising and falling. "All right," he whispered harshly. "All right." *I can stop. Sure I can.*

Right.

"No, you idiot," she said, her fingers still working at the button of his jeans. "Not later. *Now.*"

"Oh." But he lay there for a moment, sliding his fingers over her ribs, the swell of one breast brushing his knuckles. She shivered, biting her lip and arching into his touch. *Christ, I think she's responding. How did I get this goddamn lucky?* "Rowan..."

"Hmm?" She propped herself up on her elbow, the button finally popping free. He sucked in a breath. Had he forgotten to breathe? Maybe. "There it is. Look, I'm not a virgin."

What? "Christ," he said against her cheek, "do you think that *matters?*"

"I just—" Her breath came in quick, shallow gasps, she was actually blushing; he could see her cheeks turning delicately red in the dim light. Her perfume had taken on a darker, fleshy musk tone.

"No," he told her, having better luck with the zipper on her slacks. *I feel like a goddamn caveman, all I want to do is drag her off by the hair.* "Later. Talk later. Right now, kiss me."

She did, and it was all he could do to restrain himself, to slow down. He had never in his life wanted to get *inside* a woman so badly, she laughed as she wriggled free of her panties and he caught her mouth, swallowing her laughter, breathing her in as his skin slid against hers. He wanted to find out what would make her scream, wanted to pursue a particularly delicious line of inquiry about what it would be like to kiss in a straight line between the soft slopes of her breasts and the shallow curve of her belly, wanted to slide his fingers in and watch her face as she went over the edge. But there was no time for foreplay, because he was going to embarrass himself if he tried to slow down. She was on her back, silk scarves sliding underneath bare skin—*God, I can't even get her under the covers, can I?*

That thought was lost when he managed to sink down into her, tangling his fingers in her hair and finding the entrance to her body, sliding in. At least she was wet and ready. She gasped, probably not expecting this so soon, and Del muttered an apology

into the curve of her throat, tasting the sudden salt of sweat and
the spice of *her.* Her fingers slid through his hair, pulled his mouth
down on hers again, he was drowning in her, greedy with the
taste of her as he was finally, finally home.

She was hot and impossibly tight, velvet closing around him,
her back arched as she inhaled sharply. He couldn't help himself.
Sorry. I'm sorry. Christ, I should slow down. I can't. I can't. A
helpless thrust, he was too rough, a half-swallowed cry caught in
her throat and guilt flooded him. *Too fast. I'm sorry, Rowan, sorry.*
But as sorry as he was, his body wasn't sorry at all. His hips
jerked forward again, and he was buried inside her, impossibly
deep.

And he wanted *more.*

Then her mind opened under his, the shock of her pleasure
exploding against his nerves in a feedback loop, drowning him
further. He forgot everything but the taste of her, anticipating her
next move. Her fingernails drove sharp diamond points of pain
into his back. He gave another deep thrust, and then another. Her
mouth broke free and she whispered his name.

"Sorry," he gasped against her throat.

"Sorry? What the hell *for?*" And she actually giggled, her
amusement sliding through him, wine-red, wine-dark, a curious
comfort. Her fingers softened, and she made a slight beckoning
movement with her hips that set off a most interesting chain
reaction in the velvet grip of her muscles around him.

"I can't—"

"And they think you're so controlled." Another husky laugh,
another beckoning little movement, and he lost himself, slipping
below the surface of her mind, pouring into her. He thrust again,
a nice long stroke that cut her laughter off in mid-gasp. *That* was
satisfying, and he did it again.

"I *am* controlled," he managed through clenched teeth. *I
should have done this months ago. You have no idea how long
I've waited for you.*

Her breathing quickened, and he caught the rhythm, her
pleasure spilling through him, turning his body into an instrument,
something to be used for her. He was too close to the edge,
straining to hold on. It wasn't fair to go too fast. He wanted her to
enjoy it, goddammit.

But she moved again, writhing suppleness under him, and he
tipped over into the crisis of exploding novas. His release triggered
hers, their minds dissolving together into white heat. For a single

heated moment he merged completely with her, leaving his body behind and simply drowning in the dark silken depths of her talent and her body at the same time.

Time came back, invaded the world again. He collapsed against her, sweat mingling between their bodies. He buried his face against her throat, breathing in the musk of her arousal, and choked back tears.

"Shhh." Her fingers trailed up his back, a touch that sparked fresh fire in the base of his belly.

Again, he thought, dazed, propping himself on shaking elbows. *As soon as I can, I want to do this again. And slower. Much slower.*

"Amen to that," she murmured, catching the thought. She smoothed his hair. "Relax. We've got time."

No, he didn't have time. He was a dying man, and he wanted her, just as soon as his body would cooperate with him.

"I'm sorry," he whispered. "It should have been better. I should have taken more time."

"Don't worry. Here, move over. Talk to me a little bit."

"Christ, you want to *talk?*" He hadn't even managed to get her under the covers. Where was the control he had such a reputation for? *If this ever gets out I'm going to be a laughingstock. Then again, as long as she's here, I don't fucking care.*

"For a little while." She sounded amused. *Don't worry, you have a chance to redeem yourself.* Her voice whispered in the middle of his head, a connection solidifying. He could feel her thinking, the deep satisfied glow threading through her veins. "Then I've got other plans."

"I'm yours," he whispered. And he meant it. Just because one part of him was a little exhausted didn't mean he was without hope. He was, after all, used to thinking on his feet, and there was an extremely interesting set of ideas having to do with his mouth and a few delectable corners of her body. "Just tell me what to do."

Thirty-Four

Sleeping with a very warm male pressed against her back was proving to be impossible. Sweating, Rowan pushed the covers down and tried to wriggle away from him.

Justin made a low sleepy sound and pulled her back against him, wrapped his arm around her waist, and throwing a leg over hers for good measure. He buried his face in her hair and sighed. She hadn't slept in a bed with anyone else for…oh, it had to be nigh on six years.

The memory of her last relationship made her wince slightly. Now that she knew she wasn't crazy, that the painful chaos of normal people's thoughts was what had made her withdraw, she felt a little more charitable about all those blind dates. It hadn't been fair to them that she could read their minds.

She was too warm, and she needed to use the bathroom. She pushed at his muscled arm, getting exactly nowhere.

"Dammit," she whisper-groaned, then pushed back gently with her elbow, trying to nudge him loose.

He surfaced only long enough to pull her back against his chest, murmuring something into her hair and then passing out again. She had never seen him sleep this deeply. Dozing, yes. Sleeping sitting up in a chair, sinking down just far enough to stave off exhaustion—but not dead asleep.

That must mean he trusts me, she thought, and felt a pleased shiver trace its way down her spine.

"Justin," she whispered, "let *go* of me. I have to go to the bathroom."

He muttered into her hair again, but let her go. Rowan pushed herself up to sit on the edge of the bed.

It was proving to be a peaceful night. Nobody screaming or wounded in the infirmary, no operation going critical, nothing. Rowan took a deep breath, stretched and pushed herself up to her feet.

Naked, she padded to the bathroom, closed herself in. The darkness was immediate, womb-like.

She found the toilet by touch, relieved herself and flushed. Yawned again, bracing herself on the counter. *If I turned on the light I'd have to look at myself in the mirror, and I probably look like I've been rolling around in a bed. Good God. I knew he was capable of intense concentration, but that was something else.* She was glad of the darkness, because she was actually blushing. Just like a kid.

Justin's sleeping mind still wrapped around hers, a flicker of dreaming deep in blankness. He was sleeping so heavily she felt tempted to shake him, wake him up, make him share her insomnia. But that wasn't fair. He was exhausted. She'd felt the scars from the bullets he'd taken, and the other scars from things she couldn't even imagine, things he kept closed away but that she caught glimpses of. Glimpses of cold white rooms, of pain, of fist meeting flesh, and a soft evil voice sunk into his head like a fishhook; glimpses of a sick, shaky feeling as a needle was thrust into his arm.

Sigma.

Rowan drew in a gasping breath. Her fingers found the light switch. She flicked it on, blinked against the sudden onslaught, her eyes watering.

Her reflection blinked back at her. She *was* blushing, her cheeks crimson. Her collarbones and ribs stood out starkly, her cheekbones high and too gaunt. She wasn't efficient and tough like Catherine, whose muscles moved smoothly under her pale skin. She wasn't even like Kate, knowledgeable about psychic talent and completely unflappable. Rowan had no illusions about her own usefulness on any of the "operations." She would, as Henderson said, get someone killed. Or herself.

A part of her wondered if she could just stay here at Headquarters, the only safe space she had ever found. They didn't mock her here, or point at her. But the breathless awe some of them regarded her with was almost as bad. She thought privately that some of that awe—most of it, probably—was the fact that she seemed to be able to handle Justin.

Memory rose.

Rowan's eyes squeezed shut against the light. Her father's surprised face, the small gurgling sound he'd made. Hilary vanishing. Broken glass and terror and the popping sounds of gunfire. Cold air.

She shook the memories free, feeling Justin's uneasiness. He was on the verge of waking up, deep sleep turning to dreaming, his mind reaching for hers. The dream was sharp and hurtful, something burning in his arm, screaming and darkness, and blood threading down from his ribs.

Rowan shut off the light, opened the bathroom door and padded across the room. There was a little ambient light in here, at least she could see the white sheets. She sat down on the bed. "Justin," she said quietly, touching his hand.

The dream halted, changed. He sank back down into sleep, but his fingers curled through hers and held on. Rowan sighed.

It's official, she thought. *I am going to do whatever I can to make them pay. Not just for Daddy and for Hilary, but for Justin too. They could have killed him. And Boomer and Eleanor, and Bobby and Annika…and everyone. Sigma's evil, and they have to be stopped. And if I have this talent, this gift, I have to use it to stop them. So tomorrow, I start training. No more messing around.*

The resolve took place right under her breastbone, in the same place she had buried the truth about her talent since she was five years old. That resolve had carried her through years of learning to be invisible, hanging on grimly while other people's emotions buffeted her from every side, carried her through the wrenching grief of her mother's death and the inevitable heartbreak of her father's relentless aging.

Okay, she thought, her fingers tight in Justin's sleeping hand. *No more messing around.*

Thirty-Five

"Would you look at that," Henderson said.

"Makes you want to sing, doesn't it?" Delgado's mouth twitched into a half-smile.

Below the observation deck, the shooting gallery resounded with the sound of gunfire. Three of the twelve lanes were taken—two by members of Annika's team, and the third by Rowan and Brew.

Rowan nodded at something Brew said, lifted the Glock in one clean motion, and squeezed off six more shots in a row. Then she glanced at Brew, smiling. The tall man hit the button to bring the target up to their booth, and then gently clapped her on the shoulder, Justin noticed. She must have done well. Brew was a patient, careful teacher, almost as good as Del himself.

"I don't know what you did," Henderson answered, "but good work. Kate tells me she's never seen such intense work from a trainee. And Catherine tells me Rowan's doing all right on the decks. *Knows enough to get out of the fuckin' way,* I believe was Cath's estimation of her skill."

Justin shrugged. "Rowan's doing all the work. Not me."

"How did you convince her to take classes again? She's up for graduation. Kate says there's nothing more she needs except field experience." The old man leaned against a concrete pillar, watching Rowan as Brew clipped another target in and hit the button. Rowan, her fingers moving quickly, reloaded.

Delgado's mouth was dry. He shifted slightly to ease his sore shoulder. He'd run a new batch of recruits through a combat-training course last weekend and taken a stray amateur shot. Rowan had been invaluable during the class. "I didn't 'convince' her. I just kind of put the question to her in terms she could understand."

Admit it, Delgado. You have no idea what suddenly made her snap out of it. Unless it was tumbling into bed with you. Have I infected her with my own anger?

"Well, whatever you did, it's working. Yoshi's got a kit all ready for her. How's she coming along in combat training?"

"Okay." He watched her lift the gun, take her stance habitually, felt the fierce one-pointed concentration spreading out from her. The observation deck was far above the lanes, and bulletproof. He could see everything going on down there, but still, it made him nervous. The thought of her around that much live fire made his spine go cold. "She still flinches a little. I don't think she's ready."

"If she's not ready now, she won't ever be." Henderson's eyes were on him. "You're not letting your emotional involvement with her jeopardize her training, are you?"

"Of course not." *I'm lying. Call me on it. I don't want her out there, General. Not even with a whole team's worth of backup.* "Fuck it. Look, I want her on standby. Permanently."

"Reason?" Henderson's iron-gray eyebrow arched, his thin mouth quirking slightly.

"If she goes out, I'll have to spend half my time worrying about her," Delgado said. "Adding her to the team will diminish my capability." The words felt odd in his mouth. He would never have admitted this if he had to look at Henderson. They both watched as Rowan fired a few more times, just like a pro, her stance braced but easy. He would have been proud of her skill, except that every day brought her closer to becoming a full-fledged operative.

"I don't believe that."

"You want to hang someone's life on it?" Delgado shifted his weight, his eyes dropping down to follow Rowan as she checked the gun and racked it. She and Brew went about cleaning up the booth. Brewster made a comment and she laughed, the sound echoing sharply off the gallery's walls. "I'd like her on standby."

"Overruled," Henderson said. "I'm sorry, Del. She's good for the team, and you've never cracked under pressure before. You'll do fine."

"As long as you're aware I'm going to be looking out for her."

"How would that be any different than Zeke and Cath? This isn't Sigma, Del. We don't split up budding relationships."

"It's not budding anymore." He saw Brewster touch her shoulder as they headed for the safe zone. She didn't flinch. Instead, she laughed, covering her mouth. Even through the safety glasses and earpieces she was gorgeous. Today she wore a blue tank top with a picture of a Buddha on it, borrowed from Catherine, and a pair of worn jeans. Now that he knew what her skin felt like against his fingers, now that he knew what it was like to sink into her and feel the clean depths of her mind closing over him, her body tightening around him as she cried out softly, arching her back, it was even more difficult to keep his mind on his work.

Or anything else, for that matter.

"You think you need to tell me that? I could set my clock by you, Delgado. All I have to do is find out where Rowan's gonna be. They're calling you 'Rowan's shadow' now." Henderson waved him away. "Go on, you're due in combat training with your lady love. Go work it out. I'll see you in briefing in three hours."

"Briefing for what?" Delgado uncoiled himself and stalked toward the door.

"The next job, what do you think? There's a Sig installation in Florida we're going to take a look at. We've also got some field testing that needs to be done, and Kate thinks Rowan can help."

Delgado looked back over his shoulder. "Don't wreck my reputation, General."

"Ha. Wild horses won't drag your little secret out of me, I promise. Get me that workup on the Broward facility, will you?"

"Ten-four." Del closed the door to the observation deck and stood for a moment, his hands flexing into fists.

Christ, what have I done?

He'd maneuvered her into wanting to be an operative to give her something to care about, to pull her out of that numb grief of hers. Now he was seeing the consequences. Would he be able to protect her?

I got her into this, I have to take care of her, he thought. Then the deeper, mocking voice of his conscience spoke up. *What, you thought she wouldn't ever come out and play as an operative? You thought she'd never reach this point?*

The thing was, he hadn't thought she'd reach this point so *fast.* She'd thrown herself into being a trainee instead of a neophyte with such fierce determination, it made him a little uneasy. What would happen once she channeled all that energy into fighting Sigma? She was likely to become obsessed.

I'm a fine one to talk about obsession, he thought, setting off for the transports. *I'm obsessed myself.*

The transport was empty, since the gallery was at the farthest edge of Headquarters. He leaned against the wall and ran through Rowan's training in his head, one more time.

Kate said there was nothing more to teach her. Brew had let her rack her own gun. Catherine had given her grudging stamp of approval, and Yoshi had a kit all ready for her. And Del?

I don't want her anywhere near an operation, he admitted to himself. *I don't want her shot at, or trying to open a door while the Sigs bear down on us, I don't know how she'll act under pressure.*

Except he did. She would be as clear-eyed and calm as he trained her to be. It was up to him.

"Christ," he muttered.

When he reached the *dojo*, he was in a fine black mood. Rowan was waiting—or not exactly. She was in the same tank top and a pair of loose black silk pants, sparring.

With Ellis, whose lanky frame was wrapped in a white *gi*.

Ellis was one of Blake's surviving team members, one who didn't need training. He was good in a fight, quick and vicious. Delgado almost wanted to stride across the room, wrench Rowan away and yell, *What do you think you're doing?* Instead he faded into the shadows by the entrance from the men's locker room to watch, driving his nails into his palms.

Rowan balanced on the balls of her feet. Ellis moved in on her, not precisely rushing, but quickly enough that she stepped back, grabbing his wrist, and socking her hip into his midriff as he flew around her, hitting the mat perfectly, bouncing up.

Rowan evidently expected that, because she relaxed, her back to Ellis, a smile on her face.

Then he grabbed her.

Delgado's heart leapt into his throat.

One strike, two—Rowan's body moved without thought, stamping down on Ellis's foot, driving her elbow back into his midriff until the breath *whooshed* out of the tall man. He didn't let up, though, dragging her backwards, and Delgado took a step forward. *If she starts to panic—*

She kicked, then went still, her luminous eyes flaring, and Ellis dropped her. "Ow!" he yelled, shaking his hand out. She'd bitten him.

Rowan whirled, her knee coming up. He barely fended her off. Then he instinctively threw an elbow—and caught her in the face.

Rowan went down hard, and Delgado was striding across

the floor, rage hot under his skin.

Then she leapt to her feet. Blood dripped down her upper lip, she threw four punches in a row, Ellis shuffling back, blocking. But Del could see how much it cost him, how he was scrambling to stay ahead of her.

This has gone far enough. Delgado didn't break stride. Ellis's eyes flicked up past Rowan's shoulder, saw him coming, and she was on him in that instant, driving him to the ground and giving him a short jab to the ribs. Blood flew—*her* blood. From her nose. Maybe it was even broken.

"Got you!" she crowed, her legs tangled with Ellis's. "Ouch. *Ow!"*

Delgado set his heels, grabbed her arm, and hauled her up. Ellis rolled, came up in a ready stance. Del ran his gaze over the man and noticed he was wincing. He'd be bruised. Rowan had gotten in a few good shots.

"I don't recall putting you on the roster," Del said mildly enough, as if his fury wasn't painting the air red.

"I was early," she said. "Ellis offered to give me a bout." Her eyes were shining, the tank top spotted with blood. More dripped from her nose—at least it wasn't a gusher. "I got him!"

"Good for you," he said, hating himself for what he was about to do. "Think you could take me? Sigs work in pairs, and they won't give you a chance to catch your breath."

The challenge in his tone was something new, and he was sure his eyes were flat and cold. *I can't do this,* he thought, and closed himself up tighter than a fist. She wouldn't be able to read him—not until the anger went away. Anger was the best fuel, and the only thing that let him close her out. *She's not ready; she's not ready. She'll hate me for this.*

Rowan tore her arm out of his hand and punched him.

Reflex took care of blocking, deflecting the strike. It was a good one, all her weight behind it, she stepped aside like he'd taught her, changing the arc of her movement so he couldn't catch her and throw her off-guard. Delgado moved in on her, pressing her, no time to respond, her own arm came up as he gave her a half-strike punch. She kicked for his knee, but he moved, knowing each move she would make before she made it.

Every move but the one she used—electricity crackling, and his arm going momentarily numb.

He backed up a step, two. "Where'd you learn that?"

"Boomer showed me," she said, panting, her ribs flaring, dried blood crusting on her face and sweat damping her hair. "It's easy. He calls it a 'crackle.'"

He started circling, not watching the tank top clinging to her chest, not hearing Ellis's low tuneless whistle as he watched Delgado move in on her. They were starting to draw a little crowd, like most good sparring matches did. *This one's Del versus his girlfriend, and Del looks pissed*, he thought sardonically, hearing the words as if they were someone else gossiping. More grist for the rumor mill.

Rowan tracked just like he'd taught her—good girl. He moved forward slightly, and she countered, playing through the sequence.

"Nice."

"Thanks." Her eyes were shuttered, dark. "You look mad."

She's trying to get into your head. He moved, a flurry of strikes she managed to block, but he was bigger and he pressed her mercilessly, all the way across the mat. She threw one or two halfhearted punches, not enough to hurt him. He was pressing her too hard.

One small miscalculation and he had her, locking her arm and spinning her, his arm across her throat. She kicked, but he was ready for that. He twisted her other arm, not hard enough to really hurt her, just enough to make her feel it, clinically noting that she went limp in his arms, her ribs heaving. "I don't think you're ready," he said in her ear, feeling her shiver slightly as his breath caressed her skin. "Not yet."

"Not for you, maybe," she shot back, her free hand hooked over his arm, as if she would try to pull his forearm away. "But for Sigma? Yeah."

"I don't think so," he said, his tone dropping intimately. He couldn't help it. The heat of her against him reminded him of other things. What was it about her that could deprive him of all good sense and caution?

"Kate told me there's nothing else she can teach me," she replied, then ever so subtly, instead of going limp she leaned back into him, as if they were playing a game. A deeper kind of game that would end with his hands on her in a different way.

Oh, no you don't, angel. Delgado didn't have to take a deep breath, but he did, searching for control. He wanted to let go of her, apologize, suggest a trip into town for dinner—

but no. Here in the practice room, there was no room for *friend*. It was one of the first things Sigma had taught him, and the lesson ran deep.

"Can you let go?" she asked, finally. "I'm getting a little tired of this."

He released her—but not right away, just to drive home the fact that he *could* keep her. "You're still sloppy."

"I'm ready," she parried, rubbing at her arm. "Even if you don't want to think so."

"We'll see. Yoshi has a kit packed for you. We'll pick it up tomorrow. For right now, we'll start with the heavy bag."

A flash of surprise crossed her face. *Oh, no, I'm not going to let you off easy, angel. I'm going to have to be twice as harsh as anything you're likely to find out there—and they won't stop because you're tired and bloody and hungry.* "Heavy bag," she echoed, and her face closed like a door. She couldn't keep him out of her head—not completely, not with them sharing a bed every night. But both of them avoided contact, and it was almost as good.

"What are you standing around for?" he barked. "*Move, girl!*"

Her eyes flared. "Make me," she flung back at him, her hands on her hips. "What is *wrong* with you?"

He took two steps and had her in an armlock, ignoring the sudden gasps from their audience, marched her across the *dojo* to the line of heavy bags, then shook her a little before letting her loose. "Let's see you do the standard, operative," he said crisply. "And the longer you fight me, the longer you'll be here."

Her nostrils flared and her chin lifted. She wiped at the blood on her face, smearing it across one cheek. Delgado's heart began to ache.

Without another word, she spun on her heel and attacked the heavy bag. Delgado looked up, seeing shocked faces and slack jaws. He narrowed his eyes.

People scurried back to what they had been doing, except for Ellis, who watched Rowan as she worked the heavy bag. He looked shocked, eyeing her as if she was a new species, one he wasn't quite sure was poisonous or not. Del looked back at her and saw, without much surprise, that her face was set and flushed. Her training held, though—she wasn't emitting waves of anger or distress.

"Is that the best you can do?" he snarled, hating himself.
The skin over her knuckles on both hands left bloody prints
on the bag. Her hands were almost blurring, she cursed at him
with an inventiveness he found grimly amusing right before
he decided to stop this. It had gone far enough. He'd made his
point.

"Rowan—" he began, and she whirled away from the bag,
her ponytail whipping.

"I *hate* you!" she screamed, her voice bouncing off the
mats and the ceiling, drilling through the whispers. "I wish I'd
never seen you!"

He stood rooted to the spot while she gave the heavy bag
one last kick—good solid contact, her boot thudding onto heavy
vinyl and the entire bag shuddering like a side of beef on a
conveyer belt—and stalked past him, her hands and face
bloody, and her head held high.

Well, the little voice in his head said clinically, *looks like
it's no warm bed for you tonight, Del. Straight to the doghouse.
What the hell's gotten into you?*

Thirty-Six

Her hands ached, but they were steady. Rowan dabbed at her lacerated knuckles with a cotton ball soaked in antiseptic, hissing softly. "That stings." Her eyes watered, and she set her jaw. A single tear from the stinging rolled down her cheek.

"Bet it does." Catherine popped her bubble-gum. She leaned against the bathroom door, electric light glowing off her vinyl pants and skintight *Ambrixes* T-shirt. Her nose-ring glittered. "You're serious? Del did that?"

"I did it. On the heavy bag. But he kind of pushed me into it." Rowan sighed, tossed the bloody cotton ball into the wastebasket, and picked a fresh one, dipping it in the antiseptic. "I've never seen him like that before. He saw me sparring with Ellis and just kind of went…"

"Was that before you got your nose socked or after?"

"After. Ellis accidentally got me in the face."

Cath and Zeke's bathroom was cluttered with different kinds of scented soap, and towels hung everywhere, not to mention bits of hand-washing hung up. It was messy, but comforting.

"Oh, God." Catherine rolled her eyes. "Ellis popped you on the nose and Del saw it?"

"He might have." Rowan dabbed gently. Another tear trickled down her cheek, her eyes watering from the stinging. "My nose isn't broken though, just bloody. Thanks for asking."

"What did he do? Is Ellis in the infirmary? How many punches?" Catherine's Mohawk nodded cheerfully as she eyed the pile of cotton balls. "Wow."

"He didn't do anything to Ellis, he just sparred with me— ran me ragged. Then he set me to the heavy bag. I think I lost my temper."

"So what *happened*? Talking to you is like pulling teeth." Cath rolled her eyes again dramatically, doing her best to look like a sarcastic teenager—and succeeding pretty well, since she was under twenty and her tone was heavily weighted with irony.

"If you'd quit interrupting, I could tell you." Rowan finished dabbing at her knuckles. "There, that's the best I can do for right now. Anyway, I kicked the heavy bag, shouted something not very nice, and left."

"That's it?" Cath's jaw dropped. "That's all? You didn't throw anything? Zap him? *Anything?*"

"I kind of doubt 'zapping' Justin would be a good idea. I did shock him while we were sparring." Rowan's tone was dry and unamused. "I need some advice here, Cath, and I have to admit I'm not getting any." *You're as bad as Hilary,* she thought, and stopped, waiting for the burst of pain. It came, but it was strangely muted.

"Personally I think you're crazy for dating him anyway, but that's just me." Cath popped her gum again. Rowan swept the bloody cotton balls together tossed them into the trash. Bandaging would do no good. She'd heal quickly anyway; she always did.

"Why does everyone assume I'm dating him?" Rowan capped the antiseptic and hauled herself up off the toilet lid to put the bottle away in the mirrored cabinet. Catherine's bathroom was, of course, decorated with a lava lamp and a print of Frankenstein. Half-empty bottles of nail polish in different shades scattered over the counter, and an ammo belt hung by the door.

"Maybe because you're sleeping with him?" Cath said sweetly.

"Oh, for God's sake." Rowan sighed. "When did everyone get so interested in my life?"

"You're a very interesting girl, sweetie. Here's a shirt." Catherine held up a green-and-white lump of material. "Need some pants?"

"No, there's not much blood on these, I'll wear them. I'm starving." Rowan examined her sports bra in the mirror—one or two spots of blood, that was all. She took the shirt and held it up. "Good God. Where did you get a Lucky Care Bear T-shirt?"

"Oh, around and about. Let's see how it looks." Catherine's eyes were sparkling under their heavy coat of eyeliner. "Yum. Makes your tits look cute and perky."

"It's too small," Rowan complained, then had to grab at the counter as a wave of dizziness swept her.

"Ro? You okay?" The younger woman's voice sounded very far away. "Ro?"

"I'm fine," Rowan said dreamily. "Fine. I promise I'm fine. Just tired and hungry, that's all." When Rowan opened her eyes, she saw Catherine examining her, eyes narrowed and cherry-painted mouth pursed.

"You look like you've just seen a ghost. And believe me, I should know."

Rowan shrugged. Catherine and Zeke's suite had two bathrooms, a long brown velvet couch, and psychedelic posters on each wall. No plants except for a cactus on Zeke's bedside table. Magazines and dirty clothes were scattered everywhere. A stick of strawberry incense fumed in a holder on Catherine's worktable.

For someone with such a precise, detail-oriented mind, she certainly is messy. Rowan caught herself smiling as she scanned the room. It was full of life and the stamp of Catherine's personality. "I suppose I'm just a little surprised. I didn't expect Justin to act that way."

"What way? Like a jerk with a jealous streak?" Cath rested one hand on a cocked hip and regarded Rowan with a very adult and bitter half-smile.

"Jealous?" Rowan touched her nose delicately with her fingertips. It wasn't swelling much. Catherine had insisted on applying ice and dosing Rowan with ibuprofen. "I don't think he's ever—"

"Oh, yeah. He's jealous. Come on, Price, he doesn't let you go *anywhere* alone. I'm surprised you can visit the bathroom by yourself. Del probably saw Ellis getting sweaty with you and went into he-man mode. It happens."

"I'm sure it does." Rowan pulled the hem of the T-shirt down and gave herself a final once-over in the full-length mirror Catherine had draped a black feather boa over. "I just don't see Justin as the jealous type."

"You're dense." Catherine padded over to the unmade king-size bed, dropped down, and began working her feet into her boots.

I look like I've been in a fight, Rowan thought, leaning close to the mirror. She had a raccoon-mask of bruising around both eyes, and her nose was a little swollen. It had been a good hit, but the swelling was already beginning to go down. It smarted, though. The only problem with healing rapidly was that most of the pain was compressed into a shorter time. *Well, what do you know? I was in a fight. Me, the sissy girl who ran away from every schoolyard brawl. Imagine that.*

"I probably am," she murmured, touching her split lower lip. "Ellis got me a good one, but I won the fight."

"I was *talking* about *Delgado*, Rowan." Catherine couldn't have sounded any more sarcastic if she'd tried, which was in and of itself a compliment. "You're hopeless."

"Catherine...how did *you* get into the Society?" It wasn't the right time to ask, but Rowan was curious.

The younger girl paused, her fingers tangled in a boot lace. "Sigma snatched me from the playground at Sacred Heart," she said finally, tonelessly, tossing her head slightly. *Like she's tossing a ponytail,* Rowan realized, and shuddered. Sometimes Catherine seemed no more than a very scared child, for all her toughness. "They nabbed me and put me in a holding tank. They ever tell you about Sig holding tanks? They're padded and circular, with a drain in one corner so you can piss. But the top is Plexiglass and always dark. You can't tell if you're being observed or not. The lights are fluorescent, and they never go off. I was in there for about sixteen hours before the door was blown and Del and Henderson came in. They got me out. On the way out we passed the Sig who was coming to shoot me full of Zed. He had forty hypodermics. Someone had broken his neck. Probably Del." She paused, yanked the boot lace tight, and tied it swiftly. "Guess why they wanted me."

"Probably something to do with your telekinesis," Rowan guessed.

"Yeah. I used to make pebbles and rocks rise up off the playground and smack the other kids. Wasn't very nice. And the nuns reported it to the priest, who reported it to Rome, but somehow Sigma found out about it." She shook her head, her Mohawk—now tipped with crimson—shivering. "Del was first in the door. I threw myself on him, and he put me in an armlock and said, 'If you want to get out of here, come with me'."

Rowan let out a soft breath. Cath shivered. She bounced up from the bed, her booted feet hitting the floor with a thud. "Grab a coat. I want to smoke a cig topside, okay?"

Rowan shook her head. "What an awful habit," she said, but she found her camel coat hanging on the rack by the door. "What's my coat doing here?"

"You left it that afternoon we played pinochle, remember? Hand me my scarf. I'm hungry too, so let's hurry. Wonder what's for dinner tonight?"

"Probably spaghetti." Rowan handed over the long, striped Dr. Who scarf and shrugged into her coat, wincing as a few more bruises made themselves apparent. Justin hadn't been kind.

Neither was I, she thought, and sighed. At least he'd been smart enough to leave her alone. She was a lot calmer now. Calm enough to feel a little guilty over the way she'd screamed at him.

Catherine chattered the entire way up to the surface, her silver jewelry flashing and hoop earrings shivering. Rowan made the appropriate noises, feeling her mood lighten. The girl meant well. For all her punk bravado she was actually a very sensitive, intelligent young lady. And she was trying to make Rowan feel better.

Hilary would have snorted and dragged Rowan out for a night on the town, dancing and drinking and overriding Rowan's good-natured complaints. Thinking about Hilary sent the usual pain through her chest; a pain that seemed to be getting…if not less sharp, then at least easier to bear.

Hil would have chided Rowan into calling Delgado, and she would have bought a carton of ice cream and raged against jealous men and insisted Rowan tell her every detail.

Rowan shook her head, dislodging the thought. Catherine, busy talking about parallel processing and gigs of RAM, didn't notice.

When they stepped out through the steel-reinforced doors, dusk was beginning to creep into the sky and between the buildings. Catherine flicked her cigarette lighter and lit her smoke, taking a long drag. "God, I've been dying for this," she said. "You want one?"

Rowan shook her head. It was late March but still chilly, the sky clear, though the grass was wet from this morning's rainfall. Pockets of snow still held on in deeply shaded corners, eroded from the rain and the ground slowly warming up. Venus glimmered in the sky. Rowan could still hear her father's voice telling her about the stars. "No thanks." Her breath plumed in the air, as if she was smoking too.

"How about you? How did you get here?" Catherine's eyes glinted. She hopped down the steps, then wrestled herself up to sit on the low stone wall next to the carved lion. The lion's paw rested on a stone urn frothing with ivy. "I only heard about half of the story from Del."

Rowan shrugged. "I saw a light in an abandoned house and thought it was kids playing around for Halloween," she said slowly. "Then I ran across Justin. When he said you were parapsychology investigators, I freaked out. I couldn't have anyone suspecting what I was."

"You blew out the instruments, you know. Without even trying. It was weird." Catherine frowned and took another drag. "We weren't sure if you were government or not. Del looked like he'd been hit with a two-by-four. I think he already had a case for you."

"Well, the next time I saw him two Sigs were trying to kidnap me in a parking lot. He chased them off and got invited to dinner." *He probably 'pushed' Dad,* Rowan realized, remembering her father's odd insistence. "Then he came to dinner—and so did Sigma. They shot my father and my best friend."

"God, I'm sorry." Catherine looked aghast. "I didn't hear that part. I just heard Del snatched you from a Sig team and dragged you halfway across the country before it was safe to bring you in."

Rowan shrugged, crossing her arms over her breasts and hugging herself. Her left arm twinged—she had a bruise on her bicep. As gentle as he'd tried to be, Justin had still hurt her.

Maybe that's a lesson.

"I hate those fucking Sigs." Catherine blew out a long jet stream of smoke. "Brew says they're just guys doing their jobs, most of 'em. I say, so were the Nazis. It doesn't make them any better."

Rowan leaned against the stone lion, ignoring the chill seeping through her coat. Nausea rose briefly under her breastbone. She took a deep breath, the back of her neck prickling. "I agree."

"You okay?" Catherine stubbed her cigarette on the lion's paw and tossed the remainder into a coffee can set to the side. "You look kind of pale."

"I'm always pale." Rowan attempted a cheerful tone. "I think my blood sugar's bottoming out. Let's go eat."

Catherine slid her arm through Rowan's and grinned down at her. "Good idea, sistah. If it's spaghetti, I want tons of garlic bread."

"Meatballs," Rowan agreed, good-naturedly. "Sounds great."

Thirty-Seven

He stood in the dark, staring out through the French doors, listening to the subliminal sounds of Headquarters. He'd chosen this room because it was far away from the bustle of others, and he wasn't immersed in the chatter of other minds out here. And the light from the windows, light any time he wanted it, a room where he could shut and lock the door at any moment, a bathroom to himself—all these things had been more precious than he had ever dreamed. Just being able to lock a door was like every Christmas he'd ever had rolled into one.

His memory of the first year at Headquarters was a blur of prowling the corridors fighting the burning need for Zed, sometimes holing up in a faraway lonely spot to curl in a ball and sob while the agony of breaking the addiction tore through him. When he had finally recovered enough to be useful, Henderson had suggested he find some rooms he liked; Delgado had used them sparingly in the years since, not bothering to hang anything on the walls, not daring to make anything about them personal.

Now the room was alive with reminders of Rowan. Plants and bookcases, one of her fluttering blue scarves wrapped around the bedstead, a stack of art books she'd bought at the used bookstore in town holding up a terra cotta pot with a blooming blue orchid. More than that, though, was the smell of her clinging to the air; a scent so faint he doubted anyone else would recognize it.

Delgado filled his lungs with that subliminal smell. Sooner or later she'd come back, unless she was going to abandon everything in here.

His conscience pricked him. He should be standing guard, watching over her. He'd promised she wasn't going anywhere alone. But nothing had happened, and Delgado, for all his quiet snooping, hadn't found anything to make him think Jilssen was anything more than simply obsessed with Rowan's talents. And besides, she was angry; she wouldn't appreciate him following her around.

I hate you! I wish I'd never seen you! Her voice echoed down into the dark well of his brain. Had he *ever* thought she would understand?

She'll come back eventually, he told himself. *Then you*

can apologize. Apologize? Hell, you can get down on your knees and beg. She's got a soft spot; you can use that. You're an idiot, Delgado, the biggest idiot on the face of the Earth.

"I don't care," he muttered, his breath fogging the glass. "Don't care. If I'm cruel here, she'll be ready for out there. Facing *them*."

That wasn't training, the sharp calculating voice he hated echoed inside his head. *You were jealous. You saw her sparring with Ellis, and you're jealous of anyone who gets that much of her time. Hell, you're even jealous of her patients. You're obsessed, Del, and you miscalculated bigtime.*

"She'll forgive me." He didn't care that he was talking to himself; here at Headquarters it was practically required to mutter to yourself and look grim. Some of the telepaths had to subvocalize to make their talents work.

What if she doesn't? She's never yelled at anyone like that before. She told you she hated you.

"She doesn't hate anyone, that's her problem."

Still, you've done a good job of teaching her to hate Sigma, haven't you? What if she uses that lesson on you?

"She'll forgive me."

Maybe she won't. Maybe this will be the thing that shows her what you are. Who you are. And you pushed her, Delgado, you pushed her right over the edge.

Shadows lengthened, dusk turning into night. The fields surrounding Headquarters fell under folds of darkness. Past dinnertime. Where was she?

If he *reached*, he could probably tell. But that was a violation of her privacy. Just because she shared a space of her mind with him didn't mean she wanted him spying on her...even if she was the only thing he could think about.

The only thing he could *care* about.

Even if he was worried, standing in front of the French doors, trying not to strain for the sound of footsteps in the hall outside. Worried enough to make a fist. Worried enough to curse under his breath, touching the fogged glass, and tracing the letters with a fingertip. *R. O. W.*

Footsteps outside, a low laugh, and the door slid aside. The air inside the room tightened in anticipation. "Let me grab my purse," she said over her shoulder as she entered.

Delgado's shoulders tensed. He stared at the fog on the glass, his breath drawing a vapor curtain over the world outside.

The light flicked on, blazing, and he turned around, trying not to blink as it stung his eyes.

"Justin," she said, quietly. She didn't sound happy. There was a raccoon-mask of yellow-green bruising over both her eyes, and the bridge of her nose looked a little swollen. She had her purse, was digging in it. Had he frightened her? Couldn't she tell he was in here waiting for her? "We're going to town, some emergency snack cravings. You...um, you want to come?"

How does she manage to do that, rob me of every good, sensible, logical thought? He closed his mouth with a snap. A green and white shirt with a teddy bear printed on it stretched across her breasts, the bear had a four-leaf clover painted on its belly. She pushed a few stray strands of pale hair back, tucking them behind her ears. Then she ducked into the bathroom, and he heard her moving, the clatter of something dropped in the sink.

She came out, sliding a second earring in—a silver Celtic cross, swinging gently. "Justin?" she prompted, pulling her coat up over her shoulders, her purse safely stowed under it. "Cath wants Pop Tarts and I was thinking of a cheap bottle of wine and some Cheetos. Brew says he has to return some movies, and Yoshi wants a beer. Are you coming?"

He managed to find his voice. "Do you want me to come?" *I sound like a teenage boy,* he thought, and took a step away from the French door. *Please, Rowan. Forgive me.*

She shrugged, her face closing, the glitter draining from her eyes. "You don't have to," she said, and someone knocked on the door. She turned away, her boot heel scraping on the floor.

"I'll come," he said. "Just let me get my coat. Can I? I mean...Rowan?"

"Well, then, come on." She tapped her toe, cocking her head to the side. "I didn't think you'd be up here," she said as he ripped his jacket off the hanger and shrugged into it, automatically easing the coat over his rig.

"I was waiting for you. I'm sorry. I'm an idiot."

"I know you're an idiot," she said sharply, and turned on her heel, her pale hair flaring out in a luscious wave. "Come on."

It was a good thing he was wearing his boots, he reflected. She might have left him behind otherwise.

Waiting in the hall were Brew and Catherine, Brew's wire rim glasses glinting in the hall light. "You coming, Del? Good thing Henderson's getting the van." There was an edge of uneasiness in his clipped British voice. Catherine threw Delgado a pointed look, eyebrows raised, and slid her arm through Rowan's.

Rowan's hair glowed, and he searched for something polite and normal to say. "Well, I've been wanting to go into town for a beer myself." It was the only thing he could think of. Rowan and Catherine were heading down the hall already, arm in arm like schoolgirl chums.

"Come on, mate," Brew said. "Beer it is. I've talked the ladies into stopping by a little bar on Sixth Street. You can buy her a drink and try your luck."

"Am I that transparent?" Del muttered.

"Not to most. Don't worry, she hasn't said a word about it."

"Great." *That could mean she's too angry to speak*, he thought.

"Yeah. She even insisted we come up here and see if you were in, so we could invite you along." Brew's white teeth flashed in a grin. He rolled his shoulders back under his bomber jacket. "A good sign, eh?"

"Maybe." Del kept his tone clipped. *How about that? Five minutes ago I wanted to smash everything I saw. Now I feel like laughing.*

He was actually relieved.

Thirty-Eight

Rowan's headache got worse as they took the freeway into the city. Henderson drove, Brew rode shotgun, and Rowan was in the middle row window seat, Catherine and Yoshi beside her; Justin and Zeke shared the back seat. Catherine chattered, Yoshi hummed an odd discordant song to himself, and Rowan tried to listen to Catherine through the pain that seemed to force diamond needles through her head.

Then, as if she had passed through a wall, the headache faded between one mile marker and the next. Rowan let out a short breath and felt Justin's silent presence in the seat behind her. It was oddly comforting, she had to admit it. They had started calling him "Rowan's shadow," she'd heard it whispered behind her back. It seemed they weren't so scared of what Rowan could do anymore; she was a known quantity. All the uneasy glances at her were a result of Justin's presence. They seemed far more frightened of him than of anything Rowan could do.

He shifted behind her, and she felt the movement. Trying to keep him out of the corner of her mind he inhabited was impossible. Even when he didn't press, like he had this entire afternoon, she still felt him like a nagging, lingering toothache. Only he didn't hurt her—it was as if he was a part of her, and if she tried to block him away he was still there. Like a phantom limb.

Just as she thought it, Henderson took an off ramp, swerving to avoid something. "Look at that," he said. "Bad driving strikes again."

"Almost merged right into that semi. Wonder if he's drunk?" Brew shook his head. "Little bit o' bad karma there."

"Karma?" Catherine snorted, leaning forward, her Mohawk nodding. "There's no such thing."

Rowan dropped her head and covered her face with her hands. Her eyes and nose throbbed, healing. Being around the others helped—they were a cohesive unit, and she was a part of it. She'd never been a part of anything before, except her own family.

Memory rose. Daddy's face, the little gurgle in his chest...

No. She wouldn't let it happen. Not to any of them. Not to Justin, not to Catherine, not to *any* of them. She would fight with every ounce of her being to protect them.

And if Justin didn't think she was ready...

He's wrong. I'm ready.

Why would he act that way? How could he be jealous?

Not jealous, she realized. He hadn't struck out at Ellis. He'd pushed *her.*

There is no "friend" in the practice room, he'd told her once, lying next to her with his hand spread against her hip, warm and forgiving. *They taught me that.*

A dawning realization made her take her hands away from her face. Catherine was staring at her. "You okay?"

"I just had an idea," Rowan said softly. Cath blinked, then reached over and caught Rowan's chin, her fingernails scraping slightly.

"Christ, you've healed up. That's pretty powerful mojo you've got, baby."

"Really?" Rowan glanced down at her lacerated knuckles. They now looked smoother, as if the scrapes were weeks old instead of hours. "That's a good thing, isn't it?"

"Wow," Cath breathed. "That's *incredible.*"

"If that's why my head was hurting, I'd rather it didn't happen." Rowan stared at the back of Henderson's head as he drove. Her gaze suddenly clouded.

She felt something else, then, Delgado's hand on her nape. His fingers closed, hard and warm, and his strength flooded her. "Your head's hurting?"

"It was. But not now." Rowan's eyes narrowed. Something was wrong.

Her stomach rose sharp and sour. She closed her eyes, searching for the source of the disturbance.

Immediately Justin was there. *I'll anchor you. Go as deep as you need to.* He didn't care that she'd shouted that she hated him, and he didn't care that she hadn't been kind to him. He just offered his strength, a hot tide of it pouring into her spine, wrapping around the core of her.

I don't know what's wrong, she thought disjointedly. "Something's *wrong,*" she said. "My head hurt, and then..."

Does it feel like Sigs?

"We're not under attack," Brew said. "If we were, I'd know."

"I'd trust Rowan's senses," Yoshi said quietly. "Let her work."

"What should we do?" Zeke piped up.

"Quiet." Henderson sounded crisp. "Del?"

"Hang on." He sounded funny, almost dreamy, disconnected. "Rowan, move a little bit. *Here*." And he *pushed*, to show her.

She followed—and lost it. The sense of nausea drained away. "It's gone," she said. "I'm sorry. Maybe it was something else."

Henderson was quiet.

"I'm sorry," Del said, and Cath gasped as if he'd sworn. His fingers were still clasped around Rowan's nape, warm and comforting. "I should have just let you do it."

"It wasn't you. Whatever it was, it's gone now." She paused. "Don't pay any attention." She tried to say it lightly, failed. "Maybe it's nothing." *I'm jumping at shadows. And here I thought I was so competent.*

"Not likely," Henderson said finally, braking and pulling into a parking lot. "Let's be circumspect tonight, ladies and gents. It's 2100. Rendezvous by 2300, and everybody go with a buddy or two. You got me?"

Murmurs of assent, Brew pulled the door open and cold air sparkled into the van. Rowan stayed where she was. Zeke helped Cath out, Brew scanned the parking lot, and Yoshi exchanged a few words with Henderson. They were all waiting, despite Henderson's orders to rendezvous. It seemed that whatever Henderson's Brigade did tonight, they would do it together.

"Ro?" Justin's voice was soft. His hand slid away from the back of her neck.

"I'm here," she said. He didn't feel angry. Didn't sound angry either.

"You coming?"

"If I stay here, will you go?"

"No." Now she could almost hear him smiling. "I don't want a beer that badly. But you'll break Brew's heart."

"I guess I'd better go, then." She moved across the seat and hopped out, catching her balance. Instinct made her glance around—the parking lot was on Eighth Street. She had a pretty good grasp of this part of the city by now, having come for shopping trips and supply runs with Cath and Justin so many times.

Justin unfolded himself from the black van, turning to close the side door. He paused just slightly, his awareness scanning the perimeter. "Looks clear," he muttered.

Cath slid her arm through Rowan's. "Come on. Let's go to the grocery store. If we get our junk food, we can all go to a bar."

"You're too young," Brew shot back from Rowan's other side.

"Says *you*."

"Children, children." Rowan was still trying for a light tone. She felt Justin behind her, suddenly thoughtful, a deep well of silence.

Rowan's shadow.

"Okay, Mom." Cath rolled her eyes.

"How did we every get along without you?" Yoshi asked dryly.

"You just sort of blundered along." Rowan rolled her eyes. The sudden burst of laughter—even Henderson made a sound of amusement—rewarded her. But in the middle of the laughter, a sudden uneasy feeling made Rowan almost stumble, as if a cold finger had traced up her spine.

She stopped dead, closed her eyes. Brew halted after realizing she'd stopped, Justin stepped up behind her.

"Row—" Cath began.

Delgado clapped his hand over her mouth. "Shhh. Gather up and give her some cover."

Rowan's eyes flew open. "We have to go back," she heard herself say. Her voice rang against pavement and fell flat into the gutter. The parking lot was deserted, the van crouching in a pool of shadow. "We have to go back *now*."

"Why?" Zeke asked. "Goddammit! Why didn't you say something before?"

"We've got to go *back*," Rowan insisted, suddenly absolutely certain. "Now. *Now*."

"Back to where?" Henderson asked.

"Back to Headquarters. Something's wrong. We don't have much time." *I sound so certain.*

Rowan flinched, feeling Justin's fingers close over her shoulder, steadying her. "Everyone back to the car," he said. "She can feel Sigs, so let's be safe."

"Let's move, troops," Henderson said, and it was official.

"Awww, *crap*." Cath sighed. "I was looking forward to Pop Tarts."

"Hurry," Rowan pleaded, and they all started back toward the van, Justin's arm coming over her shoulders. She tilted forward, walking quickly and unsteadily, and he pulled her back.

"We *are* hurrying, angel. Just relax. We'll get there in time."

He sounded so utterly certain she almost believed him.

Thirty-Nine

Nobody said anything on the way back. Rowan shook with distress the closer they drew to home; Justin set his jaw. This was an enemy he couldn't fight, so he simply offered his strength, sitting in the back seat with her, Brew doing his best to shield her from the other side.

When they took the off ramp, he reached over the back seat and brought out the emergency kit. "Everyone arm up," he said, and started handing out the guns. Rowan accepted a Glock, and the small sounds of checking clips and chambering rounds resounded through the tense silence. Next came the comm-links fitted in everyone's ear

"Well," Yoshi said from the front passenger seat. "The place still seems to be standing. I don't see any smoking craters."

"It may only look safe," Delgado supplied.

"You're paranoid," Zeke piped up.

"It doesn't mean they're not out to get us."

"Can we have a little less chatter?" Henderson asked, turning to the right and flicking the headlights off. Delgado felt a sudden flare of gratefulness—the old man had believed Rowan without question. "I'm going to use the access road. I hope nobody wore heels."

"I left mine at home," Brew cracked, and Catherine giggled.

Delgado felt Rowan stiffen. "Can't you feel that?" she whispered.

"What?" he whispered back, his mouth close to her ear. She shivered.

"Exactly," she said. "It's too quiet."

"No psychic chatter," Brew supplied helpfully. "We're too far out to feel it, Rowan."

"Something's happened. We're too late." She was cheesy-pale in the darkness. He felt the waves of trembling gripping her, the shortness of her breath, and wished he could *push* her into fearlessness. Instead, he sank into his link with her, feeling her headache and nausea as if it was his own. *Christ, if she feels like that no wonder she thinks something's wrong.* He took the pain for her, took it and took it until she went limp against his side, curling into him. A small thread of nasty satisfaction curled through him. She hated him, but he could still comfort her.

"General?" Brew, with the quiet tone he used very seldom.

"Brew?"

"I'm getting it, too."

"Could just be static from her." Zeke shifted in his seat.

"It's not." Delgado heard the clipped tone in his own voice and realized something was bothering him too. "The lights," he said. "The lights should be on. There's no glow."

He was right. If it wasn't for the almost full moon overhead, Henderson would have been unable to drive without the headlights.

"I know," Henderson said. "But thanks anyway."

"What could take the grid *and* the backups out?" Catherine shivered. "I hope nobody's stuck on the transports."

"If they are, they're relatively safe," Delgado pointed out. "It takes time to crack a transport line."

"What do you think's happened?" Cath turned around to look at Delgado. "Rowan? What do you think?"

"I don't know," she said miserably, her breath hitching. Henderson cut the ignition, rolling to a stop and then slipping the van into "park" without touching the brakes.

"Hear that?" he asked, and the entire van went silent.

A faint noise filtered through. Delgado's skin went cold, then roughened with instinctive goose flesh. "Choppers," he said against Rowan's temple, then inhaled the clean scent of her hair. "Christ."

"What is it?" Cath was still twisted in her seat, looking at Rowan, who slumped into Delgado's side, her head hanging. The gun was in Rowan's hand, pointed at the floor with fingers locked outside the trigger, just in case.

"What else?" Henderson said quietly. "Sigma."

"How?" Yoshi shifted slightly, uncomfortable without his computer. "And what are we going to do?"

"Go in or go to ground," Delgado said. "That's the question."

"Something terrible's happened," Rowan whispered. "If there's someone alive in there..."

Silence. The entire group waited.

"We'll recon," Henderson said heavily. "If it's an attack, we'll be needed to cover an exit so we can get the noncoms out. And if it isn't, if it's just a power failure, they'll need Rowan to calm everyone down."

"It's not a power failure," Rowan said suddenly, quietly. A terrible certainty colored her voice.

The thudding of helicopters faded a little, then returned louder than ever. "Sweeps," Delgado said. "It's Sigma."

Nobody said a word.

"All right," Henderson said. "Del, you cover Rowan. Rowan, you sense anyone, point 'em out to Del and let him take care of it. Rest of you, let's spread out and go in quick and quiet. It's maximum prejudice."

Catherine swore, but nobody else said anything. *Don't worry,* Del thought, laying the words gently in Rowan's mind—as gently as he could.

That's like telling me not to breathe. No matter how much her body rebelled against the nearness of Sigma's presence, her mental tone was strong and clear. He pressed a kiss against her temple; nobody else would see in the darkness.

Zeke carefully, slowly, slid the handle of the door up. There was a slight click. "Anyone out there?" he whispered.

"No," Rowan whispered back. "I don't feel anyone. Not close."

"Okay." He tapped his comm-link and eased the door open. Chill air poured into the car. For such a large man, he moved lightly, sliding out of the van, kneeling down and sweeping the opposite side of the road with his gun.

Cath went next. Henderson climbed out of his seat and out through the side door. Then Yoshi opened his door and seemed almost to vanish. Brew slid out, and Del gave Rowan a gentle push.

Go on, angel. Don't worry, I'm here. He followed her as she moved slowly, her boots shushing on the wet pavement as she moved to the side and crouched down, pale hair glimmering in the moonlight.

That hair of hers is going to make things difficult, he thought, but Cath handed Rowan a scarf, which she knotted around her head with no comment.

They went around both sides of the van and across the drainage ditch, boots slipping in slush-snow. Delgado steadied Rowan when she slipped on the frost-rimed grass. His heart sped up, not quite racing but not resting either. He promised himself he would let nothing hurt her.

There was an empty field here, and they slid over it in waves, taking care to move in an unpredictable pattern, Rowan moving like an automaton. All her attention was taken with fighting off the urge to throw up or scream at the tearing, jagged pain in her head and the twisting nausea. *Why do Sigs affect her that way?*

What is it about them? Just the danger, or something else? It wasn't the first time he'd wondered. *Is it the migmeters or something else?*

Slowly, they crept up on the easternmost edge of Headquarters. Everything was dark. Every building, every light that should have been showing paths over the quad or the basketball court was out. Delgado could feel no ripple of emotion in the air around them. It was as if everyone had left and the last person had shut off the lights.

They skirted the east main building and started for the cover of a short laurel hedge. It was a gamble—a crossfire from the buildings could pin them down for mop-up. Henderson was obviously trusting Rowan's acuity.

Henderson froze. Delgado went down to one knee, instinctively grabbing Rowan's wrist. She let out a short, sharp sound.

They hit the ground, Zeke's leather jacket creaking. All except Rowan, whose knees seemed to have locked.

A small flicker of light showed in the north building.

Flashlight, Del thought. *Something's not right.*

"Trap!" Rowan might have thought she was screaming, but all that came out was a choked whisper. "Go back! Go *back!*"

The sound of the choppers coming back for another sweep got louder. Henderson was already scrambling back, cutting for the edge of the south building that would shield them from being seen and also let them access the transport net through an access hatch—Delgado knew this, because it was what *he* would do. Cath ran after him, followed by Zeke, who ran sideways, a gun in each hand. Brew and Yoshi were twin shadows.

Del curled up to his feet. He yanked on Rowan's arm, felt her stumble. She was trying to do something, as if lifting a massive weight with her mind. *Pushing,* with all her strength.

There was a sharp cry from the north building, and Rowan let out a soft sound of pain. "Leave them!" he whisper-yelled at her, yanking her along savagely. She stumbled again, he righted her, and something zinged across the quad.

Del didn't hesitate. He pushed her in front of him and almost returned fire before Henderson hissed a sharp command, freezing his finger on the trigger. Rowan stumbled around the side of the building and almost fell into Zeke's arms. The massive man grabbed Del's shirt and hauled him in just as more bullets chewed the air behind him.

"Let them think we're unarmed," Henderson said, brief and clipped.

They could have shot her! Delgado swallowed the instant flare of rage. He wanted to sink his hands in the throat of the man who had shot at her, wanted to hold him down and use a knife, wanted to—

Justin! I need you. She was fighting something huge, little hitching sounds of effort coming from her as she wrestled with it.

He threw every spare ounce of power he had into the link with her, his hand clamped around her arm and Zeke dragging her from the other side. The scarf came free and her pale hair trailed on a faint chill breeze as the sound of choppers roared overhead.

Henderson reached the access hatch, knelt down, and keyed in the security code. Miracle of miracles, it opened, a round slice of metal. The old man covered them as Catherine scrambled down into darkness. So did Yoshi, followed by Brew, Del pushed Rowan at Zeke. "Get her down!" he said, and looked up just as the choppers roared overhead.

Rowan half fell into the access hatch, and he knew she was safe. Zeke followed, then Henderson.

Light poured down, blinding him. Delgado went into a fighting crouch, then rolled as bullets dug into the frozen earth. *Clumsy, sloppy. I'd take that kid to the range and make him practice.*

He felt Rowan's instinctive horrified cry and her talent coiling, striking like a snake. The light above them yawed, and Del saw Henderson vanish down the hole. "Come *on*, Del!" Henderson's voice crackled over the comm-link.

"Go," Del said. The chopper veered off, but another one was coming. He could see what they couldn't, a line of dark shapes coming over the quad, lit by the backwash of light from four choppers sweeping in from the west. "I'll cover you. Get to an exit."

"Del, come *on*. That's an order!"

"Hurry up, old man. Get Rowan out." Del's eyes had just begun to come back after the assault of light. The chopper that had spotted them veered crazily toward the field.

Justin! Her mental cry was sharp and despairing. Every cell in his body wanted to turn back, go down the hole. But a quick calculation of the numbers told him that the Sigs would pour down the hole, and it would become a desperate fight in the dark.

Go, angel. I'll see you soon. He kicked the access hatch shut, fired a round into the keypad, and took a deep breath. The Sigs were almost around the corner—even he could sense them now.

Justin! Stop it! Come on!

"Can't even if I wanted to, angel," he muttered, bending almost double and running for the building. "Go. For God's sake, old man, get her out."

He reached the back door just as the first Sig came around the corner, spraying the area around the hatch with gunfire. Del slipped into the darkness, leaving the door open slightly, peering out, gun held ready.

The smell was something he recognized, a stench that rose around him. No wonder Rowan hadn't sensed anything. He glanced back at the hallway, lit by a soft red glowstick clutched in someone's hand. Someone's dead limp hand.

Dead bodies.

His gorge rose briefly, pointlessly. An assault like this would have taken phenomenal resources to crack the shields, dampers, and countermeasures. Why hadn't anyone been alerted? Why hadn't the fail-safes gone off, and all team leaders been alerted?

Traitor. Someone must have shut down the grids. Either that or Sigma had sent a fucking army.

"General," he said into the comm-link, "I'm inside the south building. Looks like an abattoir. Everyone's iced."

"What?"

"Someone blew the safety grid from inside, General, I bet you dollars to doughnuts." He pitched his voice low. "I'm going to do a sweep, see if I can pick any—"

Thwish. He felt the spear of ice bury itself in his back.

What the—He reached behind his back with his free hand, a slim metal wand tipped with something very sharp.

The tranquilizer dart came free in his hand, and he stared at it for a moment, his entire body suddenly numb.

Justin! Justin! NO! Rowan's horrified scream.

"Tranquilizer…dart…Get…her…out…" Delgado said, and passed out.

Forty

"Well, isn't this a fucked-up situation," Henderson said in the darkness.

Rowan shuddered. The blackness closed around her, a claustrophobic trap even though the tunnel was wide enough for a transport and a narrow walkway on either side. Henderson's Brigade walked single file: Henderson, Brew, Cath, Rowan, Yoshi, Zeke.

Justin, she keened, tears slicking her cheeks. Her head hurt from *pushing* both the helicopter pilot and the other Sigma psychics. She had fought off their combined mental weight, keeping them blind to her as long as she could until it was too late.

Sobs rose up in her chest. She stayed fiercely silent.

"What's up?" Brew's quiet voice.

"We have to decide. Go back toward the central hub and see what we can salvage, if they've cleared out, or take our luck with outside."

Silence again. Rowan leaned against the wall. She had never felt so tired. Even her *hair* hurt. "Everyone they had," she murmured.

"What, Rowan?" Henderson, suddenly attentive.

"Back there. After we saw the flashlight. It felt like they had a large group of psychics there, trying to pin us down." Her voice was flat, exhausted.

"Were they working through someone?" he asked.

"I don't know." She closed her eyes. Pinwheels and sparks of false light flared through the darkness. "I couldn't tell. I was busy trying to hold them off."

"Christ," Brew said. "Bloody fucking hell."

"Don't freak out," Cath hissed.

"Shut up." This from Yoshi. They were all claustrophobic. Fear began to taint the air, a sharp acrid smell.

Rowan dragged in a deep breath. "Let's just calm down," she said, hearing the false serenity in her tone. It was hard to reach that place of tranquility that let her heal people, but she took another breath and prayed for it.

It came. Finally. She felt the fear fade, stroking at its edges, soothing it away.

"What do you think we should do?" Cath asked.

Is she asking me? I don't have any clue. Justin. Justin.
"I'd say we should go back and get him," she said slowly.

"No," Henderson vetoed immediately. "We go on and hope nobody's found the exit."

"What if they have?" Rowan asked, then clamped her mouth shut.

"Then we're dead." Henderson moved briefly. "Everyone, hand on shoulder. Let's go."

The sound of their footsteps fell into a well of dark silence. Rowan reached out for Justin, again, felt nothing. An *absence.* "He said tranquilizer dart." Her voice was ragged. "Why would they do that?"

"He's valuable," Yoshi said. "He was one of their best operatives, and they need to figure out how he escaped them."

"Not to mention the fact he's been linked to you," Henderson said. "And if they can break him, they can root out any Society cells they find."

Rowan swallowed a sob, willed her mouth to shut.

They trooped on in silence until Henderson halted. "Here it is," he said. "Rowan, can you do one more thing?"

She felt pale as glass, past exhaustion and in a sort of enervated haze. "I think I can," she said, hearing her voice crack and hating it. Why couldn't she be strong? Like Justin, like Cath? *I thought I was so ready. I was so sure I was ready for this.*

"Good. Scan out there and tell me if anyone's waiting to surprise us."

Rowan closed her eyes. Yoshi's hand tightened slightly on her shoulder. It wasn't Justin's support, but it did make her feel a little better. She took another deep breath, centered herself, and cast her awareness out the way Kate had taught her.

Kate. Was she dead? Justin had said something about everyone being dead.

Contact.

—what the—

—it's me—

—oh God—

Rowan sagged in relief. "It's Eleanor. And Boomer, and Bobby, a couple others. No Sigs that I can feel."

"Good." Henderson felt for the keypad.

Rowan, worn thin and exhausted, felt a shock-blast of

worry and tight-throat claustrophobia, awe and fear and terror combined. She drowned in Cath's emotions for a moment, her knees buckling.

"Careful, Ro." Yoshi dug his fingers into her shoulder. The grating pain helped, gave her a focus. She closed her eyes and stumbled out, her hand on Cath's shoulder.

It was a good thing her eyes were closed. Light played over her face. She flinched. Blinked.

"Dammit, Boomer, turn that off. Are they following you?" Eleanor lowered the machine gun from her shoulder.

"Rowan!" Bobby cried.

"We need to move," Henderson barked crisply. "Any other survivors?"

"Not that we saw," Eleanor said heavily. "We were in the infirmary looking for Rowan. Boomer had one of his presentiments. They came to the infirmary last. If it wasn't for Bobby, they'd have caught us too."

"The infirmary last? That makes no sense." Zeke's dirt-smudged face swung around, and he looked at Rowan.

No. Oh, no.

"Oh, my God," she whispered. "Why? All that, just for me?"

"I doubt you were more than a secondary objective." Henderson glanced at the small, ragged group, and Rowan looked around.

Boomer. Eleanor. Bobby. Emily, whose round face was terribly pale, a bandage glaring white around her head. A tall thin young man with his arm in a sling. She dredged up his name—*Eric.* Tamara, one of Lyle's team, her red hair caked with mud and her face covered in dried blood, her eyes terribly shocked. Garth, another one of Lyle's team, his arm around Tamara's shoulders, wincing whenever he took a deep breath. And last of all, little Melissa, her eyes wide as she held Bobby's hand, her blond hair in two pigtails falling down her back.

And Henderson's Brigade. Minus one.

They were in a small stand of pine trees, the clean fragrance of pine rising and swamping them. The chill wind after the confines of the tunnel was like heaven, no matter that her teeth almost immediately began chattering. Yoshi, right next to her, curled his hand around her upper arm and peered at her face. "General? She's going into shock."

Zeke slid his leather jacket off, draping it over Rowan's

camel coat. It was warmer, and she blinked at him gratefully.

"All right," Henderson said. "We've got to get out of here. Can everyone walk?"

Murmurs of assent.

"Brew? Which way to the road? We'll parallel, come into town, get some shelter, and send someone for a cache." Henderson started giving orders, and Rowan simply stood and stared at the yawning hole that was the end of the transport tunnel. Any moment she expected to see Justin emerge, maybe bloody but still alive, his dark eyes meeting hers as they always did.

I never even told him how much he means to me, she thought, and shivered harder.

"Rowan?" Henderson was right next to her. Cath and Zeke pushed the round metal door closed. Yoshi lay his hand over the keypad once it was closed, his eyes closing and a small sound of effort coming from him. Electricity crackled. Rowan suddenly understood—he was scrambling the lock.

She blinked up at Henderson's lined face. "He's not coming, is he?"

"Don't underestimate him," the General replied softly. "If there's a way, he'll come back to you. You did good work, keeping them off us. Good job, operative."

Bile rose in Rowan's throat. She hadn't done anything but screw up. She hadn't realized it was a trap until it was too late, the combined weight of the Sigma psychics keeping her blind and deaf. She'd screwed up when it counted.

"Don't blame yourself," Henderson said. "It will poison you. And I need you if I'm going to get everybody out of this."

Her eyes met his, startled. "You don't—" she began, but he shook his head, laying a finger against his lips. Rowan shut up.

"Right. Let's move out. Everyone pick a partner and buddy up. Brew, Yoshi, you two take Rowan. If she starts fading give her a glucose tab and call a rest stop. Cath, Zeke, take the kids. All right, everyone. Let's go. Quiet and quick as we can now."

Moments later, the small stand of pines was empty.

Forty-One

Consciousness. Fuzzy, fading. Restraints. Wrist, elbow, knees, ankles, boots bound together, gag in the mouth. Blindfold. Arms twisted behind his back savagely.

First thought: *They must have a high opinion of me.*

Second thought: *Rowan. Did she get out?*

He wished he had even a quarter of her talent, so he could tell for sure. He lay perfectly still, trussed up, his arm bent back uncomfortably under him, his back strained. He was on something hard and cold, metal. Thrumming metal.

A chopper.

"He's awake." A familiar, whistling voice.

Jilssen.

Rage woke down in the depths of Delgado's bones. He pushed it down. He had to *think*.

But the fuzziness of the tranquilizer was still on him, and the thought that Jilssen was here, that Jilssen had been trying to get Rowan into a telem rig—maybe one tuned to broadcast her location—that Jilssen had been stalking her through Headquarters, blinded him momentarily.

The thought that Jilssen might have turned the security grid off with his clearance was almost as bad.

A boot in his ribs. "Stay still, Delgado," a gruff male voice warned him. He placed the voice—up above him, crouched over.

Del *reached*.

The man stumbled backward as Del's mental fingers curved into his brain, striking unerringly. He could have squeezed the man's mind for information, but instead he simply burst all the locks and smashed through, vandalizing, striking back.

Shouts. The metal floor tipping. Delgado found another mind, curiously unprotected, and forced his way in like a battering ram. The first man was screaming, clawing at his own eyes. The second stumbled toward Delgado, compelled, ready to cut his bonds and set him loose.

If he hadn't been so slow, so fuzzy from the tranquilizer, it might have worked.

Something jabbed into his arm. Del twisted, trying to strike out, and went limp, a terrible slow creeping fire invading his body.

NO. NO. NO—

"Now." Jilssen's voice, hot and rancid in his ear. "I've wanted to do that for *so* long."

It was Zed. He would know that feeling anywhere, the slow fire taking over muscle and nerves, the languor, the utter lethargic incapableness.

Fight it, fight it. But with what? He'd kicked it once, and almost gone mad, had no illusions about doing it again.

Rowan.

The sight of her running on the track, her pale hair a banner on the breeze she made, lips moving silently with the song in her headphones. The quick intelligence in her wide green eyes. The feel of her skin against his fingertips, her sleeping curled against him, barely even breathing, trusting him to keep her safe. Shuddering, arched beneath him, her mind open to his.

Her last despairing cry for him.

Did they know she could cure a Zed addiction? Did Jilssen know?

He gave himself one more moment to remember her face, then gathered everything together, hurrying, hurrying.

He locked his memories of her away while he could, pushing them deep into the most guarded recesses of his brain. Then he slammed the door on them, closing away the sight of her face in the hard, cold, secret part of himself—and before the Zed could reach his head and shut him down, he did the only thing he could.

He *pushed* one last time, arching and screaming as the compulsion turned inward, tearing through his own brain, a feedback squeal of nerves and neurons pushed too far.

Then he passed out, before the drug could reach his brain.

***

When he came to again, it was to fuzzy white light. Too white, too bright, sterile.

Del opened one eye. Then the other. Braced himself.

Sigma has me, he thought as the door whooshed open. They must have been waiting for him to wake up.

Delgado blinked.

The man was tall, white-haired, and dressed in a white linen suit. The face was familiar—he had, after all, seen it in his nightmares for years. Bland and middle-aged, a regular nose, dead dark eyes, hair in a white buzz-cut.

"Well, well." Colonel Anton tilted his head slightly. "Agent Breaker. What a pleasant reunion. You've done a little bit of damage, old son." His voice was kindly, avuncular, as he limped into the room, leaning heavily on the cane. His freshly-polished shoes squeaked against the whiteness.

There was an IV pole right next to Delgado. The slow, creeping fire of Zed slid through his fingers, up his arms. He blinked, trying to remember…what?

For a moment he had it—a flash of green eyes, something—

Then it was gone. He stared at Anton, willing himself to remain perfectly still. If the man tried to use telepathy on him, the feedback would be excruciating for both of them.

"Andrews mentioned he'd seen you again. You've been a very naughty boy."

Del searched for words. "Go fuck yourself," he rasped, his tongue thick and useless, slurred with the Zed. It was so hard to care about anything when it had its claws in you. But when they took the needle out, he'd only have a short time before he started to unravel without it. Oldest trick in the book—get your unwilling operative hooked. Classic.

"Now," Anton said, "we're going to have a little talk about Miss Price. And then you're going to go back into training. You've gone a bit soft. Then you'll start a regular routine of work until your Talent or your body gives out. There is…" Here the colonel paused for effect. "…no hope for you."

Del blinked at him again. *I will do whatever I have to do to escape you,* he thought.

The colonel settled himself, legs braced, leaning on his cane. "Where is Rowan Price?"

Delgado shook his head. *Who?*

"Do you want to be tortured? We can go that route again."

He cleared his throat. "Whatever you're asking me," he said slowly, slurred with the drug, "makes no sense. I remember *pushing* myself to forget."

Anton stared at him for a moment, then turned on his heel. His cane thumped against the floor.

Just before he reached the door, he paused.

"Training starts tomorrow, Agent Breaker. And the first thing you'll be doing is hunting down whatever rats escaped our cleanup."

Colonel Anton limped out of the room.

The door hissed shut.

Del closed his eyes. The Zed reached his head, and everything else faded away.

Forty-Two

The buried cache of weapons, rations, cash and clothes was undisturbed, and Cath, Zeke, and Eleanor brought it back to the small house. There was even a small plastic box that held car keys, Yoshi told Rowan that the cars were at a warehouse in the city waiting for pickup.

The small house Henderson had the keys for was empty except for a few mattresses in each room, but Rowan didn't care. She dropped down on one mattress in the living room and was instantly asleep. She dreamed of blank white walls and something like icy lava eating through her arms and legs.

When she awakened fourteen hours later, the house was transformed into an impromptu command center. Yoshi was perched on a chair, looking a lot more comfortable now that he had a computer. He tapped at the keys and murmured to himself. Cath handed Eleanor a cup of something that smelled like coffee, and Bobby was busy sorting ammunition into different boxes. The others were probably out getting supplies or in other rooms, working away like busy little bees.

Henderson looked down at her from where he sat, hunched over a table with a map and a cell phone on it. There were markers on the map, little lead weights painted different colors. "Morning, Rowan. Want some coffee?"

She opened her mouth to say yes, but nothing came out. Instead, she levered herself to her feet and found the bathroom, stumbling out of the living room. It was a relief to close herself in a separate room and relieve herself, and the sound of the flushing toilet covered the low sobbing noise she made. There were paper towels stacked near the sink, and she washed her face with cold water and patted it dry. She ran her fingers back through her tangled hair, grimacing. The hum of dampers was normal, now, and she was no longer a wildly-emitting distress beacon.

Rowan looked up into the mirror. Her eyes had giant dark circles under them and her hands shook.

Justin.

She opened the bathroom door and walked like a robot down the hall and into the living room again. The shades were drawn tight, slivers of sunlight falling through the cracks. The house was warm, and Rowan collapsed on the mattress again, staring fixedly at all the activity around her.

Cath brought her a cup of coffee. "Drink. You drained yourself last night. You'll need food too. Come on, drink."

Rowan obediently drank.

The coffee was hot and sweet. Rowan sighed as the sugar and caffeine began to sink in. Henderson made more notations on the map, then rolled it up and turned to look at her.

She met his steel-colored eyes squarely, and waited for condemnation.

"You saved lives last night, Rowan," he said finally. "We wouldn't be here if you hadn't done what you did."

She cleared her throat, a sad little sound. "I cost you your best operative, General. And I didn't see the trap in time."

Henderson actually sighed, rubbing at his eyes. His gray hair was wildly mussed, he was missing his steel-rimmed glasses, and his clothes were rumpled and wrinkled around his spare frame. For someone who was usually so precise, the change was shocking. "If Del's alive, he'll come back for you, Rowan. And they won't kill him."

"Why not?" she asked dully, staring into her coffee cup.

"They need him to hunt us." Henderson got up, the chair creaking. "Now drink your coffee and eat something. I need you to help me get everyone to safety and figure out how to rebuild. Delgado needs you, too. If he comes back and finds out you've done something silly, he'll be very unhappy with me."

She knew he was only using it to needle her, but it worked. She felt the sharp prick of irritation and took another gulp of the hot coffee. Cath brought her—wonder of wonder—two strawberry Pop Tarts.

"I'm making toast and eggs, but you can start on that. You need sugar or you'll develop a backlash headache." Cath's Mohawk was sadly bedraggled, but her violet eyes were clear. "That was some good work last night."

"I failed," Rowan answered. "And Justin..."

Cath shook her head. "Quit it. Don't mope, Ro. I hate mopers. We need you to do some of your fancy work for us. Garth's leg is bleeding again, and Melissa...well, she's retreating. We *need* you."

Justin needs me too. Rowan's conscience struggled. They'd shot him with a tranquilizer dart. And she'd dreamed of white walls, and something burning...

"I'll stay until Garth and Melissa are better," she said slowly. "But I have to find Justin. He'd find me."

"Shit, the man's got nine lives." Cath shrugged. "I gotta go, my eggs are burning. Just...just don't do anything stupid, okay, Ro?"

"Of course not," Rowan murmured, looking back down into her coffee cup.

I'm going to find him, she thought, feeling icy resolve close over her heart. *He'd find me.*

No matter what it takes, I'm going to find him.

The other thought that lay just under the surface of her consciousness frightened her.

And God help anyone in my way.

To Be Continued...

Excerpt from Hunter, Healer
Coming October, 2005

Green eyes, wide and dark, she stood with Andrews's hand around her upper arm. Motionless, she was too sedated to recognize the danger, trusting Delgado completely.

He wasn't ready for that.

Pale hair, laying damp and dark against her forehead. More rain kissing her skin and sliding into Del's eyes. Stay still, *he thought.* Just stay still. *Moving, every muscle strained, every nerve screaming.* Stay still until I can get to you.

Andrews sneering, certain he had both of them—but Delgado whirled, throwing the knife. His other hand came up, the weight of the gun strangely familiar, the bullet took out the other Sig as the knife buried itself in Andrews's shoulder with a meaty thunk. Rowan made a thin noise and swayed again.

He caught her arm. "Are you all right? Rowan? Goddammit, Rowan, talk to me."

Agent Breaker woke up, his arm flung across his face and the dream fading into unreality. Again. The metal shelf was hard underneath him, and he strained as he did every morning to *remember*.

It didn't work. Whatever he'd done to himself appeared to be permanent. Even the Colonel's star psions couldn't reverse it, and the Colonel seemed a little upset. This Price girl, whoever she was, managed to hop one step ahead of every Sigma trick. They seemed to blame Del for that too.

If he'd trained her, he'd done it well.

The door to the concrete cube they called a room slid aside, and Del curled up to sit on the bed, a hand closing around a knife-hilt. It was damp and chilly down here, but he didn't care. The bed was a single metal shelf, the cube had a drain in one corner, and two blankets and a bare light bulb were recently accorded luxuries. The single metal bar for exercise—pull-ups, inverts, and the like—sliced across the cell, low enough that he had to duck to avoid it. This room wasn't made for comfort.

Not like a room he remembered with scarves scattered over the bedstead, books jumbled on shelves, and a clean warm perfume in the air. Sunlight fell through the window and French

door of that room in the most secret corner of his mind. Del
had the idea that if he waited long enough, was still and silent
enough, he might catch a glimpse of whoever owned that
room—maybe the woman they were so eager to find. It never
happened, but that room had held him during the worst of the
beatings and the deepest of the drug-induced questioning
sessions.

That room had saved his sanity.

Andrews leaned against the doorjamb, without Jilssen for
once. "Hey." His deceptively-sleepy blue eyes under short
wheat-gold hair moved over the concrete cube, as if Del was
holding contraband in some corner.

He was, but he wasn't about to let the Colonel's second-
in-command know it. "Hey," he returned, the knife lifting a
little, playing through the sequence that would end with it
whipping through the air and burying itself in the lean man's
throat. It would be immensely satisfying to see Andrews's eyes
bug out and hear him choking on steel, maybe with his fingers
scrabbling at the hilt while Del moved in on him. Del could
strip him of weapons and grab his magkey, but there were armed
guards at both ends of all the corridors, as well as the security
net and the trackers.

*Don't forget the trackers. Wait for your time, Agent Breaker.
Just wait.*

Where was Jilssen? The traitorous doctor who had allowed
Sigma to take Society Headquarters had been coming around
less and less—maybe because of the way Del stared at him,
aching to tear the man's throat out. It didn't matter—Jilssen
was a small problem in the scheme of things. Sooner or later
Del would have his opportunity. Of that he was sure. Patience
brought a man everything he needed, especially when there
was nothing left but endurance and the dream of revenge.

Andrews shrugged under the supple, oiled leather of his
rig,. Del had copied the pattern for the rigs for the Society. He
could remember that clearly. He'd altered them to make them
easier and lighter, a few material adjustments. He remembered
buckling a rig on someone, testing it. She'd been a little shorter
than the usual woman and her nearness had made his hands
shake imperceptibly.

Who? He shook the memory away. His hair was cut short
now, none of the longhair crap the Society let its members
indulge in. Del had never gone in for that, but his hair *had*

been longer when he'd come in. He remembered that, remembered the click and buzz of the electric razor against his scalp. So he'd been growing it out, he guessed. Something to do with the hole in his memory.

His arm itched, the creeping fire of Zed wearing off. They'd drugged him hard, always asking the same question.

Where is Rowan Price? Whoever she was, they wanted her badly.

That was enough to make Del hope they didn't find her.

"We've got jump-off in forty. Get your ass up. You're coming topside with me. We've got a snatch and grab to do."

"Fine." Delgado coiled himself to his feet and noticed Andrews tense, his muscled shoulders rolling under a black T-shirt. "Who we grabbing?"

Andrews stepped back. He might look lazy, but he was ready. Del wondered if his shoulder was hurting from the old knife wound. The blond man's lip curled as he looked over the inside of the concrete cube. Del didn't rate even a mattress pad yet; he might not ever. They were confusing his inability to remember with stubbornness. Del didn't blame them. If he'd had a choice, it *would* have been stubbornness.

"Some psion the freaks have been courting. We've got a shot to bring in a whole busload of them. Including the golden girl who's been running me around the goddamn country."

Del let one corner of his mouth tilt up into a smile. He seemed to remember a time when a smile had started to feel natural. But he was back in Sigma now. Every expression, the most minute of facial tics, was a weapon or a betrayal now. You never knew who was watching, who would report what, or when the fist would come down hard.

I never really thought I'd escape, he realized, as he did every day. *I was just waiting for them to scoop me back up. Deep down, I knew it. Knew this would happen.* "She's been putting you through your paces, huh?" *The more I hear about this woman, the more I like her, you son of a bitch.*

"Oh, yeah. It's almost like hunting you, you sarcastic fucker. Come on, we've got to kit you out." Andrews didn't sound happy.

Of course not. For three months this Price had been eluding him, slipping through his fingers like water. Sigma couldn't exterminate the last few vestiges of the Society, no matter how hard they tried. Delgado's knowledge of the ragtag assortment of psionics and their usual procedures hadn't helped as much as Colonel Anton had hoped. Despite picking his brain for every scrap of information that could be gotten out while a cocktail of Zed and Sodium Pentothal was forcibly pumped into Del's veins, the Colonel was no closer to eradicating the persistent thorn in Sigma's side.

And the Society had even started, incredibly, to fight back. A whole Sigma snatch team had disappeared off the map a month past Del's recapture. Civilian psions Sigma had targeted for acquisition suddenly vanished, reappearing fitted out like Society members, recruiting new psions and damaging Sigma with a persistent guerilla war. Slowly, incredibly, and successfully, the Society had managed to stay together and fight the massive tentacles of a well-funded black-ops government agency.

Del kept his face a mask and silently cheered. He gave all the information he could—he had no choice, not if he wanted to end up anything other than a brain-wiped, Zed-shattered hulk. And the beatings hadn't helped. Andrews was sadistic, and his trained bullyboys not much better. Del didn't want to give them any more reason to pummel him. He'd just barely gotten over the last goddamn thrashing they'd given him.

So Anton was letting Delgado out to play, was he?

I can use this. Maybe escape.

But if he escaped, how would he break the Zed habit? He wasn't sure he could do it again. Once was enough for *that* particular hell, thank you very much. The drug was meant to give you withdrawal so bad you'd do anything for another hit, and without a full detox unit to help him through the worst of the physiological effects he might find himself in an even worse place than he already was now. Strange as *that* sounded.

And if he escaped, where would he go? How the hell could *he* find the Society?

More importantly, would they trust him once he found them? Probably not.

He slid off the bed, his rig coming with him. He buckled it on, rolling his shoulders to make sure it fit right. Slid the knife back into its sheath. Giving him a few weapons didn't matter. One man, no matter how gifted or well-trained, couldn't extricate himself from a full-size Sig installation. It would be insanity even to try. "Well, we'd better go, right?"

"We'd better. You think you can bring this girl in, Del?"

I'd rather firebomb this whole goddamn place and dance on your burning grave, you sadistic son of a bitch.

"If I trained her like you say, I should be able to."

But if I do find her, I'm not bringing her in. I'm going to help her get so far away you'll never find her.

"You better be careful," Andrews said. The bastard was smirking, his blue eyes alive as if he was contemplating someone's pain. Probably Del's. "If she keeps this up the Colonel might decide she's better dead, even if she is a golden girl. Jilssen has a hard time convincing him to bring her in alive anyway."

Del shrugged. "If I cared, I wouldn't be here." *I escaped you once before.* But he was past lying to himself, and the thought was merely reflexive. Empty bravado wouldn't help him.

What would help him was finding the genius who could outthink Sigma, hold the shattered Society together, and direct an organization like this back from the brink of disaster. A genius like that might have an idea or two Del could use.

A genius like that might be able to help Del figure out what he'd done to his own head, and what he couldn't remember. Andrews laughed, sidling back out the door. "Yeah, sure you don't care. Come on, Breaker. For this assignment, your ass is mine."

"Color me excited," Del mumbled, and followed him out the door into the blinding white-tiled corridor beyond. They were underground in the high security warrens, armed guards with personal dampers everywhere and trackers in special cells on every level. Someone down the hall screamed—probably undergoing their first reeducation session. Zed and a beating, just the right way to wake up in the morning.

Sigma. Back home in the bad old cradle. They were going to send him out on an assignment for the first time since his recapture. And any assignment, however well-planned it was, might offer Del a chance to do something other than keep being a Sigma lapdog.

Excitement rose at the thought, but his training clamped down, regulating his pulse back to a steady even thudding. Even a heartbeat could give him away.

That was just a vanishing possibility, though. It was far more likely that Anton and Andrews were going to use Del like a ferret in a hole to smoke out any Society operatives possible. They had all the weight of the government behind them, and they had learned a few things since Del's last escape. Whoever this Price girl was, she was still playing in a rigged game. Del's unwilling acquiescence to Sigma might be the thing that tipped the balance against her.

Whoever you are, Price, keep running, he thought. *I hope I did train you, I really do. 'Cause that's the only thing that's going to save you if they somehow make me hunt you down.*

Society #1

4-12-14

B N N
SAINTCROW

SEP 0 9 2016

Printed in the United States
49436LVS00006B

9 781933 417585